The
MAJESTIES

—

The MAJESTIES

❖ *A Novel* ❖

TIFFANY TSAO

ATRIA BOOKS

New York   London   Toronto   Sydney   New Delhi

ATRIA
BOOKS

An Imprint of Simon & Schuster, Inc.
1230 Avenue of the Americas
New York, NY 10020

Originally published in Australia in 2018 by Penguin Random House Australia
as *Under Your Wings*

First Atria Books hardcover edition January 2020

ATRIA B O O K S and colophon are trademarks of Simon & Schuster, Inc.

For information about special discounts for bulk purchases, please contact Simon & Schuster Special Sales at 1-866-506-1949 or business@simonandschuster.com.

The Simon & Schuster Speakers Bureau can bring authors to your live event. For more information or to book an event, contact the Simon & Schuster Speakers Bureau at 1-866-248-3049 or visit our website at www.simonspeakers.com.

Interior design by A. Kathryn Barrett

Manufactured in the United States of America

1   3   5   7   9   10   8   6   4   2

Library of Congress Cataloging-in-Publication Data

Names: Tsao, Tiffany, author.
Title: The majesties: a novel / Tiffany Tsao.
Other titles: Under your wings
Description: First Atria Books hardcover edition. | New York: Atria Books, 2020.
Identifiers: LCCN 2019010114| ISBN 9781982115500 (hardcover) | ISBN 9781982115517 (pbk.)

ISBN 978-1-9821-1550-0
ISBN 978-1-9821-1552-4 (ebook)

For Amanda

Keep me as the apple of your eye;
hide me in the shadow of your wings . . .

—*Psalm 17:8*

The
MAJESTIES

WHEN YOUR SISTER murders three hundred people, you can't help but wonder why—especially if you were one of the intended victims—though I do forgive her, if you can believe it. I tried my best to deny the strength of family ties when everyone was still alive, but now I realize the truth of the cliché: Blood does run thick. Even if poison trumps all.

It was caught on surveillance tape, so there's no denying that Estella was the culprit. I haven't seen the footage myself—can't see at all in my present condition—but I can imagine it with great clarity. At the mouth of the corridor leading from the hotel ballroom to the adjoining kitchen, my sister appears. The angle of the camera makes it difficult to see her face, obscured by the enormous hair-sprayed chignon atop her head, but I'd recognize those calves anywhere—peasant's legs, our mother always jokingly called them, disproportionately bulky for Estella's otherwise slender frame. Graceful in stilettos, despite her country-bumpkin appendages, she glides out of one camera's purview into another's. My mind's eye sees her in the kitchen now, speaking to one of the staff, who grants her immediate entry upon learning that she's Irwan Sulinado's granddaughter. Graciously, she offers a pretext (a mission to reassure a germophobic aunt, perhaps—any excuse would have served since, in Indonesia, the wealthy don't need reasons). They allow her free passage, "*Silakan, Ibu*"—ma'am, as you please—and let her sail on, past flaming woks and stainless-steel bins of presliced meats and vegetables, fielding deferential nods from surprised and frazzled cooks. Only when they resume their duties does she strike, pulling a tiny vial from inside the high, stiff collar of her silk cheongsam and scattering its contents into the great steaming tureen of shark's fin soup with a flick of a jade-bangled wrist.

I'm making this whole scene up, of course, except for the cheongsam: a gorgeous gold-and-emerald affair covered in delicate coiling vines that she'd bought years ago on vacation in Shanghai. That's where my mind beats out the security cameras; such fine embroidery would never have registered on tape. Similarly, I bet the recording didn't catch the resolution in her step, the hardness in her jaw, the murderous glint in her eye that also went unnoticed by all the family members and friends in attendance that night—and, to my shame, me. I've replayed the evening dozens of times in my head, and I'm sure of it: There was nothing out of the ordinary about her except that she was in exceptionally good spirits, which I'd attributed to her downing two flutes of champagne before the traditional first course of peach-shaped birthday buns had made its way to the banquet tables.

"Gwendolyn. Doll," she'd whispered in my ear, giggling. She split a bun along its rose-tinted cleft, and dark lotus-seed paste oozed out.

"I always get a kick out of these," she confided. "Don't you think they look like blushing butts filled with . . ."

That set me giggling too. A fine way for two women in their early thirties to behave. Truth be told, I might have drunk my champagne too quickly as well.

You'd understand why, after sharing a sisterly moment such as this, I'd be baffled that Estella would want to kill me, or any of us, or, for that matter, herself. I think that's why I'm not as angry as I probably should be. If she'd poisoned us all and spared her own life, it would have been unforgivable. But no, she wanted us dead and she wanted herself dead, and now only I am alive. If you can call it that.

It seems like ages ago that I learned I was the only survivor. It's hard to keep track of time in my condition, so I can't provide an exact hour or date, but it was after I'd woken up, gasping into emptiness, and screamed and screamed and nobody came. It was after the footsteps eventually arrived and, ignoring my cries for help, someone readjusted my body, tinkered with the beeping thing at my side, and departed. It was an eternity after that—an endless cycle of being awake and terrified, of calling out in vain to whoever shifted me and rustled around my prone body, punctuated by bouts of exhausted sleep. It was even after I'd stopped calling out at all. (They couldn't hear me. I finally came to terms with that.)

I found out what Estella had done only when two women came in and, while attending to me, began to talk to each other. I hadn't heard voices for so long that my ears didn't comprehend at first what they were saying. Gradually, words began to form out of the babble.

". . . Estella Wirono. Granddaughter of the Chinese tycoon Irwan Sulinado. Put it in the shark's fin soup. The footage was all over the news."

"How many were poisoned?"

"Around three hundred."

"How many survivors?"

"Only one."

"A shame," the second voice said sorrowfully.

Then they left me to my desolation.

Estella's apology—her dying words—made sense after that. The chaos of the evening flooded back to me: The shrieking of the first victims as they began to choke and twitch, to retch and collapse, followed by a different sort of cry—the belated realization that one's life is about to end. The hotel ballroom spinning madly. Guests staggering to their feet, trailing tablecloths in clenched fists. Wineglasses and plates of Peking duck crashing to the black-and-gold-carpeted floor. Gerry Sukamto trying to control unwieldy fingers long enough to dial a number on his mobile phone. Leonard's mother convulsing on her knees, attempting to pray. Our cousin Marina crawling feebly toward one of the exits, sobbing with fear, the front of her evening gown drenched in vomit. The tiny bodies littered around the children's table, their nannies desperately trying to wake them up.

I remember turning to my grandfather's table and seeing the birthday boy lying limp in his chair. My stepgrandmother slumped in his lap, her powdered, chubby face crushed against his crotch.

That was when I lost myself in my own shaking and heaving. My cheek hit the ground. And there Estella lay as well, twitching, watching me, us watching each other. She reached for me, her arm creeping across the carpet so slowly it was difficult to tell it was moving at all. I tried to say something—what, I don't know—but it dribbled from the corner of my lips in a weak groan.

Then she mouthed something. I didn't understand. She mouthed it again: "Forgive me."

What for? I wondered, before slipping into oblivion.

Now I know.

And as I said, I do—forgive her, I mean. I love her too much to do otherwise. But I still want to know why she did it. It's only natural. I have little else to wonder about these days.

I didn't anticipate ending like this. Who would? I've always known I would die someday, ideally after seventy, but before the point where I'd have to hire a nurse to spoon-feed me chicken congee and then clean my gums with a wet rag. The grim possibility of dying young also crossed my mind from time to time: a car accident, a plane crash, a terminal illness. But this—this hovering in blackness, this stretch of in-between, alive and dead and neither—this I never dreamed possible. Yet here I am.

Perhaps it's just as well that I have so much time on my hands, even though I have no way of measuring its passing. And perhaps it's also right that I have no visitors and, hence, no distractions: Everyone who would have taken the trouble to look in on me regularly is dead. It's peaceful, though. A far cry from running Bagatelle, to be sure, but this way I can devote time to contemplating what Estella did, and coming to some understanding of it. In fact, the more I dwell on my circumstances, the more I realize the importance of the task before me—the task that only I am capable of carrying out. Who knew Estella more intimately than I? Who loved her more deeply? The answer to all this, if there is one, almost certainly lies with me. And call me crazy, but I'm positive it's crouching in plain sight, waiting to be recognized for what it is.

"THEY'VE PUT ME in charge of creating a photo slideshow for Opa's birthday dinner." The tone in which Estella delivered her announcement told me she wasn't particularly enthused.

"Photos from the past," she went on. "Opa as a boy. Opa as a teenager. Opa and Oma getting married. Opa and Oma and the kids. Significant events. Funny candid shots. That sort of thing."

I shrugged. "It's Opa's eightieth. Very auspicious. We have a few weeks to go. Might as well pull out all the stops."

"Did you say 'we'?" she asked with a smile.

I corrected myself. "You all. I'd help, but Bagatelle can't run itself."

"I know. I figured you'd be too busy. They know I don't have much to occupy me at Mutiara, so I don't have an excuse."

"You don't want to do it. That's a valid reason."

"Too late." She sighed. "Tante Margaret asked if I would, and I said yes. It's fine. I really shouldn't complain. It's not that big a deal. Maybe it'll be fun, digging through old photos and all that."

"What else are you helping out with? I thought Tante Margaret was supposed to be in charge of organizing the whole thing."

Tante Margaret wasn't the oldest of our grandparents' children, but that didn't stop her from being the bossiest. Estella laughed. "Yes, she's in charge, all right. She's delegated everything: mostly to me and the cousins, though Ma's pitching in too. Christina and Christopher are ordering the cake and party favors; Ma and I have arranged the venue and catering; Benedict, Jennifer, and Theresa are tackling the seating chart— Tante Margaret figured that three brains should be able to prevent social mismatches and hurt feelings. Marina's taken care of the invitations, as

I'm sure you've seen—engraved glass slabs in velvet boxes; what was she thinking? Even lazy Ricky's playing a part; Om Benny's agreed to fly him out from the US for the occasion. And now I'm supposed to see to entertainment. So far, it's the slideshow and an emcee. Maybe a singer or a band . . ."

Just listening to all this made me immensely bored. I stifled a yawn. "So send Tante Margaret a text message and tell her you've done enough."

"It's a bit more complicated than that. Apparently, Tante Betty really wanted to do the slideshow, but Tante Margaret was worried she'd make a mess of it like she does everything else. So to spare Tante Betty's feelings, she said that I had my heart set on it."

I rolled my eyes. "As the older generation, you'd think they'd be more mature."

"You know how it is with Tante Betty. She's been touchy about everything since Opa handed Om Benny the reins."

"The decision was made five years ago," I observed. "You'd think she'd make her peace with it."

Estella shrugged. "Frankly, I'm still not sure if she understands why Opa chose Om Benny and not her."

Our aunt may have been the eldest child, but her knack for screwing everything up had made our uncle—the capable eldest son—the most logical heir to Opa's throne. The choice had been a wise one. With Om Benny at the helm, Sulinado Group was doing better than ever. Our family conglomerate had bounced back with astonishing vigor from the monetary crisis that hit the country in late 1997. Synthetic textiles were what we were best known for, but our holdings in natural fabric manufacturing, agriculture, and natural resource extraction were now performing handsomely. Last year, we broke into *Forbes Asia*'s Top Sixty Richest Families in Indonesia list at number fifty-seven.

This was all in spite of Tante Betty. Her track record of failed projects was enough to make anyone's hair stand on end: the cotton plantation, the oil refinery disaster, the debacle with the meatpacking plant . . .

Our coffees arrived. "It's just a slideshow," murmured Estella, sipping her cappuccino with a frown. "What a ridiculous thing to lie about."

"What's the alternative?" I chuckled. "Telling Tante Betty the truth? Has honesty ever been our family's way?"

Ever so slightly, Estella's shoulders slumped. I always forgot: Our family's aversion to directness pained her more than it did me. As if to distract herself, she let her gaze drift to our surroundings, starting overhead with the high vaulted ceilings, their surfaces frescoed in blue sky, leafy branches, and yellow songbirds in midflight, and hung with chandeliers of rose crystal. From there, her eyes traveled down the walls—an honest vanilla hue—and across the pale parquet floor to the rest of the dining room: the ornately carved chairs upholstered in mossy velvet, the glass tables laid with cream-colored cloths and blue hydrangeas in squat crystal vases. There were barely any other diners. Prenoon brunches were a habit we'd picked up during our undergrad days in the US, and though the restaurant opened at 11 a.m. on weekends, few civilized members of our set ever ventured out before midday. I noticed Estella scanning for familiar faces nonetheless.

"No one we know," I said to save her the trouble, and she breathed an infinitesimal sigh of relief. Estella was so conscious of familial responsibilities and social protocol, she found it difficult to relax completely around anyone of our acquaintance.

"The renovations look good," she murmured, bringing her attention back to where we were sitting, by the floor-to-ceiling windows overlooking the iconic Hotel Indonesia roundabout outside. "Elegant. Tasteful. Not like before."

I pretended to be astonished. "What, you didn't like it? The purple leather? The Versace-print carpet? What's wrong with a bit of Vegas charm?"

Estella chuckled, which made me happy. I liked to see her laugh. "I don't know what Eva was thinking," she said. "And now she's wasted eight months on redecorating, poor thing. Not to mention the money all this must have cost."

"No one asked her to start her own business. She should have gotten it right the first time."

"Not everyone's as shrewd as you, Doll."

"They should be. What's the point of being Chinese in this country if you don't live up to the stereotypes?"

Another snicker from Estella. I was on a roll.

I did have some sympathy for Eva, and not just because she was a former high school classmate and our cousin Christopher's ex-girlfriend. The interior decorator had initially quoted her three months and half the price. Eight months was a long time to be closed—especially when you were paying sky-high rent for prime glass-front property. The privilege of looking down one's nose at the dementedly happy bronze boy and girl atop the Welcome Monument didn't come cheap. But the restaurant scene in Jakarta was so cutthroat that Eva couldn't have afforded *not* to renovate Eva's. (Yes, the restaurant was named after her—not that anyone was surprised.) The past few years had seen the luxury dining scene flare up like a rash, spreading through the capital at an alarming rate. Designer burger bars, edgy coffeehouses, and nouveau-style dumpling spots had popped up all over, not to mention chic restaurants specializing in street-vendor fare sans poor sanitation and at ten times the price. All were impeccably designed; all were staffed to the hilt with young, well-mannered, well-groomed waiters and waitresses; and all, to a certain extent, were interchangeable. Owning a restaurant was an expensive headache; to break even, you really had to stand out, keep it fresh, change the menu, change the chef, make the credit card discounts attractive, sponsor events, replace the décor and the furnishings at the slightest hint of wear or tear. Hence, the recent renovation of Eva's. But any period of closure beyond four months was too long. Customers were like goats. They wandered off to graze elsewhere and forgot you ever existed. Eva's face-lift had done wonders, but was it enough to make up for lost time?

I doubted it.

"Enough about the family. And Eva," said Estella just as the waiter arrived with our lobster eggs Benedict. "Tell me what's new with Bagatelle."

"Not much since we met last Sunday."

"Don't be modest. There must be something exciting happening. Always is, isn't there?"

I couldn't help but beam. She was right. Bagatelle constantly had something new going on. It was part of the joy of starting one's own business, and Estella's eagerness for updates over our weekly brunch tête-à-têtes never failed to gratify me, especially since the rest of our family tried to pretend Bagatelle didn't exist.

I told her about the progress our scientists had made on the newest version of our serum—a minor breakthrough, but a step forward nonetheless. And I described our two most promising ideas for next year's autumn/winter lines. She listened as she did every Sunday—intently, brow furrowed, staring straight ahead, chewing and swallowing with relish as if my words heightened the pleasure of eating.

"Marvelous," she murmured when she had exhausted my store of news. "I'm so proud of you, Doll. Bagatelle's doing remarkable things."

"What's new with Mutiara?" I asked in return, a split second too late. I must have looked sheepish because she flashed me a reassuring smile.

"It's okay, Doll. We both know nothing much happens there."

True. The family had never intended for it to be an exciting holding. In fact, they'd never had any real ambitions for it at all. Sulinado Group had acquired it almost incidentally in early 1998, in the middle of the monetary crisis, when we should have been lying low like everybody else. Things were bleak across Asia, but in Indonesia, they were especially grim: The rupiah plummeted, and massive loan defaults tore the economy to shreds; the extended bloodbath on the Jakarta Stock Exchange was eventually followed by an actual bloodbath in May. Demonstrations were held; protesters were shot. Jakarta's Chinatown was set ablaze, and Suharto finally stepped down.

Acquiring in that climate seemed like madness, so in hindsight it was clear why Opa was insistent. No one in the family had realized the extent of his condition. No one knew he had a condition at all. We mistook it for the same despotic obstinacy that had been his hallmark trait for as long as any of us could remember. And so, while all the other Chinese tycoon families tucked in their feelers and withdrew into their shells, Om Benny, acting on Opa's orders, negotiated the purchase of the small silk-manufacturing company. Price wasn't an issue: The Halim family was desperate to sell. Rumors raged nonetheless: How could Sulinado Group afford to acquire at a time like this? Everyone else was eyebrow-deep in foreign loans they couldn't afford to pay off. What debts were we failing to service? What hidden offshore assets were we utilizing?

As it turned out, even in the early stages of Alzheimer's, Opa proved cleverer than all of us. When the worst was over and the ruins had stopped smoldering; when chaos retreated back into the dark crannies where it could be ignored; when the president had been replaced, and replaced, and replaced yet again; when Indonesia's economy began to stabilize and business recommenced in earnest, Mutiara lived up to its name. A pearl. Insignificant in size, yes, but with strong fundamentals and a consistently decent profit margin. It had a secret patented formula for weaving silk thread of varying thicknesses, producing an exceptionally durable yet very fine weave. More importantly, under the Halims' control, it had somehow acquired a contract with the federal government to supply silk fabric for all state and tourism bureau needs. Still more importantly, the contract had, by some miracle, retained its validity through each change in administration.

Mutiara practically ran itself. And this had made it a perfect company for Estella to run upon her reentry into our family's activities. Conveniently, the distant middle-aged relative we'd commissioned to oversee Mutiara had died suddenly of hemorrhagic dengue fever. It was the ideal situation for Estella, our mother reasoned to the rest of the clan. It would ease her into the business world without presenting her with any real difficulties. It was self-contained and uncomplicated in its operations. It was perfect.

But also boring. And if the arrangement had been an ideal one at first, especially given the tragedy of Leonard's death a year and a half into her appointment (what other business would have plodded indifferently along despite months of neglect?), it was plain to see that Estella could do with more of a challenge.

More specifically, it was plain that Estella should be running Bagatelle with me. The glimmer in her eyes whenever I caught her up on company affairs, the flush of pride in her cheeks when I related its accomplishments—could anything have been more obvious? And yet here was the strange thing: No matter how many times I urged her to join me, she always refused.

"I'd only hold you back," she'd say.

"No, you wouldn't," I'd insist.

"I mean it. If I come on board, I'll ruin everything. You need complete freedom."

"What the hell are you talking about? Come on, it'll do you good."

The debate and variations thereof would always end there, with her insisting that her noninvolvement was in Bagatelle's best interest. She was happiest admiring my triumphs and living vicariously through my success.

"Anyway," she would add, "I'm not like you. Never have been."

This was a lie. She was once. Before marriage. But it was impossible to change her mind.

Eventually, I stopped asking. I had my pride too. Bagatelle and Mutiara. They said so much about the different paths we had taken, even if we'd started out joined at the hip. Mine wound through a dark wood and up a solitary peak. Hers kept her confined to a garden maze walled by high hedges.

We'd just finished eating when the mobile phone at Estella's elbow shivered. It was Tante Margaret. She was en route to Opa's house and wanted to know if Estella could meet her there—so my sister could pick up the photos for the slideshow herself and save Tante Margaret the trouble of sending them later.

"That's fine. See you soon," said Estella, hanging up.

"Why do you always do that?" I asked.

"Do what?"

"They tell you to jump and you ask how high."

"It's called being accommodating."

"Yeah, I know." I shot her a mischievous grin. "I'm not into that. Not anymore."

"True. You're so unfilial these days, it's positively unnatural." She grinned back and shook her head. "It's probably for the best."

"It is. It keeps me from going crazy. You, on the other hand, they're driving completely mad."

She rolled her eyes. "Don't exaggerate."

"Well, you *should* set some boundaries."

"A bit late for that now," she retorted, a twang of bitterness in her voice.

I placed my hand over hers. "It's not, you know. You've oriented yourself around family your whole life—us, Leonard, your in-laws. You're only thirty-three. It's not over yet.

"Join me at Bagatelle," I almost said, pulling back in the nick of time. She'd rebuffed me already, too many times to count.

"I know, I know," she said with a sigh. "But it's not easy to break away."

"I don't see why."

"And that's a good thing." Then, in response to my puzzled look: "You not seeing, I mean. I think I have the opposite problem, Doll. I see too much. How things could be, you know? How things once were, how they might be again. It makes it hard to detach . . ."

I had no idea what she was talking about, but I made a decision. "I'm coming with you to Opa's," I declared.

"You don't need to. I'm sure you have a lot of work to do."

She was right. Two leaning towers of Bagatelle-related documents were waiting for me back at my apartment.

"It's no trouble at all," I said with a wave of my hand.

This was part of our routine, the dynamic we had settled into in recent years: Estella playing the protective sister, and me mirroring a similar protectiveness back at her, staying by her side in an effort to pry her from the family's clutches. Consequently, I visited my parents and attended family gatherings far more than I would have otherwise. I wanted to remind her by my presence that she didn't have to let others run her life.

"Well, if that's what you really want," she said. Her fingers hovered over her phone. "My car or yours? Or should we go separately?"

"We'll go in your car," I said. "I'll tell my driver to meet us there."

OPA'S HOUSE BOTH was and was not Opa's house anymore. The home we remembered from our childhood had been capacious and cluttered— an abundance of high-ceilinged space portioned into an endless series of rooms and alcoves and passages, diminished only by the innumerable objects they housed. Our late grandmother had loved material possessions, innocently, as only a rich merchant's daughter could.

When Oma was still alive, she would tell us grandchildren about exploring her father's shipping warehouses as a little girl. Her father hadn't seen the point of schooling his daughters, but he was generous with allowing them freedom when they were out of the house. As a child, she would spend whole days at the wharf, wandering amid piles of tobacco-leaf bundles and burlap sacks filled with coffee beans, sugar, and nutmeg. She would drape chains of tiny freshwater pearls around her neck and admire her reflection in propped-up panes of polished granite. She would press her cheeks against the cool of jade carvings and bury her face in folds of bright silk. Then, woozy from sniffing bottles of sandalwood oil and worn out from clambering up and down the rice-wine barrels stacked in pyramids, she would doze off. The laborers would find her atop an open flat of down pillows or curled up in a nest of packing straw. They would carefully convey her back to their boss's office, her head resting against their bony brown shoulders.

"Feelings, ideas, philosophies—they're reliable as the wind," Oma would tell us grandchildren as she sat with us in the garden or as she pottered around the kitchen, baking cakes. These were her father's wise words. She'd repeat them tenderly to us while tucking flowers behind our ears or depositing blobs of batter on our outstretched fingers and tongues. "Gold, on the other hand, and land. A roof over your head and food on the table. They keep you and your loved ones healthy and alive."

Her father was right. It was material wealth that ensured his survival and that of his family during the Japanese Occupation, and afterward too, during the tumultuous years of the country's struggle for independence from the Dutch. She recounted how her father had to draw often on those deep pockets of his: to purchase mercy from authorities, hoodlums, and anti-Chinese mobs; to keep beatings and insults to a minimum; to request that the plundering remain civilized and destruction restrained.

Having made it to adulthood on the strength of worldly goods, Oma lavished her possessions with affectionate gratitude. Although I can only speculate, perhaps it was why she didn't object to her father orchestrating her marriage to Opa, who was then an industrious but penniless clerk in her father's employ—an ambitious individual whose extraordinary shrewdness Oma's father trusted to put his daughter's inheritance to good use in order to provide for her and any offspring. I could imagine all too well young Oma marrying young Opa on compassionate grounds: How terrible for a promising young man to be poor, she must have thought. If she could furnish him with the means to achieve worldly success, then why shouldn't they be happy together?

I don't know what Oma's taste in furnishings was like when she was younger, but the Oma of our childhood had a weakness for the heavy, ornate, and downright garish. Giving such objects space in her house was her version of doing good, like adopting stray animals. "I never saw anything like it," she would say of each new acquisition once it had been delivered and unpacked. "It seemed a pity not to bring it home."

Every room was furnished in dark mahoganies and teaks. Tables and chairs lurked everywhere; in the obvious places, of course—the dining room and the kitchen, the sitting room and the veranda—but also in corridors, like guests at an overcrowded party, and behind doors as if waiting to pounce. Less prolific, but still numerous, were the glass-paned cabinets and squat sideboards, covered in reliefs and edged with flourishes and spires. Bureaus and dressers of all sizes dominated the bedrooms, their drawers either bulging with rarely used bed linens and batiks, or practically empty save for random objects kept solely because there was no reason to throw them away—marbles, rubber bands, playing cards, screws.

The ornamental items were ten times as overwhelming, unable to hide behind any ostensibly practical purpose. Dark, ponderous paintings of stormy mountain ranges, brooding forests, and thundering horse herds—all framed in intricate gilt—covered every wall, interspersed with enormous Balinese friezes depicting ceremonial processions and battles. Sculptures in marble, wood, resin, jade, and stone, ranging from the size of bowling balls to the size of full-grown men, occupied whatever free space remained. Chinese lions, horses, and ingots; moonfaced Buddhas and serene Mother Marys; locally made replicas of famous classical and Renaissance art modified for modesty's sake—Michelangelo's David in a fig leaf and Venus de Milo in a toga with arms added. And there was the favorite of us grandchildren: a wooden statue of a smiling old man about half a meter tall with an enormous bulging head and a long trailing beard. In one hand he carried a knobbly walking stick, in the other a plump peach.

"He's the god of long life," Oma would tell us. "The peach represents immortality." We were technically Christian, Oma's father having converted from Buddhism in his youth. Still, Oma would insist, "We Chinese believe in him," whenever we would ask, which was often because, like all children, we enjoyed hearing stories again and again.

"We Chinese . . ." The phrase betrayed both solidarity and distance: a faint but steady sense of kinship with an ancestral land and people whose customs and philosophies danced through our lives like shadows, rustled our daily and annual routines like delicate gusts of wind.

We grandchildren pretended we had an ancestor who looked like the statue, and developed a custom of rubbing the statue's bald head when we passed by—our childish way of honoring his memory and ensuring our own longevity. By the time Estella and I had reached our teens, the bulbous head had been burnished black by the oils from all our hot, eager palms.

The statue was gone now, along with Oma's other possessions: sold off or donated to charities and less well-to-do relations in order to make room for Opa's second wife. "New Oma," Estella and I called her. The renovation and redecoration of the old house constituted the one and only request she ever made. We resented her presumption at the time—Oma's body was barely cold in the ground—but in hindsight, I suppose we couldn't blame her. What bride, however docile in temperament, would want to spend the rest of her elderly husband's life languishing among the bric-a-brac of her deceased predecessor? And so, as a marriage present, Opa had graciously consented to the complete remodeling of his home.

It was almost cruel how the house so conspicuously symbolized everything wrong with this latest, final stage of his life. Gone was the clutter, the richness, of the old days, the old wife, even the old memories. New Oma liked "modern" things, and was also a fervent believer in something she called "minimalism"—something she picked up at the questionable interior design school Opa had paid for her to attend when she was only his mistress, when Oma proper had still been alive, and when none of us had the faintest idea of her existence. We only found out what exactly these aesthetic creeds meant after she had applied them to the house. Furniture could only be black, white, gray, or fire engine red, and had to be fitted with rods of metal. A work of art couldn't depict anything recognizable, or use more than three colors.

Our footsteps echoed as we followed Tati, one of the maids, through the cavernous foyer and formal sitting room. I had the sensation of passing through a white void populated by drifting blocks of solid color, now a prismatic umbrella stand, now a shoe cupboard disguised as a concrete block, now a side table of barbed wire and an ottoman perched on scarlet high heels. They forced the mind to hallucinate in order to stay sane.

As we crossed the larger of the two dining rooms and passed the table— all angles and glass and chrome—I couldn't help but see in its place the enormous wooden oblong slab of the old days, draped in indigo-and-white batik, and laid end to end with platters of meats and vegetables and assorted fritters, basins of steaming broths and curries and stews, tiny bowls of sauces and pickles and paste, and, on a stool of its own near Oma's seat, the gargantuan rice cooker from which she served each of us in turn.

Tati showed us into Opa's television room. He was slumped on a gray felt sofa, the transparent base of which made it look like it was hovering in midair. His eyes gazed blankly at the flat screen mounted on a wall. Tante Margaret was sitting next to him. Much to our amusement, they were watching a cooking show. Estella and I kissed him and Tante Margaret in turn, our aunt doing an admirable job of emitting disdain even as she submitted to the light peck I bestowed millimeters away from the surface of her cheek.

"How are you, Opa?" asked Estella, more for the sake of form than to elicit an actual response.

"Learning how to make croquettes?" I asked faux innocently, pointing to the screen.

The good thing about his condition was that we could be more relaxed around him—irreverent, even. In the old days, my wisecrack would have earned me a slap across the face. Now my only punishment was a sharp nudge from my sister. Opa blinked several times and turned slowly toward us, as if awaking from a nap. How shrunken he was now, this stern giant of our youth. How diminished, even if amid the sagging ruins one could still make out the hard lines. He grimaced, either at the show, my joke, our sudden presence, or all three.

"Margaret. *She* put this on," he declared accusingly.

"Stimulates the brain, Ba," said Tante Margaret in a slow, loud voice, as if he had trouble hearing. "Television's good for you."

I could have sworn the opposite was true, but I held my tongue.

"Why are you here?" Opa asked.

"I'm helping Tante Margaret put together a surprise for your birthday party." Estella tilted her head in the direction of our aunt.

Even as Opa nodded, he lost interest, turning toward the images on the television screen, letting his gaze go vacuous the second he laid eyes on them.

New Oma entered the room to greet us, the simpering smile on her face ill-suited to a woman of fifty-three. Deferential to the point of obsequiousness, she was never the materialistic slut our family had made her out to be when Opa first brought her home, mere months after Oma's death. Her status as Opa's secret concubine of twenty years constituted the only lapse in her virtue. She hadn't even been cunning enough to lay claim to Opa's wealth by bearing him any kids.

When Opa introduced New Oma to the family, all his children snubbed her, and we followed their example—as much as we were able to without incurring Opa's wrath. But she was of humble stock—a family of Chinese shopkeepers living in Medan—and so obviously intimidated by us that we found it hard to stay hostile for long. We settled on treating her as inconsequential. And she wisely continued to adopt a submissive manner around us, always averting her eyes and hardly saying a word. Admittedly, she was a good wife to Opa in those last days, though really she was more of a patient and devoted nurse.

She kissed us on our cheeks—weak, clammy smacks—folded her hands in front of her, and lowered her head. "Tati's bringing out some snacks. Would you like some coffee or tea?"

When the refreshments made their appearance, New Oma retreated to the corner and sat mute in an especially uncomfortable-looking chair with wire arms and a plexiglass back. We sat sipping coffee, nibbling at slices of tapioca cake, and chatting—mostly with Tante Margaret about various safe topics: the logistics of Opa's birthday party, gossip about families we knew, and fine dining. Even if my conversational contributions occasionally did tip toward the sarcastic, my sister did a consummate job of glossing over them and gliding us along. From time to time, Tante Margaret would dutifully try to involve Opa, who would either ignore her entirely or respond by closing his eyes.

Our aunt was looking as glamorous as ever. She was wearing a Pucci-print dress, and her hair was coiffed into a lion's mane. You'd never have guessed in a million years that she was fifty-one. With her eyes rimmed in black liner, she looked almost like a Chinese Sophia Loren, which was perhaps what she was going for, since her current husband, Salvatore (her third), was an Italian count. How they'd met, we weren't quite sure; the exact details surrounding this latest marriage were rather hazy, as were the details of her previous marriage, and her first marriage, and the divorces that had followed each one.

She certainly had a type: minor aristocrats from Europe, which wasn't that surprising when one considered how much time she spent there liaising with Sulinado Group's partners in textiles and agribusiness. The husbands were interchangeable: gray at the temples and blue in the eyes, with good looks, good manners, and expensive hobbies like polo playing and collecting seventeenth-century French cravats. I'm sure our aunt's good looks had played a role in attracting them, but her more material charms had made them especially eager to tie the knot. Poor things. The wedding vows never benefitted them as much as they'd hoped. Our aunt was far too smart not to insist on ironclad prenuptial agreements.

Tante Margaret had just started ranting about the impossibility of finding "real" cheese in Jakarta when, out of nowhere, she asked, "And how are you doing these days, Stell? Is everything okay?"

The abrupt shift startled both my sister and me. On the surface, our aunt's tone was earnest, as were her blinking eyes. The veneer of genuine concern irritated me nonetheless. As if Tante Margaret actually wanted to know. As if any of the family did. As if anyone desired an answer other than "Don't worry, I'm fine."

But as usual, Estella obliged. "Don't worry, I'm fine," she said.

I opened my mouth to say something, but Estella diverted the conversation back to the city's dearth of Roquefort suppliers.

Opa eventually nodded off to sleep, and on Tante Margaret's signal, New Oma rose and led us upstairs into a suite of empty bedrooms. They were meant for relatives or guests who wished to spend the night. No one ever did.

This corner of the house functioned as a storage area for what remained of Oma's personal possessions—the clothes, magazines, toiletries, and assorted other items that no one could be bothered to sort through after her death. They had been tossed indiscriminately into cardboard boxes, sealed with tape, and left to gather dust. New Oma led us now to a sort of oversized dressing room, judging by the built-in closets and its adjacency to a bathroom. Green curtains of rough silk framed the window on the wall to our left, and against the wall to our right were Oma's boxes, stacked in columns two meters high. In the center of the room stood an enormous lacquered armoire, decorated with peonies of gold and white. I was pleased to discover it had survived the cull; I remembered it from childhood, when it had lived in our grandparents' bedroom. After dinner, Oma would open the armoire doors wide, flop back in the armchair by the bed, and turn us loose. Spreading open brocade-bound albums and scattering unhoused photos over the plush Oriental carpet, we would assemble the jigsaw puzzle of our family's past.

"When was this, Oma? Who was this, Oma?" we would ask, our questions clamorous and insistent. Oma's laughter came in merry peals like a bell, jingly and high and sweet as a grandmother's should be.

"Let me see it," she would say. We would carry the photo in question to her and climb into her lap to nestle in the billowy folds of her batik house-dress and the soft, squishy body beneath; to inhale the rose-scented soap and talcum powder that evoked cakes and cleanliness and safety. Gently, she would take the photo from us and squint. Then the story would come: sometimes long, sometimes short, depending on the photo and the vivid-ness of her memory. At first, we would bring her photos we'd never asked about before, but after satisfying our desire for novelty, we would fall back on our favorites—the ones we had brought to her innumerable times be-fore and would bring to her innumerable times again so that we could hear from her the stories we loved best.

"Ah," she would sigh, when Tante Betty's oldest, Christopher, brought her the black-and-white portrait of Oma's family. "This is such an old one! That's me, still a girl. That's my father and mother—your great-grandfather and great-grandmother. Those are my brothers, your great-uncles. And my sisters, your great-aunts. I was . . . fourteen, fifteen? It was before I met your opa."

"What about this one, Oma?" Jennifer, Om Benny's second child, would ask. She favored the faded group shot of our youthful parents at a beach. You could glimpse the sea in the gaps between their heads—that is, if you weren't too distracted by Om Peter's sideburns.

"Oh, this one!" Oma would exclaim, pulling Jennifer toward her. "It was taken in Amsterdam. Your father had just started attending university there."

Oma's index finger traced our parents' faces from left to right, starting with the squarish young man in tiny swim briefs and ending with the stun-ning wavy-haired woman in a floral one-piece. "Benny, Peter, Betty, Mar-garet, Sandra, and Sarah. Oh, that was a beautiful day. We even brought a picnic lunch. See?" She pointed to the large cooler in the far-left corner. "But do you know what happened?"

"What happened? What happened?" we would chorus on cue.

"We spread out mats and laid out all the food. There were three roast chickens. And boiled eggs. And fresh bread to make sandwiches. And *acar*. And sliced ham. And butter cake for dessert. Yes, we spread it all out and were about to eat. And then? Whoosh! A seagull came and took a piece of cake!"

We broke into wild laughter and made whooshing sounds ourselves.

"And then?" she would continue. "Whoosh! Another seagull took some bread!"

"Whoosh! Whoosh!" we cried excitedly in between shrieks and hiccups.

"And whoosh! They kept attacking us and all us girls ran away. And the boys and your opa tried to fight them off. Your opa got so mad he threw a whole roast chicken at a seagull and smacked it in the face."

At this climactic moment, we practically collapsed into hysterics, our cheeks aching and our sides bursting. Ricky would pretend to be a seagull and Benedict would pretend to whack him in the face with a roast chicken and everyone would cackle in delight. Once our laughter had subsided, we would all congregate around the photo again, seeing in our parents' static faces the full extent of the comedy about to unfold.

The most beloved photos were of the whole family or the very old ones of Opa and Oma. The second most beloved photos were of our own parents, followed by ones of Tante Sandra, our youngest aunt, who in life had behaved more like a big sister to us than a grown-up. She died in her early twenties when I was around nine or ten. The least popular photos were of Om Peter, who taught us all how to play poker but rarely spoke to us otherwise. We didn't know back then that he wasn't Oma and Opa's biological child—that Opa's sister, already the mother of eight others, had begged her brother to take him and raise him as his own. There was a lot we didn't know back then. Even more than we didn't know later.

Estella's favorite photo was one from our parents' wedding: Ma wearing a form-fitting velvet gown of sky blue studded with sparkly stones, Ba in a white tuxedo with a black bow tie, our parents dancing together.

"We bought the dress in Paris," Oma would tell Estella. "It was our last day there and we'd already bought the wedding gown, but we couldn't find anything nice for the evening reception. We saw this one at last, in the window of a small shop, just off the main boulevard. It fit your mother perfectly."

I remember the photo even now: our mother, her hair styled in ringlets swept into a loose updo, her dainty face porcelain in its perfection, smiling up at our father, whose expression is barely visible from the angle at which the photo was shot. But we could see that he too was smiling—a happier and slimmer version of the father we knew back when we sat at our oma's feet, and decades later on that Sunday afternoon at Opa's house, as we watched New Oma stand in front of the armoire and fling open its doors. I wondered if New Oma had ever looked through all the photos— the documentation of our family's history before Opa had tacked her on as a postscript. If she had, it must have been overwhelming: like a child learning for the first time about the size of the world's population and the depths of its history, an accumulation of countless individuals and countless years towering over her like a tidal wave, ready to sweep her away.

"So many!" New Oma cried. "I'll tell Tati to get some bags." She pulled an album from its slot, sending the shelf's contents sliding to the floor in a series of loud, echoing thuds. The lid of an old shoebox fell off, scattering photos in a fan around our feet.

New Oma, Tante Margaret, and Estella crouched down to pick them up. I was about to do the same when Estella spoke.

"Doll, you should get going. You have a lot to do. I'll manage from here."

"Are you sure?"

She nodded and resumed shuffling the photos together into a neat stack.

Secretly relieved, I promptly said my good-byes and left. Tante Margaret and New Oma barely looked up, but I didn't care.

On the way home, my driver inching the car through the molasses of Jakarta traffic, I found myself haunted by the image of my sister kneeling amid the photographs, gathering up scattered fragments of the past, eyes fixed on false evidence of an idyllic family life that never actually was. It was a foreshadowing of the events that would follow soon after, with one difference: Instead of shooing me away, she would insist I accompany her on her mission, her quest—whatever you wanted to call it. And despite my better judgment, I didn't refuse her. I never could.

WHEN I FOUNDED Bagatelle, I knew full well it would affect my relationship with the family. That's partly why I started it. The events I've recounted so far—that brunch with Estella and our visit to Opa's house—paint a certain portrait of me as independent, aloof, and strong; an individualist, cunning and bold. But I wasn't always this way. It took me a long time to find myself.

For the first part of my life it didn't occur to me to try. Estella and I were so close. We did everything together, even though she was slightly older. Individualism was made even more impossible by the tightly knit family environment in which we were raised—the dinner gatherings at Opa and Oma's house at least twice a week; the get-togethers on weekends; the birthday, anniversary, and holiday celebrations; my mother and her siblings mixing in the same social circles, us cousins attending the same schools. Thinking of one's self in isolation from everyone else was very difficult to do. "I" wasn't a forbidden concept—I just never gave it much thought.

Only when Estella began dating Leonard did it become apparent how much I'd failed to cultivate an identity of my own, which is why, I think, their marriage crushed me so. For the first two and a half years after their wedding, I was reduced to being a phantom limb, sawed off from the source of my animation. I managed to finish my last year at Berkeley—what would have been *our* last year if circumstances had been otherwise. Then I came home to Jakarta and moved back in with my parents. I worked for the family as a director at PolyWangi, Sulinado Group's synthetic textiles mainstay. Now that I think more about it, I must have been severely depressed, but no one else seemed to notice, so it escaped my attention too.

My recollections of that period are hazy: I went to the office every day, ate at regular intervals, slept for long stretches at a time. I don't remember what I did on weekends. I was a shadow of my future self.

Being kept out of my sister's life by my brother-in-law (how he loathed me!) meant not really having a life of my own at all, at least not until that fateful and glorious trip when she and I ran away together to see the monarchs overwintering in Monterey County. It was then that I at last began to stir. The core idea of Bagatelle came up during the drive—as a joke. It bypassed my sister, but clung to me, like a windborne dandelion seed snagging on a twig. It fell to earth. It grew. And on its strength, so did I.

The monetary crisis struck the very next year, and I had enough sense not to act until the worst of the disaster had passed—a period of about four years. It helped that Leonard's decline occurred around the same time. His weakening hold over Estella, over everything, meant that she and I could again spend time together, even if it was never to the same extent as when we were younger. And it was Estella who kept nudging me to realize my ambitions. I'd never had any before, and though she refused to get roped in, her enthusiasm fanned Bagatelle—and me—into flame. Gradually, the outlines of Bagatelle took more definite shape, until at last I was ready to approach the family about it.

A lot of coaxing was required to get the family to provide the start-up capital. It wasn't that they were against me building my own business. God, no—that was the stuff Chinese tycoon families were made of. Rather, they took issue with the project's extreme impracticality. It was defiant of odds, reeking of overcreativity and amateur DIY spirit. It exhibited all the telltale symptoms of a shortsighted entrepreneurship that our upbringing had taught us to avoid, if not despise. "The heart is stupid. Don't follow it." That was what Opa used to say all the time before he deteriorated.

Despite their suspicions, the family decided Bagatelle would be a good learning experience for me. Om Benny, in particular, approved of the way

I was carrying out my duties at PolyWangi. Once Om Benny gave his consent, the other siblings went along with it. But you can imagine their fury when, once it became clear that Bagatelle was going to be a runaway success, I refused to link it up with the family conglomerate.

Once upon a time, their displeasure would have rattled me. But since my trip to Monterey with Estella, I'd grown thicker skin. I shrugged off Ma's wrath. The same with Om Benny, whom I informed of my decision via email. He sent a reply and it wasn't a nice one. They took issue mainly on principle—because I withheld from the communal pot, so to speak. (You'd think we were all still fresh off the boat from China, crammed in a single compound, banding together for survival.)

Word must have spread from there. Everyone except Estella settled for ignoring Bagatelle—my aunts and uncles out of indignation, and my father and cousins because of the awkwardness generated by their censure. But none of them cut me off cold or anything. Family is family, after all. As long as the same blood flowed through my veins, I was irrevocably one of their own. And who knows? Perhaps they unconsciously respected my audacity in forging ahead with an endeavor that wasn't just harebrained, but downright weird.

"Insect." The word should have wider appeal than it actually does. It's barely removed from "incense"—that sickly sweet fragrance of the spirit realm. Its near homonym "incest" has unsavory connotations, and possesses an aura of taboo. The word's plural form even sounds like "sex." And yet it remains a profoundly unsexy word. Think "insects" and a Pandora's box of ugliness opens. Disease and pestilence. Mandibles, feelers, stingers. Compound eyes. You imagine their cold multilegged bodies creepy-crawling all over you, gnawing at you or piercing your skin, dripping whatever fluids they excrete. And you shudder. That's why Bagatelle could have nothing to do with insects.

I forbade the utterance of the word in conjunction with our projects.

Anyone who said it more than twice, accidentally or otherwise, was immediately dismissed. Even scientific names—*Danaus plexippus*, *Hymenopus coronatus*, *Trypoxylus dichotomus*—were off-limit utterances unless you were one of our scientists. For Bagatelle to work, it couldn't be about changing minds. We couldn't say: "Look at these disgusting creatures. They're not so bad. Actually, they're sort of charming!" We had to transform the playing field completely, move the prospective customer into an entirely different space. "I am going to show you an exquisite object you have never seen before," we had to tell them, before stepping back and letting our product speak for itself. We weren't revolutionizing the way people saw insects. Rather, we were introducing them for the first time to the wonder of the bagatelle.

"Bagatelle": a French word. A short, sweet piece of music. Also the name of a kind of game. But more generally, something pleasant and trifling. A pretty bauble or trinket. An elegant brooch, say. A string of iridescent jewels to be worn in the hair. Fiery earrings filigreed in delicate gold-and-black filament. Imagine all of them trembling with vitality, radiating life from every joint. These were our bagatelles.

I still recall the debut of our first, our signature line—Majesty—during Paris Fashion Week. Majesty was all about bold brilliance and soft folds— the tropical jungle paired with the English countryside. And, by happy chance, it complemented Prada's autumn/winter line to a T. Miuccia graciously offered to share the runway with us, and the first bagatelles sailed forth into the world, perched atop felt fascinators and braided coils of hair, encircling tiny tartan-girded waists and breasts, adorning wrists, fingers, earlobes. The climax was superb: a pale girl with wild red hair wearing a plum-colored huntress-style ball gown. And draped around her collarbones and down her back in a jaunty yet stately half-cape was Bagatelle's most magnificent piece: a feathery necklace of burnt amber and shimmering blue punctuated with doe spots of black and white. Just when the eye had thought the feast was over, the majesties took flight, sailing up into the air and fluttering back down into their original position like a piece of fabric rippling in the wind. The applause lasted for ten minutes straight.

It was exhilarating. Too exhilarating. Caught up in the whirlwind of victory, I forgot entirely about checking in on my newly widowed sister. Despite the fact that Leonard had died only a few days before I left for Paris, I didn't call, not even once. I returned to Jakarta, assuming vaguely that her health would have improved while I was abroad. If anything, it had worsened. All her flesh had melted away. When we were young, she used to joke that she didn't have cheekbones—now they jutted from the sides of her face like the gill plates of a fish. Her hair was falling out in clumps. Her skin was so translucent you could make out every capillary. She never left her room; she hardly stirred from bed. Worst of all, an ominous serenity had settled upon her, suggesting she was on the cusp of migrating from this world to the next.

What had I been thinking, ceasing communication so entirely like that, at a time when my sister needed me the most? I'm embarrassed to admit it, but I really don't know. The only excuse I can give for my lapse is that the freedom must have gone to my head, and, intoxicated by it, I had ungratefully forgotten the person to whom I owed it. Riddled with guilt, I visited her as often as possible after I returned from Paris. Whatever time I had to spare, it was hers. We would sit together in her room and chat; she propped up on pillows in bed, I in the mauve armchair by her side. She refused to talk at any length about the tragedy that had befallen her. If storms did indeed roil inside her, on the surface she remained eerily quiescent. Whenever I dared to broach the subject of Leonard's death, she steered me away with a grace and tact that reminded me of a species of European gentleman I had come across lately in the world of high fashion—the sort who could guide a woman's movements with nothing more than his palm on the small of her back.

She insisted instead on discussing Bagatelle—and not just the splash we'd made in Paris. Her interest extended to everything: How were sales going? What other cities would we open in? What improvements had our chemists made to the control serum? What new concepts did I have in mind? Her eyes glittered with an otherworldly feverishness—the kind that blazes most brightly when set in a withered frame. I told her everything, from the most trivial minutiae concerning the day-to-day maintenance of the company and its boutiques, to the larger-than-life visions in my mind's eye that floated, like mirages, on the shimmering horizon of possibilities. I took on the role of storyteller, and she the eager child.

I explained that, if anything, the success of our Paris debut had put us under even more pressure to present a scintillating spring/summer line. Everyone would be waiting to see whether we could live up to our first collection. We already knew exactly where we were headed, of course. You'd have to be stupid to go to a war as big as this one without stocking up on ammunition. By the time the applause in Paris had ended, the relevant phone calls had already been made. When I'd stepped off the plane and into my office, prototypes were waiting on my desk.

On the one hand, our second line had to be completely different. We had to prove we weren't a one-trick pony. On the other hand, there had to be just enough that was similar to establish the foundation, the essence, of the Bagatelle brand. That was how the Houri line paraded into the world: voluptuous Old World sex kittens with sensuous protruding snouts, clad in iridescent blues and greens. Again, bagatelles, not insects. Majesties, not butterflies. Houris, not weevils.

Our quarterly profits went through the roof. Houris were playful, curvy, fun-sized. And like all harem girls, they were best enjoyed in numbers. People wore them in long, triple-looped chains around their necks. They stacked them on their fingers. They wound them from ankle to calf like ballet shoestrings. You had to buy at least two dozen if you wanted to bagatelle well. "That's right, Stell," I told her with some pride. "We've become a verb."

I told her that we were reasonably certain about our expansion plan as it stood, but still had some reservations. We were keeping it conservative. We'd started out in Paris, Hong Kong, and Jakarta—the first two to establish our credentials, the last because this was where our operations were based. The next few years would see boutique openings in the tried-and-true fashion capitals of the world—London, Milan, New York—along with the wealthier cities of Asia—Tokyo, Shanghai, Beijing, Seoul, maybe Singapore. In the next few years, we'd expand our offerings: women's clothing, leather goods, shoes, all designed for pairing or coordinating with specific bagatelles. After that, who knew? Homewares. Furniture. Carpets. A lower-end spin-off for the general public. A children's line. The sky was the limit.

I divulged everything to her. When Estella asked me how the bagatelle worked—a secret so closely guarded that it had been developed in stages, with no one knowing the entire sequence of the serum's recipe and application, or which chemist was working on other components of the sequence—even then, I told her what I knew.

"There are several species of fungi that prey on insects," I began, clasping my cup of green tea in both hands and letting the breath of my tale waft the rising steam across the rim. (The air-conditioning in Estella's bedroom made it feel like the interior of a fridge.) "Their tiny spores find their way into a host and there take root, multiplying, branching, spreading, but not killing right away. With ants, there's one species that works its way into the host's brain, driving its host to climb upward, higher and higher, and to clamp down on its new perch. Only then does the fungus put its victim out of its misery, bursting out of the ant's head to fruit new spores, which from their advantageous starting point can drift away on the wind, much farther than they would have ever been able to if they'd let their host die on the ground. The common name for these fungi is Cordyceps, though the term encompasses several genera."

Estella frowned. The word sounded familiar. I let her make the connection, which she did. "They sell Cordyceps in Chinese medicine stores. Ma takes it in the evenings."

"Yes, that particular variety is good for strengthening the kidneys and lungs," I affirmed. "But the fungi in their natural state are useless for Bagatelle's purposes. We've had to do a considerable amount of genetic modification using several different species."

I was no biochemist myself. But I'd picked up enough to know, roughly, how it all worked. And since I had access to all stages of the serum-manufacturing process, you could say I knew more than any of my scientists. I told her what changes we'd made to our version of the fungus to produce the exact kind of behaviors we wanted—either near immobility or certain movements in reaction to external stimuli (in the case of the climactic ending of our first show in Paris, fluttering up and down in response to a slight shrug of the shoulders). Most of our pieces were designed to be static, dormant except for a comely quivering of the body, or a flexing of the tarsi or mandibles to ensure they stayed put. But we were making new advances every day with regards to timing and precision, and who knew where we were headed next? I had plans for a collaboration with Chopard or Piaget—wrist-borne bagatelles that could tell the time with tiny diamond-encrusted twitches.

It went without saying that we had to modify the fungus so it never showed itself, never fruited, never destroyed. In fact, it did just the opposite of destroying, reducing a bagatelle's life to a state of almost complete dormancy. Each bagatelle was guaranteed to last for at least five years if given proper care. As I anticipated, our clientele didn't blink an eye. The finest of anything required care and maintenance: an Hermès leather bag, a Christian Lacroix gown, a Rolex, a Ferrari. A bagatelle didn't need much:

Each one came with a small ventilated case and a slim glass tube of odor-less, colorless nutritive mist to be spritzed on once a week. After five years, we permitted a trade-in for the same model or a newer one, provided the old one wasn't damaged.

The grace, the dignity, the humaneness of it all gave us the advantage when the inevitable protests from animal rights activists finally reared their head. This wasn't mistreatment; this was pampering. This wasn't destruction; we were caring for the bagatelles, improving their quality of life, prolonging their existences. Weren't there meatier bones to pick with real villains—the livestock industry, the furriers, the whalers? Except for a whisper in a few low-circulating magazines, the controversy never gar-nered any attention and removed itself to the furthest fringes of the collec-tive environmental activist consciousness.

The way I tell it, it sounds as if I were composed, cool, a true soldier even in the face of my sister's physical and emotional collapse. In reality, in the course of those months, I would find myself seized every now and then by feelings beyond my control. They reduced me to a blubbering mess. I implored Estella to get better, to fight whatever it was that was taking her away from the real world, from us, from the present. I begged her to revive herself and join me at Bagatelle, though she'd already said no too many times. Still, I found myself pleading, kneeling at her bedside: "Bagatelle is ours, Stell. I'm doing it for both of us."

She would only close her eyes and smile faintly. "I'm so proud of you, Doll. Please. Tell me more." It was like watching someone drown without struggling, sinking serenely to the bottom of the deep blue sea.

She did recover, obviously, and began to breathe the air of the world again, though she never quite lost that unearthly, melancholic quality. And much later, over a year after Leonard's passing, I learned that my efforts to revive her spirits hadn't been entirely in vain. In fact, she claimed that Bagatelle's success had played a huge part in bringing her back to life, at which I snorted.

"What are you talking about?" I asked. "You still won't leave the family business. You still won't join Bagatelle."

"I know," she said. "But hearing about what you've done with Bagatelle was, *is*, more than enough."

I snorted again and she gazed at me in earnest. "I'm serious. You have no idea what good I get from it. And anyway," she added after the briefest of pauses, "I think it's great that you've become so independent. You finally have a life of your own."

I continued to be perplexed about Estella's attitude toward Bagatelle—how obviously attracted she was to it, yet how adamantly she refused to come on board as my partner. But her words did confirm that my new way of life was far healthier than my old one. I was my own person now, separate from our family and no longer as dependent on her, even though I longed to bring her with me rather than leave her where she was. I was enjoying my autonomy, but I wanted to enjoy it all with her.

Only now do I realize that my desire to be with her was a weakness. It enabled Estella to pull me back in.

◆   ◆   ◆

It began with her discovery of the photo, a few days after our visit to Opa's house. I had just returned to my apartment after a long day at work and was sliding out of my heels when she called.

"Are you at home?"

"Just got back," I said. Cradling the mobile phone between my chin and shoulder, I handed my two office tote bags to the maid.

"Wow, it's almost eleven. Have you eaten?"

"My secretary ordered food in."

"What kind?"

"Oh, nothing fancy. Beef ball noodles. Deep-fried wontons. You know, working-class cuisine," I joked. I took the phone into my dressing room.

From the way she was beating around the bush, I sensed she had something important to say.

"Do you have time to talk?" she asked.

"Why, what's up?"

"It's just . . . I've been looking through the photos I brought back from Opa's place."

"And?" I unclasped the bracelet of houris from my wrist, detached them one by one, and placed them on the velvet-covered perches in their case.

"And . . . it's been more fun than I expected. Remember how much we loved going through the photos with Oma when we were little?"

"Did you find anything interesting?" I asked, prodding her toward her point.

"There's one of us next to our ant farm. We're wearing matching Minnie Mouse dresses."

"*And?*" I placed the last houri on its perch and closed the lid.

"And I found a photo that seems kind of . . . funny."

At last. I gave her another nudge. "That's what you called to tell me?" I asked, slipping off my Chanel suit jacket. "You found a funny photo?"

"No, I called to tell you that the photo has Tante Sandra in it."

"So?"

"It's a photo of her after she died."

There was no audience for it, but I arched a skeptical eyebrow nevertheless. "Well, then it can't be a photo of her after she died because she was alive when it was taken, wasn't she?"

"According to the date stamp in the bottom-right corner, it was taken in 1984."

"So?"

"Tante Sandra drowned in 1981."

At this I hesitated, but only briefly. "Date stamps can be wrong," I reasoned. "The camera was probably misprogrammed."

"Why don't you take a look for yourself?" she said, obviously irritated. "Are you coming to Gregory's birthday party tomorrow night?"

Gregory was our latest nephew. To celebrate his turning one, our cousin Marina and her husband, Yudi, were throwing a small celebration—just our family, his family, and our family friends the Sukamtos.

"I'll make a showing," I said. I knew that Estella drew a certain strength from my presence at these functions, even if she often encouraged me to avoid the clan as much as I could.

That night was different, though. I remember now how relieved she sounded to hear I'd be there.

"Wonderful," she said. "We'll talk more then."

EVERYONE SAID OUR cousin Marina was the perfect wife and mother, not so much because she was but because she expended terrific amounts of energy trying to be so. At twenty-two, she wed her high school sweetheart, Yudi Handoyo (of the real estate Handoyos). The next year, they welcomed their firstborn into the world—a girl—followed by a boy, then another girl, then, most recently, another boy. Never ambitious in the professional sense—unlike her mother, Tante Margaret—Marina threw herself wholeheartedly into housewifery, supervising a small fleet of nannies, attending classes on baking and flower arranging, and shopping constantly for homewares and clothes for Yudi and the kids.

Unfortunately, Marina's enthusiasm for domestic life was counterbalanced by the fact that she was bad at it. Sweet, scatterbrained, and nervous, she often issued conflicting commands to her nannies, which they learned over time to politely ignore (without any ill consequence because Marina always forgot what she had directed them to do in the first place). Her cakes, tarts, and cookies invariably turned out a delicate combination of underdone and overbrown. Her floral arrangements were expensive and ugly, and therefore stressful to behold. And her proficiency in shopping consisted solely of being able to purchase a large volume of items in a short period of time and have none of them match anything she already owned.

Gregory's birthday party fell completely in line with our expectations. Marina had obviously gone all out. Everything was Hawaiian-themed—or at least, what Marina believed was Hawaiian-themed. The waitstaff she'd hired for the party were in charge of making sure every adult guest was garlanded with an orchid lei on arrival and supplied with either champagne or a piña colada. There was a suckling pig turning on a spit in a corner of the garden, which was dotted with flaming tiki torches. The tablecloths were printed with hula dancers and sailboats. And through it all blew Marina like a gust of wind, ordering a waiter in midservice to make more leis; herding children indoors for dinner, then herding them outdoors again upon realizing the tables were still bare; scurrying to the kitchen to ask why the food wasn't ready yet, even though it was a full half hour before the time she'd told them to bring it out; scolding a maid for laying out blue napkins instead of green ones, and then scolding her for using green ones instead of blue.

Estella and I merely stood to one side and watched her: I with amusement, Estella with some distress. But as members of all three families continued to arrive, distracting Marina with warm greetings and conversation, our cousin began to calm down and everything assumed a less frenetic, more orderly air. By seven, all the guests were present, including the eighteen children and grandchildren of Opa's late best friend, Andries Sukamto. The garden and TV room were crawling with children and nannies. By 7:15, all the dishes were laid out on the sideboard in the formal dining room, including a traditional Javanese *nasi tumpeng* made, untraditionally, to look like a volcano. The cone of turmeric-colored rice had been dyed red at its peak and in dribbles down its slopes to simulate lava. Potato fritters had been arranged in a manner suggestive of boulders, and pieces of fried chicken tented with banana leaves to look like foothills. Plastic palm trees, hula dancers, and dinosaurs, for some reason, dotted the landscape.

We crowded around as Yudi, lifting little Gregory from the nanny's arms, began his speech.

"This," he said, gesturing with his free hand at the volcanic dish, "was all my idea." Chortles rippled through his audience, and Marina smiled nervously. "I told my wife," he continued, slowly and deliberately for maximum comic effect, "I told her, 'We must have a *tumpeng*. My one wish for this special occasion is that we have a *tumpeng*.' And you know what she said?"

Here he paused, then shifted into a nasal falsetto that sounded nothing like Marina: " 'Yu-di! *Jawa banget!*' " The guests roared at hearing Marina's complaint—But Yudi! How Javanese!

Yudi had to raise his voice over the laughter to continue with the rest of his speech: "And I said, 'Yes! My great-grandmother was Javanese! So what? And your father is Italian, so you are half *bule*. And our children are Chinese, part Italian, and part Javanese. We are a very diverse family, and I am proud of it!' " Here he seemed to flounder for a moment, as if he'd forgotten where he was going with all of this, but he pulled everything together quickly. "And we are also proud to have you all, our honored guests, here to celebrate our fourth child's birthday with us. We wish you all the best in life: good fortune, health, and happiness!"

On that concluding note, Yudi sliced off the *tumpeng*'s tip to present to his father—the oldest male and the grandfather of the birthday boy, and so the most important person there. The eating and drinking commenced in earnest.

It was a lovely speech: positive and confident and graceful. You'd never have been able to tell what a ruckus Marina's half-Caucasian heritage had caused among Yudi's family when he was first dating her. Nor would you have been able to tell that Opa and Om Benny had looked down on Yudi's family for being part Javanese (as if no drop of native *pribumi* blood coursed through our own veins). It would have taken a keen eye indeed to notice the subtle grimaces that Opa, Om Benny, and Yudi's parents made as Yudi mentioned the different races that had mingled in the creation of his little family unit.

But perhaps I only imagined the grimaces. Perhaps they were making faces about something else. Looking back, I'm more inclined to give them the benefit of the doubt, not to entertain my suspicions to their fullest, as both Estella and I were guilty of doing that night, now that I know the influence our conversation might have had on the events that followed. I wish I'd held my tongue instead of marveling with Estella, under our breaths as we ate our yellow rice and suckling pig, how Yudi perplexed us: What a genuinely loving and supportive husband he seemed, but how the sporadic bruises on Marina's body hinted otherwise. They appeared every few months: peeking out from the outlines of a sleeveless blouse like a naughty tattoo; now and then flowering on her ankle; once around her left eye, plastered over poorly with heavy makeup and a feeble excuse. We shouldn't have been so presumptuous, I tell myself now. Marina was always physically fragile, more prone to injury than most.

It was difficult not to think such thoughts, though. There was something about that evening, that party—who knows what—that brought it out, tuned it up high and shrill, that particular quality of our family and all the families with whom we associated. Estella put her finger on it when she turned to me and asked, "Remember that pond in Sweden?"

I nodded. When we were in our early teens, Opa and Oma had rented a large holiday house in the Scandinavian countryside for all their children and grandchildren. The surface of the nearby pond had just frozen over. We grandchildren squatted, mesmerized, at its edge, peering through the ice to the tangle of algae and branches and dead leaves beneath—to the dark creatures in languid motion among the sunken debris.

That was all she needed to say—*Remember that pond*—and I understood. We sat at the table, watching: the people supposedly nearest and dearest to us and each other clinking glasses and passing around food, eyes glittering and mouths wide and laughing; the children darting in and out and in between, tugging on grown-ups' arms and pant legs, cramming tidbits into their mouths and licking salty fingers before running out again into the garden. We caught flashes of the murky depths. Looking at Tante Lilly, Om Gerry Sukamto's second wife, one couldn't help but recall Tante Hannah—his first wife, divorced and replaced one day out of the blue, about whom the Sukamtos never spoke. In the brushing of Om Peter's fingertips against the shoulder of his longtime "friend" Om Andy burned tenderness mingled with resignation about what could never declare itself out loud. Around the slim waist of fifteen-year-old Pauline Sukamto clung a different silhouette, penciled in by the rumored visit to the abortion clinic in Bangkok. Sprawled over the length of a sofa was our cousin Ricky, tangible in his absence. He was in the middle of his second incarceration in a rehab clinic in Colorado.

It could drive you crazy, this double vision, one world layered on top of the other, neither of them reality.

Out of the corner of my eye, I detected motion at Estella's elbow. It was our father, wineglass in hand, the faintest trace of pink about his ears. He didn't talk much with people at events like this because they bored him, and people left him alone because he bored them. When he was young, he had been witty. Estella and I knew this because Ma told us when we were kids, always, for some reason, while she was getting ready to go out. As she sat at her vanity in her pink dressing gown, attending to her makeup and hair, we would teeter around in her Manolo Blahniks and drench ourselves in assorted perfumes.

"Your father wasn't always how he is now, you know," she would tell us over the rattle of the hair spray can. "He was so clever, so charming. But that was before you were born. Marriage." Her delicate white bosom would raise and lower itself in a wistful sigh. "Such a disappointment." (Our mother did an admirable job of keeping up facades in every other part of her life. Only when it came to our underwhelming father did she admit Estella and me backstage.)

Tycoon Daughter Weds. So read the headline of the society magazine clipping tucked into the pages of their wedding album. Estella had kept the album in her room, and we knew the story well: Twenty-one-year-old Sarah Sulinado, one of the most prominent beauties of Jakarta high society and the second-youngest child of Irwan Sulinado, founder and head of Sulinado Group, was united in marriage to Rudy Wirono, the eldest son of a journalist. The article's polite neglect of our father's details made all too clear that young Sarah had tied herself to a nonentity.

We never knew the man capable of wooing a wealthy, sophisticated heiress. Or the man strong-willed enough to insist on "Estella" for his daughter's name, even though his wife had complained that it sounded too much like "*es teler*." ("Why don't you just call her 'chocolate pudding' or 'pineapple tart' while you're at it?" she'd reportedly fumed.) To us, Ba was a mild-mannered being, whose pale skin never tanned no matter how much he golfed and whose disposition, even when he was inebriated, never caught the warmth and vivacity of the fine vintages he collected. He'd started working for the family shortly after he'd married our mother. What his job was before, we didn't know; he would always answer our questions about it with a wistful "That's all in the past." Nothing was left of his former self, as far as we could see, except for an acerbic aftertaste that lingered in remarks he made when drunk.

"Bored at your end of the table, Ba?" I asked.

He responded with a watery smile and patted Estella's hand. "Of course not. We're all having so much fun," he asserted with the barest hint of sarcasm. Then he took a sip of wine so small and quick that it might have only happened in my imagination. It took me until I was eighteen to realize our father had a "problem" and what his trick was for disguising it: One hardly ever saw him bring the glass to his lips. A diligent observer might have noticed how much alcohol he could imbibe in the course of an evening, but our father was never interesting enough to hold anyone's attention for long.

Our mother glided over, her low-backed silk dress clinging to her gaunt yellow frame, her shoulder blades swan's wings on the verge of bursting out of her back.

"Have you seen Tante Caroline?" she asked. "She looks fantastic."

Estella and I turned to look at the same time. Tante Caroline—the second-eldest Sukamto daughter, and our mother's age—was whispering something to her husband. The skin across her cheekbones was stretched taut and gleamed unnaturally, like the skin of a newly healed burn.

"Her face is so radiant, so young-looking."

Ever the good daughter, Estella gave our mother what she was looking for. "She doesn't look as young as you, Ma. And you haven't had work done."

Our mother beamed coquettishly. "Why, thank you, darling." She squeezed Estella's arm. "How are you doing? Are you tired? If you want to go home, just let your father or me know and we can leave."

A year and a half had passed since Leonard's death and our mother still treated Estella as if she were made out of bone china. It was her way of purging herself of guilt, just as she purged herself of other things she didn't want inside her.

Estella managed a smile. "I'm all right, Ma."

I patted our mother's hand, which was more like a talon, and smiled too.

"Did you enjoy dinner?" I asked sweetly, even as Estella saw through me and frowned.

"Yes! I'm stuffed," our mother asserted, rubbing the concavity of her belly.

Our father's alcoholism was consistent, whereas it was impossible to predict when Ma's eating disorder would strike. These past few months had seen it in full shine.

A spoon clinking against a glass brought conversation to a gradual halt. It was Gerry Sukamto, red in the face, steadying one hand on the table to help him rise to his feet. A panicked Tante Lilly clutched at his belt, trying to pull him back down. "A toast! To Pak Irwan!" he cried, raising his glass in the direction of my grandfather, who sat at the end of the table, dozing off. At the mention of his name, preceded by the formal honorific "Pak," Opa's ears perked up and he raised his head.

"Gerr," Tante Lilly whispered, "Gerr, not now."

"Pak Irwan," Om Gerry roared again, brushing his wife off. Already, all the guests looked uneasy. By rights, it was Yudi's father, Putra Handoyo, who should have been the object of such a gesture. Or at the very least, he shouldn't have been overlooked. The expression on his face betrayed a failed attempt at graciousness.

Om Gerry continued, "Pak Irwan, you were the best of friends with my father when he was alive. And you were the best of business partners. My father held you in the highest esteem. The day before he died, he called me to his side. 'Gerry,' he said, 'I want to tell you something. When I am gone, remember Pak Irwan and his family. We have been friends for a very long time and they have been very good to us. Don't let the friendship between the families die. Even when I'm gone, it must continue.'" Om Gerry's voice broke. He pulled a folded handkerchief from his pocket and dabbed at his eyes before resuming. "Pak Irwan. You are a good man. We are grateful for your friendship. May our families remain friends and partners for many, many more generations." He raised his glass. "To Pak Irwan!" Helpless, we all followed suit.

Our chorus of half-hearted affirmations was cut short by a frantic gurgling. It came from Opa. He was violet with rage, trying to speak.

When the word finally came, it was barely audible: "Liar." A hiss. He repeated it more loudly. "Liar!" And again, his voice ascending into a madman's shriek. "Liar! Liar! How dare you, you snake! Lies! Lies! Nothing but lies!"

With a sudden jerk, he pushed his chair back from the table and tried to struggle to his feet.

"Lies! Lies!" he continued to cry as Om Gerry's face turned the color of cigar ash. New Oma, Om Benny, and our mother attempted to calm him, but to no avail. Finally, they managed to bundle him off into the next room. Om Gerry lowered himself into his chair, his spirits considerably dampened.

"Told you so," Tante Lilly whispered. "What's the point?"

Only Yudi's father seemed more at ease than before, the faintest of smug smiles around his puckered mouth. Gradually, conversation resumed.

Catching my eye, Estella nodded in the direction of the doorway. Excusing ourselves to our father with murmurs about fresh air, we exited toward the garden and made our way across the lawn to the pool.

"What was that about?" Estella mused.

"Do you really need to ask?" I replied.

But even as I tried to brush the incident aside, the history behind Opa's outburst pursued us as we walked away from the house.

The affair was convoluted to begin with, but now, thanks to Opa's condition and the death of Om Gerry's father, Opa Andries, it had become impossible to resolve. Back in 1995, Opa Andries had asked our opa for a special favor in return for a cut of the net gains the favor would bring about. Not long afterward, however, Opa Andries had died—of a brain tumor the size of a baby's fist.

Om Gerry upheld his father's part of the bargain—or so he claimed. Opa said the sum was far below the agreed amount. It was entirely possible that Opa was right: Gerry Sukamto was prone to duplicity, even with those whom he considered allies. Yet it was also possible that Opa was mistaken: Perhaps the Alzheimer's had already begun to set in.

The agreement had never been written down, and lacking proof, Opa had no alternative but to accept the sum Om Gerry offered. But the grudge remained. It sank its teeth into Opa's memory and refused to let go, holding fast to the disintegrating scraps.

His children prudently paid no mind, more than eager to relegate the incident to the nebulous past, for the favor had been of a dubious nature: convincing villagers to relinquish their land. Opa had probably done no more than assign the task to some eager underling, who in turn had enlisted the cooperation of either local thugs or police. Even if this sort of thing was common practice when it came to clearing land, exposing wrongdoing was all the rage in Indonesia nowadays. Our family didn't want to deal with a news story, a court case, or both. Scandal was to be avoided at all costs.

As if trying to distance herself from the knowledge of these events, Estella quickened her pace. I was forced to break out of my saunter in order to keep up, but as we neared the pool—designed to resemble a tranquil lagoon—she seemed to relax. Rocks both imitation and real surrounded the kidney-shaped body of water. At the far end gushed a waterfall. Short spiky palms and feathery ferns gave the whole setup a primeval feel. Something made ripples at our feet: a lone frog, swimming repeatedly into the pool wall in an effort to reach dry land.

With one fluid movement, Estella drew three photos from her purse, and I walked over to one of the garden lights to better examine them. Given our silence and how we had slipped away from the party, anyone would have thought we were engaged in espionage.

"The first one is from London," she said, looking over my shoulder.

The large family excursions we took during our childhood tended to blend into each other, but I knew which trip she was referring to. Estella and I must have been seven or eight at the time. Our parents had allowed all of us children to stay by ourselves in our own suite. I remembered Christina accidentally tearing down a curtain during one of our rowdier games, and Ricky ordering sirloin steak and hot chocolate from room service three times a day.

And I remembered Tante Sandra. The image I held in my hands was instantly familiar, right down to the outfit she wore: blue velvet bell-bottoms and a high-necked blouse of emerald green. Her hair was long and wavy, and her makeup dramatic—smoky eyes and electric-pink lips, complemented by large gold hoops in her ears. The photo had her standing in front of Buckingham Palace next to one of its iconic guards, and I could practically hear her voice lowered in a mischievous whisper, daring us to poke him from behind. A mixture of adrenaline and adoration flooded my body, as if I were a child again, reliving that moment.

"Brings back memories, doesn't it?" said Estella. "She would've been nineteen. Take a look at the next one, from two years later. It was taken when she was twenty-one."

Twenty-one—no mistaking that. The photo showed her about to blow out the candles on an enormous chocolate-frosted creation heaped with whipped cream, chocolate curls, and maraschino cherries. Black forest, I surmised—one of Oma's specialties. In the center was a pair of candles, one a squat "2" and the other a "1." There were more candles, skinny and striped, staked around the cake's perimeter, as if more flames meant more festivity. Our aunt seemed subdued, especially in comparison to the first photo, though she was still wearing makeup and had clearly taken the trouble to curl and blow-dry her hair. She was smiling, but there was the slightest trace of a furrow between her eyebrows.

"I don't remember this," I remarked. "Were we there?"

"I don't remember either," Estella admitted.

That was the problem with large families: too many birthdays.

"Now look at the last one," instructed Estella.

I did. My eyes were immediately drawn to the photo's bottom right-hand corner. Sure enough, it was as Estella had said: six orange numbers indicating that the picture had been taken on March 21, 1984. Well after Tante Sandra's death, and yet there she was, beyond a doubt—standing against a backdrop of jagged reddish cliffs. But something about her was off, though I couldn't place what. It wasn't that she looked older than she did in the second photo. In fact, she looked almost identical because of the angle of the shot—minimal makeup, hair around the same length but not overly styled, that same smiling yet faintly troubled expression on her face.

"Where did you find this?" I asked.

"In one of the shoeboxes with a lot of other photos. Random ones—all taken at different times in different places. But it's the only one of Tante Sandra like this. I looked through all of them."

"Where was it taken?"

"I don't know. A desert, from the looks of it."

"Have you shown it to Ma?"

"Yes. I pointed out the year too. She said what you said: The date settings on the camera must have been wrong."

"It's not unlikely. Did you ask Ba what he thought?"

Our father was more prone to lapses in discretion. As a consequence, he sometimes told us the truth.

Estella nodded. "He didn't seem to think the date was any cause for suspicion either."

"So why do you?" I asked, studying the photo again, and as I did so, I found myself answering my own question. The longer I gazed at our aunt, the more justifiable my sister's misgivings seemed to become—as if I were being pulled into line with her way of thinking, her point of view. The sense that something was off about the picture strengthened, and I attempted to figure out exactly what was wrong with it, what was wrong with *her*. It came into focus, and I quickly articulated it, as if I were worried it would disappear once more.

"What's that mark on her neck?" I asked, pointing to a purple blotch above our aunt's left collarbone. I leaned in closer and squinted, trying to discern whether it was part of the photo or a flaw in the way the film had been developed. It was hard to tell for sure.

"So you think it's strange too," she crowed. "I noticed it only after I called you."

"Did you ask Ma and Ba about *this*? Did they have anything to say?" I asked.

"Ma said the film must have been poorly processed. Ba suggested it was a hickey and laughed."

I squinted again at the blotch—a dark island in a sea of unblemished skin. "It looks more like a scar—a grease burn, maybe," I observed, noting the irregular borders.

"That's what I think," said Estella.

I frowned. "Tante Sandra didn't have a mark there."

"I know."

The blotch was like the date stamp—proof that our aunt had lived beyond her supposed expiration, and yet not really proof at all.

"Photos aren't always accurate," I said, trying to retreat once more. "Remember the family portrait that used to hang above the sofa in Opa and Oma's house? Back when Oma was alive?"

A ray of levity pierced the clouds. "The one where Tante Margaret looks like she has a double chin?" Estella said with a guffaw.

I nodded. "And where Om Peter is picking his nose."

"Of all the shots the photographer took, Oma insisted it was the best one."

"It was. By her standards. She said someone's eyes were closed in all the others."

"Who hired that guy anyway?"

"Who else?" I laughed.

Estella groaned when she remembered. "Tante Betty. He was her sister-in-law's son."

We chuckled together for a while, but Estella wouldn't be distracted. Taking the photos from me, she lay them side by side on one of the deck chairs so we could better compare them: no trace in the first two of any blemish on Tante Sandra's neck.

The orange numerals in the corner of the last photo took on a diabolical glow. "I see your point, *maybe*," I conceded, "but I don't know how it would be possible. Oma was there when Tante Sandra died. She saw her drown."

It was why Oma forbade us grandchildren to swim in the sea, although, naturally, we still did so on the sly. "I've lost one child already. I can't lose another." That was what she would say whenever one of us begged her to change her mind, her voice hoarsening with grief, her eyes filming over with tears. Our clandestine frolics in the waves were hopelessly ruined; with each splash, we knew we were breaking our grandmother's heart.

Supposing for a moment Estella's suspicions were correct, that our aunt hadn't drowned after all. How could it be explained? Did she fake her death? Had our *family* faked her death? And if either was true, then why?

"I don't know," Estella murmured, as if reading my mind. "But there's more to this. I'm positive."

"There's always more to everything with our family. What can we do?" I attempted a casual shrug.

When she turned her eyes on me, they were strangely bright. "We could find her."

I laughed. "Find her? You can't be serious. Where? How?"

As the words flew out of my mouth, I realized how far downstream I'd been borne on the current of her speculation. "Assuming that she's alive," I added hastily, "which she's not."

If she heard my addendum, she didn't acknowledge it. "There must be some way," she muttered, peering into the water as if the answer lay in its chlorinated depths. The bluish glow from the pool lights turned her face the color of a sick moon.

"Even if we could find her, why go to the trouble?" I reasoned, continuing to entertain her unlikely hypothesis against my better judgment. "What does it matter now if she's alive?"

Estella frowned. "Aren't you tired of all this, though?" She gestured toward the house, the party still in full swing. "All the secrets we keep? Everyone acting as if everything is all right? As if we aren't rotting away on the inside?"

I smiled. "It doesn't bother me as long as I don't let it. Detach! That's what you tell me to do. You should take your own advice."

"I wish I could, but you know I can't."

I sighed. "And what's the alternative?"

"Redemption."

The word startled me. "What?"

"Redemption. You know. So we can change. Be better. Honest. Open. Like normal people."

Everything she'd just said, it was all too familiar. "Redemption"—one of Leonard's favorite words. I refrained from comment and tried to focus on the matter at hand.

"So you think finding Tante Sandra, *if* she happens to still be alive, will somehow bring . . . change?" I asked. I couldn't bring myself to use that other word.

"Maybe."

"How?"

Estella's brow furrowed. "Tante Sandra was different. You know that. She was always better. More real. *True.*" Her voice dropped to a whisper. "Finding this photo—it's made me wonder: Maybe we wouldn't have become this bad if Tante Sandra were still around."

I knew by "we," she meant the family. Opa's demented shrieks seemed to ring in the air: *Lies! Nothing but lies!*

Estella gave a bitter laugh. "And who knows? If Tante Sandra had been there, maybe things with Leonard wouldn't have turned out the way they did."

I contemplated this. Perhaps my sister was right. I recalled the qualities of the aunt we had so admired as children: her candor and compassion; her refusal to pretend that everything was okay; the way she wore her heart on her sleeve, even around us kids. At the very least she would have been a moderating influence on the family's tendencies toward secrecy and self-deception. And maybe she really could have prevented the tragedy that befell Estella and Leonard—she'd never have let things get so out of hand.

"So you're saying that if Tante Sandra's alive, she'll save us," I concluded, meaning to sound derisive, but with hope creeping into my words nonetheless.

Estella smiled. "If there's anything left to save."

"Well, let me know when you find her address," I joked, shaking myself free of her spell.

She glared at me defiantly. "I will," she replied.

"Tante? Tante?"

We turned around. It was Melissa, one of our nieces—Theresa's kid. She was five, but liked to act younger because she thought it was cute.

"What are you doing?" she asked us as Estella swept up the photos and stuffed them back into her purse.

"Getting fresh air," Estella answered.

Melissa broke into a gap-toothed grin. "Are you going to jump in the pool?" she asked.

Estella smiled. "No, Melissa."

But Melissa's imagination had been kindled and her grin grew wider. "Are you going to drown yourself?"

This made both of us laugh. "No, Melissa," Estella said again, eyes gleaming. "I'm going to drown . . . *you!*" She caught Melissa in her arms and made as if to drag her toward the pool. Our niece shrieked with delight.

Once we had tickled Melissa to within an inch of her life, the three of us walked back across the lawn to the house.

Family life had some high points, for all our faults.

ESTELLA SHOWED UP with the letters a few days later, when I was making my weekly rounds of the Bagatelle laboratories. Such regular visits were hardly expected of me as the founder and CEO, but I made them part of my duties. I found the ambience of the labs invigorating—stretches of sterile white space sliced cleanly at intervals by countertops of stainless steel. Blank and thus brimming with potential, they were the voids into which my scientists brought forth new, wondrous forms of life.

I'd been inspecting a lineup of silkworm corpses in their open petri dish coffins when a voice at my elbow murmured, "So this is where the magic happens."

It was Estella. Out of the corner of my eye I saw a door shut, and my secretary disappearing behind it. She must have shown my sister in. I had no time to register surprise. Without skipping a beat, Estella surveyed the tiny bodies on the counter and spoke.

"*Bombyx mori*," she observed. My eyebrows flew upward. I hadn't thought that Estella would have retained what we'd learned in those entomology classes so long ago. But then I recalled that she was, after all, in the silk-weaving business. If there was any scientific name she should remember, this would have been the one.

"I suppose you see a lot of them at Mutiara."

"Some," she said. "Since we source most of our cocoons from China, we have no reason to keep large numbers. But we do raise some of our own, along with a local silkworm species—*Cricula trifenestrata*. It doesn't hurt to experiment a bit."

Her eyes roamed over the dead caterpillars, each trailing a long orange protuberance of similar shape and size. It was difficult to tell whether they were silkworms sprouting fungi, or fungi sprouting silkworms.

"Collateral damage," I explained. Bagatelle had started a new project, the goal being to come up with a genetically modified strain of Cordyceps fungus that would double, ideally triple, the bagatelle's life span. The way to do this, at least in theory, was to alter the way the fungus worked. In the current version of the serum, the fungus took over the bagatelle's entire nervous system. But we wanted to place limits on the fungus: restrict it to only a portion of the brain.

Estella sped the train of thought to its logical conclusion. "Leaving part of the brain untouched will lessen the physiological toll on the bagatelle."

"And the mental toll too," I said with a smile. I often forgot how sharp my sister could be. "We're dealing with the mind here, so the mental is the physical."

"Any success?"

"Not quite yet. But we're making progress. So they tell me. It's more complicated than we'd anticipated."

I showed her to another room, where we kept a few terrariums, and I motioned for her to look inside one of them. The floor was covered with mulberry leaves and silkworms engaged in the act of ceaseless chewing. You could hear the shredding and mashing of leaf membrane through the mesh tops of the glass tanks.

We peered closer and, without me pointing them out, they attracted Estella's attention immediately: lone individuals that had crawled up the twigs propped against the terrarium walls. High above the teeming masses below, raising themselves up on their hind feet, they bobbed and wriggled, as if under the control of some invisible crazed puppeteer.

"Cordyceps did this? Really?" Estella asked, wrinkling her brow.

I nodded. "These are test subjects for the new serum. We're not there yet, but we're getting close."

"Ah." The sigh escaped her, the satisfactory hiss of an opened bottle of soft drink, a balloon that had been holding its breath, the happy sound Oma used to make whenever we grandchildren would fling ourselves at her and hug her knees. Estella was home, and she had just realized it. I too realized something: It was the first time Estella had ever visited Bagatelle.

"What are you doing here, anyway?" I asked, sounding more hostile than I intended. I should have been thrilled to have her there, yet I was startled by her sudden appearance in what I had come to regard as my domain.

She beamed. "I found out where Tante Sandra lives."

We retired to the leather lounge set in my office. My secretary brought us coffee. Estella placed the envelopes on the table—two of them, both opened, both addressed to our grandmother.

From one of Oma's boxes, she explained. After she had finished selecting and scanning photos for the birthday slideshow, she'd gone to Opa's house to return them. Opa had been napping. New Oma had been out. Tati and the houseboy had helped convey the heavy paper bags upstairs. Then, at Estella's bidding, they had left her alone.

Once she'd returned the photos to the armoire, Estella had turned her attention to Oma's boxes. The first one yielded a compressed wad of leather handbags spotted with white mold. The second, an assortment of ancient toiletries, among them a plastic bottle of lavender hand lotion, Oma's signature talcum powder, a cracked heel of soap, and a glass vial of fluid that had separated into a heavy black goop and a buoyant amber film.

Estella had always possessed an instinct for the systematic: the arrangement of our stuffed animals according to height on our bedroom shelves; the transferal of equations and definitions onto color-coded cards before tests, first during high school, then in our first year at Berkeley; and, when we volunteered at the Essig Museum of Entomology on campus, the memorization of the scientific names of insects, all the species in a genus, all the genera in a family. I should have taken this into account when I'd made the joke about her letting me know once she'd found our aunt's address.

I could follow her reasoning. Assuming that the photograph of Tante Sandra *had* been taken after her death, how would such a photo find its way into Oma's collection? Who had seen Tante Sandra last, and who had proclaimed her dead?

These questions yielded the same answer: Oma. And Estella had headed straight to the only logical place to look for proof of my aunt's survival. In that room, Estella had set to work. Slitting open boxes. Unpacking. Examining. Repacking. Setting to one side. Reaching for the next box. Repeating this process. She combed through women's magazines and cookbooks, notebooks and receipts, birthday cards and letters with such great care it would have made any archaeologist proud. The sun yielded to night, the ashen daylight that streamed in through the window replaced by the miserly glow of a single low-watt bulb (all the other lights had burned out and never been replaced). New Oma returned home and poked her head in to ask if Estella wanted dinner. Upon having the offer declined, New Oma meekly withdrew. Minutes later—or was it an hour?—Estella finally found what she was looking for.

The two envelopes were tucked away in a spiral-bound notebook of handwritten recipes, between a steamed strawberry pudding and a Dutch-style macaroni casserole. They contained letters, if the term even applied to such short missives. The first read, *I'm well. Sandra*—followed by an address. The second was similar—*I'm well. Have moved. Sandra*—and gave another address in the same city in California.

I studied the letters now, along with their enclosing envelopes, postmarked respectively August 23, 1982, and April 5, 1984. The envelopes themselves bore no sender's name or return address. The information contained in the letters had been meant solely for Oma's eyes.

As I held the second letter in my hands, Estella leaned over and pointed triumphantly at the last three lines:

2307 Rockaway Drive
Bakersfield, CA 93304
USA

Then she leaned back in her chair and placed her hands on the armrests as if she were laying claim to a throne.

"So that photo you found. The one dated 1984 . . ." I murmured, still in shock at what Estella had unearthed.

Estella completed my sentence. "Probably came with the letter you're holding. But why bother with educated guesses when we can ask Tante Sandra in person?"

I blinked. "What?"

"We leave on Friday," she declared cheerily. "I've asked my secretary to book us a flight to Los Angeles. Bakersfield is only a few hours' drive north from there."

"Friday? That's in three days!"

"I know!" she exclaimed. "I can't wait! Just think, Doll! We have a chance to find Tante Sandra. *Tante Sandra!* Don't you remember? How different she was from the rest of them? Like—"

"Drops of dew." The words sprang from my lips automatically—the corny line we'd come up with as children to express what made our aunt so wonderful: the freshness and purity she exuded, the clarity and simplicity of her speech and actions. Our other aunts and uncles, our parents—they had an opaqueness to them. Most grown-ups did. They asked you inane questions about how you were doing in school and what your hobbies were, and when you answered or tried to make conversation in return, they smiled for no reason and barely heard what you were saying. Tante Sandra, on the other hand, had genuinely listened—to your fears about ghosts and theories about intelligent alien life; to your design plans for the house you would live in when you grew up, and what you had just learned about bees from the book you read in the school library. It went in both directions too. Where other grown-ups only knew how to interrogate, Tante Sandra had thought nothing of pouring herself out to you. At least that's how I remembered it. And even when she left for boarding school, followed by university, whenever she came back it felt as if she'd never been away.

Opa and Oma had been far from consistent when it came to their children's education. Oma left all the decisions to her husband, who acted on the latest advice he received from his business friends, as if the quality of schools, like the stock market, changed from day to day. Tante Betty and Om Benny they sent to university in Amsterdam. Om Peter stayed local— a University of Indonesia man. They sent our mother to Perth for both her high school and tertiary education, and Tante Margaret to an elite institution in Switzerland, then to Germany to finish up. Our youngest aunt, like our mother, was shipped off to a girls' boarding school in Australia, but for no discernible reason, she was sent to the other side of the country, to Melbourne.

Tante Sandra was the baby of Oma's children, a full ten years younger than our mother. Perhaps this difference in age between her and her siblings accounted for her tendency to treat us kids as her peers. One of my earliest and fondest memories is of Estella and me sitting on our aunt's bed at Opa's house, watching her unpack, wide-eyed at the stories she'd brought back from her first year abroad. About breaking curfew and her first taste of beer. About her crush on the handsome French teacher. About how she'd cried herself to sleep every night for the first month and dreamed of nothing but home cooking.

She drowned when we were very young—we hadn't even reached our teens. And it was she who had opened our childish eyes to how much we didn't know about our family: the false walls and secret passages, the trapdoors and hidden nooks around and upon which the edifice of our collective life was built.

Even now, from the confines of my comatose state, scouring my brain for memories from this hospital bed, I can only come up with a few recollections, more fragments than scenes, as if glimpsed in passing from a speeding car. For example, a worry she voiced out loud about Om Peter's gambling debts during a game of checkers on a rainy day. Or the time she dared to tell Om Benny off for being so mean to Tante Betty. Or what she said one weekend while we were watching TV at Opa's house: "Don't be too hard on your mother. She's always lived in Margaret's shadow."

I remember too a hotel room—maybe in Monte Carlo, where the hotel would host our family on the house as long as Opa and our parents hit the gambling tables with abandon. Tante Sandra was curled up on the bed in a fluffy white bathrobe, crying. Something about Opa being a vicious and dangerous man. Something about not knowing how Oma could stand being married to him. The revelation of it: that Opa was not just stern, but *bad*; that he could or should be reviled.

And then there's this one isolated fragment, more vivid but more incomprehensible than the rest. I can't account for it at all. A hotel as well, this time in a luxurious ladies' room with floors and countertops of pink marble, and a separate powder room with enormous mirrors and upholstered ottomans. An evening function of some sort. A wedding reception for one of the families we knew, perhaps. That would explain the height of her hair and her strapless forest-green evening gown, though it doesn't explain her sitting there looking listless, staring dully at her reflection. Or her turning to ask us, bizarrely, "Do you ever feel bad about being Chinese?"

I'm misremembering the question. I must be. It makes no sense at all. But I dredge up these imperfect recollections to illuminate, if only for my own benefit, how my sister convinced me to embark on that impromptu mission to find our long-lost aunt. Estella's invocation of what Tante Sandra once meant to us—frankness, guilelessness, innocence even— threw me off balance. I found myself swaying in her direction.

"She's alive," I whispered, the miraculousness of it bowling me over anew.

"And you will come with me, won't you?" urged Estella. "I can't do anything without your help. Look at what's happened to me every time we've been apart: when I let Leonard come between us; even that short time when you went away to Paris. I need you, Doll. I always have."

There was an intensity in her expression—an energy I hadn't seen in her for a long time. It was an Estella I'd almost forgotten existed. The sight moved me, and her pleading did so even more. Call me a fool, but I was flattered. Until now, I had always been the one tugging at her elbow, trying to drag her away from the family so she and I could live our own lives. Now the tables had turned: There she was, in my company headquarters, on my turf, attempting to win *me* over. I knew helping her search for Tante Sandra would mean entangling myself once again in the family web. But my sister was hard to resist, as was the prospect of being reunited with the aunt we had so idolized when we were kids. I tried to imagine what Tante Sandra was like now, but all I could come up with was what she was like back then: wholesome and lovely and sincere and everything we aspired to be when we grew up into young women ourselves.

"It's possible that she's moved again," I said, struggling to remain sensible.

"True," Estella acknowledged.

"But let's say we do find her. What then?"

"Tell her the family needs her," Estella replied promptly. "Ask her to come back."

"What makes you so sure that she'd want to? From these letters, it seems like she disappeared on purpose, that she didn't want to be found."

"She doesn't know how much worse we've become," Estella said, shaking her head. "Not if Oma was the only one in contact with her. Oma's been dead for almost fifteen years."

"Even if we do convince her to return, what would she do? How would she make a difference, exactly?"

"How does a breath of fresh air make a difference?"

And believe it or not, that silly answer worked. I finally capitulated to the romance of her nonlogic.

"Fine, I'll come," I said. And as her face broke into a grin, I rose and walked to the great glass windows behind my desk. She'd won me over, and for some reason I felt the urge to reestablish my autonomy, as if distancing myself physically from her would help.

She walked two steps behind me. "Great view," she said, following my gaze across the city skyline.

"The view's never good in Jakarta," I demurred, secretly pleased. "It doesn't matter how high up you go."

We stood there for a good while, contemplating the high-rises and shantytowns, the roads jammed with traffic and the trash-choked canals. Arteries of sooty green snaked through the gaps, sometimes pooling in a sorry excuse for a park. Here and there peeped the silver cupola of a neighborhood mosque, attempting to catch the sun's rays through the smog. Billboards dotted the landscape too—advertising cigarettes and swanky real estate, margarine and coffee—the images plastered on them corroded by the city's toxic fumes.

At the center of it all, at least from where we stood, was a man-made lake, or a reservoir, or who knew what the proper term was, its water an unholy shade of brown, its shores a combination of concrete barrier and heaps of rubbish. Scrawny figures in floppy hats stood on these banks, fishing with long poles for debris and sometimes casting nets to haul in their catch. Suddenly, the oblong piece of machinery set in the middle of the lake began to quake, and as its mechanical teeth churned the water, a thick black substance rose to the surface. From our glass-walled, air-conditioned perch, it looked like tar.

What a contrast to the desert landscape of Tante Sandra's photo, the cloudless blue sky and the red cliffs and plateaus vulnerable in their barrenness, like the open palm of an outstretched hand. I remember feeling fleetingly and inexplicably that of course it made sense—of course our youngest aunt belonged not here but against the backdrop of that uncontaminated expanse.

"You should get back to work," whispered Estella excitedly. She gave me an affectionate squeeze on the arm. "I'll let you know once the flight details are confirmed." She returned the letters to her purse.

I offered to walk her out. "Don't trouble yourself," she said happily. "I know the way."

"DOLL, LOOK," ESTELLA whispered, gently sliding the headphones from my ears. She nodded toward the window on our left. "It's snow."

I paused my movie and leaned over to look with her at the white blankness stretching below us, interrupted every so often by patches of ice-blue water.

"We're crossing Antarctica," I said to her solemnly, as I was supposed to, in this game we hadn't played for years.

It hadn't started as a game. When we were little, we had genuinely believed we were seeing snowy lands. The view was even better from the windows near the giant mechanical doors, next to where the flight attendants sat. "Snow!" we would point out to them, and they would part their cherry-red lips in a laugh.

The fact that they never corrected us proved we were right, as did the indulgent nods of our nanny, although once during one of Ba's periodic visitations from first class, he had the nerve to inform us that they were clouds.

They can't be clouds, we'd protested with certainty. Clouds are fluffy and round. It's snow, right? We hailed a passing flight attendant to ask and she nodded and smiled. "See, Ba? Snow." And he had smiled too and slipped us some chocolates wrapped in a cloth napkin before passing back through the pleated purple curtain to join our mother.

We never minded sitting apart from them. Life had always been so ordered—with separate accommodations and activities for grown-ups and children—allowing each party to do what pleased them best. Grown-ups sat at the table inside restaurants; children, under Nanny's watchful eye, ran about outside. Grown-ups spent weekend mornings unconscious in cold, lightless rooms; children watched cartoons on TV and coaxed Nanny into making pancakes. At hotels, grown-ups went for massages and spa treatments. Children splashed around in the pool, and Nanny ordered them cheeseburgers and fries. The same separation applied on long-haul flights.

When we were older and quieter, our parents told us, we could sit up front as well. And we nodded pleasantly, not wanting to hurt their feelings by saying that we would probably never want to. The few times we had visited first class, we'd found it boring. We weren't allowed to run up and down the aisles there, or even talk much: the flight attendants were much stricter than those in the back. We were confined to sitting at our parents' feet, coloring pictures or playing cards, or else fiddling with the hole-riddled plastic boxes and pegs we invariably received on every flight—a game called Mastermind that we wouldn't figure out how to play until we were older, when we finally accrued the patience to read the accompanying instruction sheet.

The economy-class cabin, on the other hand, was a playground—the secret warrens where the leg room was supposed to be, the amusing metal-lic click of the little ashtrays embedded in the armrests, the round button that compressed softly whenever we wanted to lower and raise and lower and raise and lower and raise the backs of our seats. Even the food was fun: It came in little plastic boxes and didn't taste like real food, so Nanny let us do all sorts of things with it. We made smoothies of orange juice, cof-fee creamer, and rice, and urged Nanny to try our concoctions, which she did with an infinitesimal sip and an approving murmur. We crumbled the crackers and strewed them up and down the aisles like Hansel and Gretel. We created men, or at least the heads of men, embedding olive eyeballs and soggy carrot mouths in bread rolls. We helped Nanny slip the metal teaspoons into her purse. (She said they were perfect for stirring tea and coffee. The teaspoons we and our parents used at home were the same size, but naturally, she wasn't allowed to use those.)

The long flights were magical for Estella and me: All time blended together, so nobody could tell when it was or what anyone should be doing. We played by artificial light and fell asleep in the flickering gray glow of a silent movie. We woke at intervals and curled ourselves into different configurations, or fought for the blankets, or sleepily pulled on the headphones to tune in to one of the in-flight radio channels. We never asked if we were almost there because we knew we never were. Perpetually, we were still far away, still soaring over the lands of snow.

Even as adults, on that flight to LA, knowing full well that our father had been right and what passed beneath us were clouds, I found it hard not to believe my eyes. The white windswept plains, the banks, the rifts, the peaks—all said plainly, "Land." But to pass into adulthood is to attain the knowledge that you must sever believing and seeing from each other.

"Do you really think we'll find her?" I asked, readjusting my goose-down duvet, pressing my call button to ask for another cup of green tea. We'd long outgrown our fondness for economy class.

"I certainly hope so," said Estella. Then the childlike glow faded from her expression and her voice turned to lead. "To be honest, I don't know what I'll do if we don't."

She was thinking about dinner with our parents the night before, during which she'd told them about our trip.

"You're leaving tomorrow?" our mother had exclaimed. "Why didn't you say anything?"

Estella had tried to affect nonchalance. "It's only for a few days," she'd explained.

"A shopping trip. That's all," I'd piped up.

At this, our mother nodded approvingly and recommenced pretending to eat. "That's wonderful," she said. Then, addressing my sister: "I'm glad you're treating yourself. You've been moping about for far too long."

Ma's insensitivity never ceased to amaze me. For a moment, Ba's eyes flashed as if he were going to intervene and, briefly, I was grateful, even if his attempts often made things worse. But I was mistaken. He merely let Ma continue, oblivious to the wound she had inflicted.

"Do you remember Tante Susie?" she asked, conveying a single grain of rice to her lips with her spoon.

"The short one with big hair?" I chimed in, taking over for Estella and me. I sensed where this was leading and I didn't like it.

"No, that's Susie Onkowijoyo. The other one—Susie Sutanto. Her family owns the Angsa hotel chain? Her son Octavius went to school with you."

"What about her?" I asked.

"Octavius just got divorced."

"So?"

"So nothing," said Ma, trying to sound innocent. "I thought you'd like to know, that's all. Just something to keep in mind."

As she spoke, she turned to Estella. And when no one said anything, she pressed on, mistaking silence for a sign that things were going well. I used to wonder how someone so clueless could have been such a successful socialite in her youth. But then again, looks and money—money especially—more than made up for lack of tact.

"Stell, I know you're still recovering from Len's death. We all are, I daresay. But you should keep an open mind."

She hadn't really said that, had she? It was like something out of a bad dream. Ba's face paled.

"*You're* still recovering?" I sputtered on my sister's behalf.

Ma stared at me in confusion. "Yes, of course," she replied. "It wasn't easy for any of us. And he *was* my son-in-law, after all."

I was practically choking at that point. I wanted to say something, to yell even, but hadn't the faintest clue where to start.

Then Estella began to cry. Startled, Ma began patting her hand. Even our father sprang into action, reaching for the bottle and topping up her glass.

"Oh no. I'm sorry, dear," Ma said hurriedly, "I didn't mean to upset you. I just want the best for you, that's all. I didn't know you were still so sensitive about it. I won't mention it again, I promise."

It was the sincerity of her alarm that made it all the more terrible. And though she hastily moved on to another subject, she must have still been feeling repentant when dinner was over because, before retiring upstairs, she said to us by way of good night, "Have fun in LA, okay? Splurge." As if we'd ever been encouraged to do otherwise.

Ba's usual after-dinner custom was to beat a hasty retreat to his wine cellar, but tonight he lingered long enough to give us limp hugs.

"Your mother means well," he said, voice trailing away, taking its leave in advance of its owner.

His words were hardly consoling. And despite Estella's attempts to inject our mission with fresh enthusiasm, the horror caused by that exchange with our mother had followed us onto the plane and was crossing the Pacific with us.

"I still can't believe it," muttered Estella, looking out the window again. "To hear Ma talk, you'd think that nothing was ever wrong. That Leonard and I were . . . *happy* or something. That everything was fine up until the day he died."

"I know," I said. "But then again, what should we expect? Isn't this how the family deals with everything? We're so good at hiding the bad stuff, we manage to fool ourselves." I meant this last sentence as a joke, but there was too much truth in it.

"We have to find Tante Sandra," Estella declared. And I detected a new note in her voice—a combination of resolve and fatigue. She spoke in the same way someone stranded in the desert might about getting out alive: urging herself to succeed despite being weakened already by thirst and heat and the grinning specter of death.

Silence again. Then, out of nowhere, those words. Hysterical, I would have called them, if they hadn't been uttered in such a soft voice: "God, we're so screwed up, Doll. How did we ever get this way?"

Binge-watching movies dulled our sorrows. Estella dozed off, as did I. We slept through breakfast, as we'd told the flight attendants to let us do, and woke to gentle voices informing us we would be landing soon.

The sun was an angry welt on the horizon when the plane touched down. Nevertheless, our hearts leapt, responding as if it were a sunrise, though we knew it was actually evening and that soon it would be dark. By my newly adjusted watch it was a quarter to five. Outside, the stocky silhouettes of airport workers lumbered around on the tarmac.

It took over an hour for us to get through immigration. And by the time the porter had collected our bags and we stepped outside, it was so dark that it might as well have been the dead of night.

"I like cold weather," Estella remarked with a yawn as we rode the shuttle bus to the car rental lot. She flexed her neck from side to side and adjusted the fur-trimmed collar of her down vest.

"You do realize that when we were at Berkeley, all you did was complain about the cold."

"Northern California is too chilly. Southern California is just right."

How long had it been since we'd last talked about our college days? They seemed so irrelevant now, so far away and fantastic, that they simply never came up anymore. But we were in America again. And whenever I landed on American soil, I felt it, whatever "it" was—the "it" that made me feel like I'd been released from one of those flesh-tinted girdles that fat women wore. My stomach, lungs, and heart reinflated. A breeze ran through my ribs, making them tingle and flutter. I felt vulnerable, but also inexplicably hopeful. Endless promise and possibility rose up from the earth and permeated the air.

Since she was far more familiar with the city's geography, Estella offered to drive to the hotel.

"What time is it?" she asked as we loaded our suitcases into our rented sedan.

I told her and she grimaced. "Still rush hour," she said. Without another word she slipped into the driver's seat and, avoiding the 405 altogether, drove us north up La Cienega. We had both made regular trips to LA while we were at Berkeley: There had been too many friends and relatives attending school or vacationing in the City of Angels for us not to spend at least a few weeks there every year. But by the end of our sophomore year, Estella had been flying down every other weekend to visit Leonard. And after she and Leonard got married, because her in-laws had a house there, she visited two or three times a year.

We careened past freeway exits and halted for red lights beside stucco-walled strip malls and surprisingly familiar signs: *Hollywood Nails, Chik-A-Dee Chicken, Togo's, Best Buy, Vacuums Plus, Godzilla Sushi.* It's amazing what memories the mind conceals. I recognized them all: the red-letter bubbles of WIG WORLD, the twenty-four-hour Tastee Donuts, the quirky handbag store next door to Reuben's Deli.

Neither of us had ever stayed at the Beverly Tree Plaza before, but we had wanted to avoid running into anyone we knew, so the usual high-profile luxury hotels were all out of the question. Estella had remembered our old high school friend Nikki mentioning, ages ago, that she'd stayed there while having her eyelids done. She'd made her first wide-eyed debut at a mutual friend's baby shower, smiling sweetly and batting her eyes.

Our second cousin Hwa had been in attendance too, and she'd shrieked and clapped her hands in delight. "They're so big! You look like a Japanese manga character!"

Nikki beamed. "I know!"

"The folds are so fine," Hwa gushed, admiring the surgeon's handiwork. "He must be really top-notch. You know, my sister's friend got her eyes done in Japan—everyone was raving about Japanese plastic surgery—and her eyelid folds are so thick, they look pregnant."

Everybody laughed.

Aubrey, Gerry Sukamto's niece, was there too (we really did live in a small world). "You know what you should have said?" she drawled, "'*Darling*, I love your eyelids. When are they due?'"

This elicited a fresh roar from the room. Blinking innocently, Aubrey strutted around, running her hands over her own imaginary baby bump. "'*Darling*,' you should have said, 'if one of them is a girl, can you please name her after me?'"

It was Hwa who coaxed the rest of the details out of Nikki, including where she had stayed: the Beverly Tree Plaza, its suites small and shabby, but, importantly, with no other Indonesians around.

"I don't care who knows about me fixing my eyelids," Nikki had declared, "but I didn't want anyone to see me before the scars had healed!"

When we arrived, our room was more or less what we expected, given what Nikki had said. The furniture was opulent, but frayed. The ivory shag carpet looked like it smelled of cat. It was the kind of place where you could imagine rich old ladies taking up residence. I tipped the bellboy, and Estella unlaced her boots and flopped down on the pink chintz sofa.

"I'm starving," she stated.

"Me too," I said.

"Where do you want to eat dinner?"

"I don't know."

"Barbecue in Koreatown?"

"Ugh. Too heavy. Also too far."

"How about Ramayani in Westwood?"

I stared at her incredulously. "You're joking, right? We just got here. What are you, a villager? Can't live without Indonesian food for one day?"

"I *was* just joking," Estella said defensively. "Let's go someplace close by."

We both fell silent, trying to decipher the yearnings of our stomachs.

"How about Matsuhisa?" Estella asked.

"Funny," I said with a smile. "I was about to say the same thing."

Something suddenly came to mind.

"Will it be all right for you, though?" I asked.

She laughed—a kind of laugh I hadn't heard from her for a while. Silvery and easy. It was how she used to laugh long ago, long before.

"Don't be silly, Doll. I'll be fine."

❖   ❖   ❖

Nothing had changed at Matsuhisa. But then again, nothing ever did. Not its cramped foyer or unpretentious interior; not the demographics of the waitstaff: Asian or Eurasian, attractive and young. The same painted silhouettes of diners adorned the walls, frozen midgesticulation, teacups glued to lips, chopsticks eternally aloft—easily mistaken for real shadows until you noticed they never moved. Matsuhisa was far humbler in appearance than the offshoots spawned by its owner-chef's success. The flashy nouveau Oriental interiors of the branches in New York, Las Vegas, and London tried too hard to impress. They were teenage girls in sky-high stilettos, dripping rhinestones and cheap perfume. Matsuhisa was their kimonoed grandmother, ageless, peerless, stolid, unaffected by the passing of time.

The hotel concierge told us he hadn't been able to get us a reservation before 8:30, but by the time we'd showered off the stale smell of the plane, changed into fresh clothes and driven over, we were twenty minutes late. The service was as good as we remembered. The hostess apologized even though the lateness was our fault and told us our table would be ready in a jiffy. As we stood listening to the chatter wafting around the corner from the dining area, I felt Estella's spirit curl and tighten like a prawn in a steamer.

"We can leave, you know," I offered.

"No, I want to stay," she said. "It'll be good for me. Besides, I'm not as brittle as you all think."

We tried to push it from our minds. I made a sorry joke about the display of Matsuhisa-brand salad dressings being there since the dawn of time. She made a lame attempt to laugh. It was no use of course. The memory crept in at the corners. The blasts of cold air from the front door, constantly opening and shutting, carried in the querulous voice of Leonard's mother, fearing the wind would make her ill. The hostess guiding us to our table grew bustier and blonde, transforming into the woman Leonard had ogled that night. Even what we ordered, which was what we always ordered, were the same dishes that had witnessed Estella's public shame—the yellowtail with jalapeño, the miso cod, the creamy spicy crab. Our table for two flanking the wall offered a prime vantage point from which to survey that other table where our former selves were seated: Leonard's parents to the left, our parents and me to the right, and Leonard and Estella seated across from each other in the middle, the thin line along which our two clans blurred into one.

It had been the worst of the bad times. Leonard had reached the apex of his cruelty, which had corresponded to the apex of his financial success. The Angsono family conglomerate, Sono Jaya, had made a successful incursion into instant-noodle territory. Share prices had skyrocketed and an era of expansion had begun—for the business and for Leonard's physical person. Around the same time, he had hired a personal bodybuilding trainer. Under diligent daily tutelage and a steady diet of protein shakes, Leonard had grown as hulking as a healthy water buffalo.

The transformation from man to beast had brought about some seemingly desirable changes: He drank much less and stopped staying out so late. But for the most part, the metamorphosis had been terrifying. How the chest and arms of his polo shirt had bulged that night, the embroidered polo player on his left pectoral muscle twitching, as if with suppressed excitement or fury. How all his veins protruded and throbbed, in time, it seemed, to the beating of an enormous horse's heart. Perhaps most unnerving was his face, naturally babylike with soft lips and cushiony cheeks, sitting atop that incongruously muscular body.

It had been right before Christmas—that and summer were the two high seasons for Indonesians who owned houses or condos in LA. The air was crisp and deliciously untropical. The business year was drawing to a close, and all the important projects had been wrapped up or put on hiatus so their energy could be bottled for the first quarter of the new year. The sales were on and the shopping was good. The atmosphere was wonderfully festive. Christmas-light-trimmed houses and bushes twinkled good cheer. The velvety voice of Bing Crosby could be heard everywhere, reminding listeners that Santa Claus was coming to town.

Our two families, yoked together now for three years through Estella and Leonard's marriage, were starting to settle into a certain familiarity with each other, even if the couple's relationship was showing strain. My parents and I often came to LA for the holidays, but this time we accepted the Angsonos' invitation for us to stay with them in their house.

Leonard's mother, Tante Elise, had done it up beautifully, in a combination of light woods and quaint French country prints. Naturally, whenever she and her husband came, they brought their housekeeper from Jakarta—the faithful, stocky, four-foot-high Rina. But the size of their Los Angeles house demanded its own year-round maintenance, and this was taken care of by a large-bosomed, sandy-haired woman named Patty, who, in return for a decent salary and free room and board in the house itself, was more than happy to keep things shipshape. She oversaw gardeners, scheduled repairs, and whipped up Western-style food whenever the Angsonos came to stay. Her repertoire was wonderfully American: blueberry pancakes and crispy bacon for breakfast; buttery grilled cheese sandwiches and ranch-dressed salads for lunch; crisp-edged lasagnas and tender meat loaves for dinner; and endless trays of freshly baked chocolate chip cookies. As delicious and charming as Patty's food was, there was only so much Western food a person could stand to eat, so Patty alternated cooking responsibilities with Rina, whose repertoire consisted of familiar home-style dishes—spicy curries and sweet, dark stews; noodle soups, fried rice, and stir-fries; fried chicken, fried fish, fried tofu, fried tempeh, and, if she found the right bananas at the Asian supermarket, fried banana fritters.

At Christmas, Patty was in her element. She bustled around in boxy cardigans adorned with elves and bobbly reindeer noses and ribbons. Garlands of fake fir studded with velveteen bows and glitter-dipped pinecones materialized on the stairway banisters. A wreath attached itself to the front door. A Christmas tree complete with lights and metallic balls and bronze tinsel sprang up overnight in the living room. The gas fireplace blazed from sundown to whatever time Patty decided to turn in for the night. Bowls of itty-bitty candy canes and Hershey's Kisses littered every table, counter, and shelf. It was the season to set aside differences and, accordingly, jars of swarthy molasses crinkles rubbed shoulders with jars of men and women of the gingerbread persuasion. And thrown into the mix were tins of blond snowflake-shaped sugar cookies iced in blue, points tipped with tiny silver balls of dubious edibility.

In short, during the holiday season especially, Patty ensured that the Angsono house looked, smelled, and felt like the houses of white people. I wouldn't be surprised if Patty was bringing to life her own private fantasy of all-American life as she thought it ought to be. (I dimly remember what she mentioned in passing to me once about a shiftless ex-husband, an estranged daughter, and a dingy former apartment with bad mold and faulty plumbing.) Leonard's family loved it. We loved it. All our Indonesian friends loved it. And the handful of American friends whom Leonard's parents entertained took it for granted—they were made to feel unconsciously at ease in a way that would have been impossible if not for the invisible hand of Patty.

So you see, two weeks of Yuletide comfort and joy, of inhabiting an environment that radiated happiness and warmth, had lulled us into a contented stupor that made that night's awakening at Matsuhisa all the more wrenching, as sudden as a lightning bolt on a clear day, and triggered by virtually nothing: a woman, Nordic in bone structure and good looks, passing our table and catching Leonard's appreciative gaze; Leonard's hand, as he reached for his green tea, brushing almost imperceptibly against her hip. Nothing, really. And yet Estella flashed, scrawling her temper across the sky.

"What, two women aren't enough for you? Why don't you add her to your harem?"

Our mother's warning not to air dirty laundry in public came flat and low: "Stell."

Leonard eased his massive back into his chair and narrowed his eyes. "Don't be stupid," he responded coolly. "Anyway, how do you know it's just the two of you?"

My sister's hand cracked against his cheek, a blur of manicured scarlet and diamond and gold. And then Leonard had simply taken her wrist in his and squeezed. The pink jolt that raced up her arm forced her mouth into an inaudible shriek.

"Len, don't," his father said low and sharp, rising to his feet. "Not here, Len. Not here." He sounded as if he were addressing a dog.

Ma squealed in spite of herself, hitting my father frantically on the shoulder. "Rudy! Stop it! Get him to stop it!"

Abruptly, Leonard let go. We all resumed eating. Estella, still tender, nursed her tea in silence. After five minutes, maybe seven, conversation about everyone's plans for the next few days recommenced: appointments with doctors in Beverly Hills; golf for the men, shopping for the women; meals with the friends from home who were also in town.

Nonetheless, our parents were obviously shocked by the whole thing. I wasn't. Some part of me had been expecting this all along. The eruption of physical violence had only been a matter of time, and not just because of the notes Estella had found in his briefcase. Those too had been part of the inevitable progression of their relationship into what it had been fated to become from the start. Estella and our parents had simply chosen to deceive themselves, while I never had.

The families had taken two separate cars to the restaurant, and after our mother won the fight over the bill—Leonard's parents had the tact to let her win, to let our family regain some face, appear in control—she announced that she and our father were taking Estella and me to that new gelato parlor all our LA-savvy friends had been raving about. Leonard could go back home with his parents and we'd meet them at the house. She said all this pleasantly, smoothly, as if nothing had happened.

When the valet brought the car around, our father slipped him a ten and slid into the driver's seat as if he knew where we were going, where this gelato parlor was. Our mother cheek-kissed each of the three Angsonos good-bye. The only sign that something, anything, had altered was that our mother and I had changed places, Ma sitting in the back seat next to Estella instead of in the front with my father. Our parents waved as we pulled away and Leonard's parents waved back. Only their children took part in none of this: to the casual onlooker, we must have looked like overgrown five-year-olds, petulant and up past our bedtime.

In the back seat, Ma took Estella's arm, sat stroking it consolingly, wordlessly. Humming softly to himself a tuneless tune, Ba continued to drive to who knew where.

It was Ma who spoke first. Tentatively. "Stell. Does he do this often?"

Estella didn't respond, only crossed her arms and exhaled impatiently. Ma repeated her question. "Does he do this often? You know. Hurt you?"

The car sped up. Our father was merging onto the freeway.

"No," Estella finally snapped. "No. This is the first time."

"Are you sure?" Ma asked.

Estella snorted. "Of course I'm sure."

"Why are you angry? I'm just trying to help."

"I just told you, didn't I? This is the first time. Does it matter?"

Ma's voice shrank, wounded. She began to sob, her natural inclination to play prima donna mingling with genuine maternal concern. "Of course it matters," she whimpered. "We're your parents, Stell. We love you."

Estella exhaled again and looked out the window. "How dare you," she mumbled.

"What?" asked my mother.

I turned in an attempt to catch Estella's eye, to calm her somehow, but I could see that it would be of no use. A fury had come upon her. Her face was blind and hot, and I could tell that everything was white and tingling and electric. "How *dare* you," she repeated, her whole body quivering. "As if none of it mattered until now. As if everything he's been doing up to this point hasn't mattered. And now . . . only *now* you worry about him hurting me? Only now you do something on my behalf? Only now do you dare to tell me—" she choked. "As if you didn't know before this. As if you weren't responsible for . . ." To prevent herself from breaking down, she stopped talking.

"Oh, Stell," Ma moaned, "how could we have known? You can't blame us. We did it because we loved you. You think we don't love you?"

Estella said nothing, even when Ma repeated her question. "You think we don't love you?" It was relentless, her good intentions, her desperation to absolve herself of guilt. "You think we don't love you?"

At last Estella spoke. "I know you do," she said curtly, trying to put an end to it all. Anything to end it all.

"We couldn't have known it would turn out like this, could we, Rudy? Ask your father. We couldn't have known—"

A scream. Estella's. A piercing howl to drown out Ma, Leonard, the world and time and all that had contributed to the miserable situation she found herself in. No, not to drown them out. To shatter them. To break them into pieces. To reduce them to dust to be scattered by the winds. But it was useless.

We never made it to the gelato parlor. Thank God. Our father had sense enough for that. He drove us in circles for a while, then parked the car two blocks from the Angsono house until both his daughter and his wife had finished crying. Then he started the car and took us back. When Patty innocently asked us whether we'd had a good time out (everyone else had gone to bed, or at least to their bedrooms), we all lied and said that we had. And when we went upstairs, it was implicitly understood that Estella was to sleep in my room that night.

As I said, that was the worst of the bad times. It really was. Who knew that in two years, Leonard would transform again beyond recognition? That in four he would find Jesus? Then again, Leonard was always unpredictable, a man of change eternal, evolution everlasting. If he'd lived any longer, who knows what he might have become?

"You know, even then, I didn't wish he were dead," Estella mused, dredging us up into the Leonard-less present.

I raised an eyebrow and my pair of chopsticks. "You *do* remember what you said to me that night, right? After we came back from 'gelato'? When you were lying next to me in bed?"

She frowned. I had her right where I wanted. I popped a morsel of cod into my mouth and let out a maudlin wail: " 'I wish he were dead. Oh, Doll. I wish he were dead.' "

She grinned and whacked me on the shoulder with the flat of her palm. "I did *not*!"

"Ow! Yes, you did!"

"I did not! I did not!"

But she kept hitting me and we both kept laughing because we knew it wasn't true and because I'd just said it to lighten the mood and because it was good to have a sister.

I miss her.

Hell, I'm so lonely, I miss them all: Ma and Ba, the rest of the family, even Leonard and his parents.

I'm not sure I anticipated how much nostalgia I would suffer in trying to find out why Estella did what she did. Then again, in these memories I find much-needed company, even if they are of the dead—bodies I've brought floating up, bloated faces skyward, eyeballing the stars.

"SO WHERE ARE the polar bears? It's freezing here."

Those were the words with which Leonard introduced himself, his body shivering, unaccustomed to how much colder autumn was in Berkeley than LA. At the time, he was cultivating the persona of funny guy, though he would drop this in a few months when he finally realized that humor not only didn't come easily to him—like a dog with good survival instincts, it refused to come at all.

Estella and I had just finished our first semester at Berkeley. It would have been Estella's third semester if not for Oma's sudden death. Why our grandmother kept the diagnosis a secret—not just from her children, but from her husband as well—we never knew. By the time we found out, the time for coherent explanation had passed. The cancer had multiplied, riddled her from head to toe, lodged in her lungs, her liver, her bones, her brain. We knelt, clutched, wept for Oma, but at the bedside of a stranger. She was gone in a matter of weeks. We would never understand.

No one prevented Estella from leaving for college following the funeral. Her clear-eyed sense of duty made none of that necessary. She called the admissions office to explain the situation and push back her start date by a year. They sympathized of course. The financial contribution our family had made was too generous for them not to show compassion. They even sent flowers. *Our Deepest Condolences*, the card read, toothpicked with a plastic stalk into a spray of white carnations and calla lilies.

Somehow, the family emerged from Oma's passing, and Estella and I made our way across the Pacific to Northern California. Horrified at friends' reports of the low quality of housing in Berkeley and its hippie-infested environs, our mother opted to rent us a place rather than buy one.

Engaging the services of a high-end leasing agent, the three of us dashed over for a whirlwind tour of suitable properties before settling on a newly renovated townhouse just ten minutes' walk from campus. We said we could take it immediately and pay two years' worth of rent in advance, as long as the owner didn't mind overseeing the installation of double-glazed draft-proof windows and new carpeting, which we would pay for of course.

We knew more or less what to expect, thanks to others who had gone to study in the US before us. Those on the East Coast and the handful in the Midwest complained about the biting cold and the dreary people; those out West, of life being too slow, too "laid-back"; and the brave souls who'd headed to small, isolated college towns in the middle of nowhere pined desperately for the city—for the roar of traffic, for crowded streets, for good shopping, for more than five restaurants. Everyone grumbled about the food: especially the Americanized Chinese restaurants, identifiable by menus listing unfamiliar dishes like "moo goo gai pan" and "Peking ravioli." Water chestnuts, celery, and flaccid baby corn infested every stir-fry. All the sauces except sweet-and-sour tasted the same. Takeout always came with packets of a radioactive orange gel called "duck sauce."

On the East Coast, everywhere except New York, the problem was paucity: Good Chinese food was extant but rare, and Indonesian restaurants were practically nonexistent. Consequently, East Coasters looked longingly to the golden West, whose denizens in turn pushed their plates away in mild disgust, emitting sighs homeward across the Pacific.

"It's not how the food tastes," our cousin Ricky tried to explain as we sat together on the second night of Oma's funeral wake. Ricky had come back as soon as he'd heard the news. He'd been in the middle of his sophomore year at the University of Southern California in LA, the city that boasted some of the most "authentic" Asian food in the country. "The real problem with American Chinese food is the size," he said. "Too big. Too coarse. The meat and vegetables are sliced too thick. Go out for dim sum and each *siu mai* is the size of your fist. And the portions are double the size of what you get here. Even if you avoid burgers and pizza and fries and eat only Asian food, you end up gaining weight." Ricky glanced down at his paunch, which was indeed more prominent than it had been when he'd first left for the States. Then he shrugged. "I'll lose it after college." Which he never did.

Ricky, the closest in age to us, was always the most good-natured of our cousins. And also the laziest. Too lazy even to cheat to get good grades, like a lot of the other rich Chinese-Indonesian kids did. Ricky couldn't be bothered to pay anyone to write his essays or to sit his exams. And he didn't even have the energy to copy the homework answers his friends would circulate among themselves. Still, he was smart. Even with minimal studying, he managed to squeak by every semester with Bs and Cs. Mostly Cs. Om Benny and Tante Soon Gek weren't over the moon about their son's performance, but they weren't too annoyed either. It meant it would cost them a little more money and trouble to ensure Ricky was placed in all the right internship programs. But since he was being groomed for the family business, his indifference had little effect on his future career prospects. It was the drugs that would do Ricky in—the cocaine and pills he'd discover after college, just when all of his friends were getting over them and stumbling back to their feet.

Ricky: our favorite cousin and, it turned out, the most harmful. I wouldn't go so far as to accuse him of initiating Leonard's relationship with my sister. But now, turning the matter over, I believe more hinged on Ricky than he himself, in his pleasant slack-eyed inertness, could ever have imagined. If Ricky had been a more protective older cousin, if he'd been choosier about his friends rather than just falling in with whoever happened to be at hand, if he'd had the vigilance to pass judgment on other people's choices instead of being indiscriminately happy for them no matter what they decided to do, Estella might never have ended up with Leonard. But Ricky was Ricky. And when he came to visit us during our first semester, he brought along his friend and roommate who had wanted to see San Francisco too.

We knew within a minute of meeting Leonard that he was one of our set. He spoke our language—Jakarta-slang Indonesian sprinkled liberally with English, courtesy of an elite private school education. Fair skin, slanty eyes: like us, of Chinese descent. His polo shirt and jeans were Lacoste and Armani, and on his wrist he sported a Rolex. ("Old-fashioned, I know," he'd say when people commented, "but what can I say? I like the classics.") They'd driven up in Leonard's car because Leonard had thought it would be cool to drive up and down the state.

"You know—a road trip," Leonard explained over dinner on the first night of their visit. "Like in the movies."

"Some road trip," Estella teased. "Don't those take days? Weeks? How long did it take you? Seven hours?"

"Eight," Leonard answered. "Bad traffic. Ricky wouldn't know. He slept the whole time."

"I was tired," Ricky protested languidly, nudging a blob of chèvre onto his fork prongs with his knife. "Len, you said you didn't mind me taking a nap."

We were at Chez Panisse, which we had specially booked because of Ricky's visit, not so much because Ricky had wanted to dine there (though if there was anything he did really give a damn about, it was food), but because the restaurant had a reputation and, thus, it seemed the courteous, cousinly thing to do—that is, to go out of one's way. Though the magic of Chez Panisse's ambience was lost on Ricky, whose sole focus was on the meal, it seemed to be having a favorable effect on his friend. The rustic wood interior and the warm and whisky-hued lighting, the baskets of rustic flour-dusted loaves and the wildflowers spilling out of brass tureens and

clay pots—Leonard summed these up approvingly in one word, in English: "*Cozy*," he said. "Do you come here often?"

"Not really," I said. "Once at the beginning of the school year when Ma
was settling us in, and then again a few weeks ago as a special treat."

"What was the special treat for?"

"Homesickness," said Estella.

"Well, if I lived here, I'd come every day," he blurted. "Even for takeout." It might have been funny—the idea of a college student eating at
Chez Panisse seven days a week was comically extravagant, even by the
standards of our set. But his timing was bad. As a response to my sister's
statement about missing home, the remark came off as insensitive. We
laughed feebly, as we'd been doing at his jokes since he and Ricky had
arrived a few hours earlier. And we kept it up through Saturday, Sunday,
and Monday morning—through seal watching and gummy clam chowder
at Fisherman's Wharf, through shopping in Union Square, through the
marijuana haze and faded tie-dye of Haight-Ashbury. Thankfully, the
jokes Leonard attempted came regularly but not frequently, with several
hours' space in between each one. And no wonder: It must have been very
hard work for him, now that I think about it, and now that I know he had
no sense of humor. He must have been trying to impress us. Each joke,
before he inflicted it upon us, must have spent several minutes undergoing
meticulous assembly—which is probably why he reused the polar bear
joke as we parted.

"You never showed us the polar bears," he said with a grin at Estella and
me, breathing through his mouth in deliberate puffs so they turned cloudy
in the morning air. "Call me if you're ever down in LA. We'll hang out."

"What did you think of him?" Estella asked me as we watched the car
drive away, Ricky's head already nestling in the hammock of his seat belt.

"I'm not sure," I answered.

"Really? I thought he was okay."

"Don't know. Something's not right. And his jokes were terrible."

"Well, yes. There is that."

"But there's more." I drummed my fingers against my lips, trying to locate it exactly, the thing about Leonard that was off. "Did you see him glower when you teased him about his road trip not being a real road trip?"

"Did he?"

He did. I remember how it surprised me, that sulk, vanishing even as it spread across his face, like a passing shadow. "I think so," I answered. "Briefly."

"He's not bad-looking."

I shrugged. "Could be worse. But he looks like a little kid."

"I think it's his cheeks. They make him look like a baby angel in an old European painting."

"Baby with a temper," I added.

"Well, he's friends with Ricky, so he can't be too bad," Estella mused.

Only later would we know that this conclusion couldn't have been further from the truth.

❖   ❖   ❖

The madness of the initial few weeks made it easy to forget our weekend with Ricky and Leonard. Estella and I had always had studious streaks, much to the bemusement of our family and friends. Keeping up with macroeconomics, statistics, and calculus extinguished the small spark of a social life that we'd managed to kindle during the first weeks of the semester. And the introductory-level entomology course, which we'd picked for fun, ended up taking more time and energy than we'd anticipated—not because it was difficult, but because it offered us, for the first time in our lives, an outlet for the unorthodox obsession we had developed in preadolescence.

It had started with the ant farm our father had bought us on one of his overseas business trips: a flat, transparent rectangle bordered in red plastic and divided into two. The underworld was to be filled with the packet of white sand that came with the farm, and the surface world was decorated with red plastic cutouts of a barn, a silo, and a picket fence. The instructions said to send for our ants by mail to the address listed, but Ba told us that this only worked if you lived in the US, where the manufacturer was based. So we asked Mardi, our houseboy, to collect local ants for us instead. Big ones. He did—presenting us with a glass jar of leggy auburns with blackish abdomens that he pinched between his thumb and forefinger and hurled with expert aim, one by one, into the narrow opening at the top of the farm's frame.

The instruction manual informed us that the colony would only last one to three months without a queen ant to produce eggs and give its members a sense of purpose. That was enough for us. Spellbound, we watched them tunnel through the white sand, depositing each grain in slow-growing piles on the surface before descending yet again for more. When they cleaned themselves with their mandibles, they resembled tiny armored cats, grasping threadlike legs between threadlike legs, nibbling at particles invisible to our clumsy human eyes. And to communicate with each other, they touched feelers in a wispy dance that ended with the ants brushing past one another as if they'd never exchanged intimacies in the first place.

Then, after a week, the colony began to wither. Two ants began sleeping all the time. Then five. Then more. They lay strewn all through the tunnels and on the surface. Every now and then, one would convulse before flopping down again in a crumpled heap. And when they finally gave up, their bodies would stiffen and curl into balls.

The survivors created a graveyard, hoisting the corpses in their mouths to the far corner of the surface world and dumping them there in a heap. But the disease continued to spread. Perhaps the farm's configuration was unsuited to the tropics. The underworld had always been foggy with condensation. Now, with the bodies piling up and more succumbing to illness each day, the moisture looked pestilential and unclean.

Over dinner one evening, we told our parents what was happening.

"Have you fed them enough?" our mother asked, though her expression made it obvious that she didn't want to talk about the ants at all.

We told her the manual said not to overfeed them, but she shrugged. "Did you feed them any meat? Ants like meat."

Desperate, we cast into the farm a fingernail-sized sinew of poached chicken. The few ants who were still healthy swarmed over it happily, and we were delighted that the problem had been solved.

The next morning, we discovered they too had grown sick, had plastered themselves onto the chicken flesh and were twitching like the others. The moisture had worsened, spreading to the surface as well, where the chunk of meat lay steaming in its own juices. By the next day, Death reigned supreme. We left the farm alone for a week, hoping for the miracle of mass resurrection. But then the farm began to mold over, and Nanny helped us disassemble it and wash the sand and dead bodies down the kitchen sink.

"Don't be sad," Nanny counseled. "Ants aren't very smart."

"What does that have to do with anything?" I asked.

"If the ants were smarter," Nanny replied, never skipping a beat, "they wouldn't have died so easily."

Our mother was glad that the ants were gone. She'd never concealed her belief that girls and bugs didn't mix.

"Pretty girls don't play with ants," she'd informed us when Mardi had first helped us assemble the farm. "It's weird. And ants are dirty. I don't know why your father got you that filthy thing."

The truth was, our father probably hadn't put that much thought into it. He'd likely bought it on an absentminded whim, or at the last minute from some store in an airport. Despite our mother's disgust, the ants left a deep impression on us. Even watching them die had been enthralling. Creepy-crawlies became our guilty pleasure, like the stash of Swiss chocolates Ma kept under her bed to binge on before purging. Mardi, who also helped with the gardening, proved a willing accomplice: Whenever he found an interesting specimen, dead or alive, he brought it to us for examination. One time it was a freckled green grasshopper the size of a chocolate bar. We opened the lid of the cardboard box in Estella's bedroom and recoiled at the force of the grasshopper's spring as it launched itself onto the top shelf of a bookcase. Shrieking, Estella ran for the door to call for help, but at that moment it adjusted its forewings, revealing a netting of translucent vermilion underneath. We sat back down to behold it, charmed.

Another time, Mardi presented to us, in an empty Fanta bottle, an expired carpenter bee, its wrestler's body burly and its thighs furred black, its wings dark and iridescent like polarized sunglasses. Its mouthparts were unfurled, and it looked as if it were mocking us, sticking out its tongue.

We lingered on the fringes of the soccer field at school, scouring the grass for signs of life; we borrowed from the library science books on insects and spiders. Our choice of illicit fascination was far more unconventional than those of our peers. Most of the girls were into makeup—experimenting with eye shadow and lipstick in the school bathrooms in the morning, and washing their faces clean before their drivers came to fetch them home. Rumor had it that the boys circulated porn magazines among themselves.

When we hit our midteens, Estella and I stopped indulging our insect obsession. The peer pressure had proved too much for us, and though our friends hadn't dropped us, they had started making fun. Someone had slipped a bottle of anti-lice shampoo into Estella's backpack one day. Another time we were standing around during lunch break when some jerk dumped a whole Ziplock bag of dead flies on our heads. Anyway, the hobby had reached the limits of its expansion, seemed stunted somehow: There were only so many dead bugs we could collect, only so much we could learn from the limited selection of books available to us.

But then came college and, with it, the freedom to expand one's mind, to let it ooze in whatever direction it fancied. At least, that was how the American kids saw it. Their eagerness was contagious.

"Seriously?!" exclaimed a senior girl in a blue bandana and a yellow T-shirt that read GOT RICE? We were at a freshman-orientation pizza party thrown by BASA—the Berkeley Asian Students Association—and we'd just told her what classes we'd signed up for: all economics-major requirements.

"Take a fun class. Live a little," she counseled earnestly. "They're always the ones that end up changing your life. Am I right, Ray?"

The guy next to her ran his hand over his buzz cut as he took a swig of Sprite. "Yeah, totally. I'm an electrical engineering major, and the best class I took as a freshman was Classical Philosophy with Professor Bergson. Awesome teacher, if you're interested. It really blew my mind."

I'm not sure if the class on insects was mind-blowing, per se, but it felt—I don't know how else to put it—like relief. Like cool water on a patch of skin that had itched for so long we had learned to take its itching as part and parcel of existence.

We threw ourselves wholeheartedly into doing well in entomology, even as we sought to remain diligent in our other areas of study. Staying on top of all the coursework was challenging, and Estella and I, without really meaning to, became recluses. It didn't help that other Indonesians—at least those we were used to having as friends (i.e., mostly Chinese, and of a certain social class)—were far less thick on the ground at Berkeley than in places like LA or Boston. No one of our family's acquaintance was there, nor was anyone else from our high school. On the whole, we kept to ourselves.

We did attend the occasional BASA event: dumpling-making study breaks, or bowling with bubble tea afterward. We also had a bewildering coffee with a brunette named Kelly from our statistics class. After she talked at us for ten minutes straight about anime, we realized she thought we were Japanese. Not living in student housing made avoiding the company of others all too easy. When we weren't in class, we were studying at home, or studying in a café, or eating out with each other, or, toward the end of the semester, volunteering at the Essig Museum of Entomology—learning to properly pin, label, and classify insects; inspecting drawers of specimens for signs of infestation by dermestids.

The family was still too shaken by Oma's death to contemplate vacationing abroad that winter, so Estella and I flew down to LA after exams to stay with Ricky for a week. From there, the three of us would fly back to Jakarta together. Ricky was still renting an apartment with Leonard, and entering their world from ours was like being thrust out of a cave into broad daylight. Somehow, and probably through no contribution of Ricky's apart from his careless affability, the two had become a sort of social epicenter for the wealthy Chinese-Indonesian students in the area. People hung out at their place around the clock, often under the pretense of studying, but more often they watched movies and simmered in the Jacuzzi, shot pool and played cards, draped themselves in bunches around the living room and kitchen and bedrooms, chatting animatedly and laughing. Food streamed in like tap water: delivery boys bearing boxes and containers of all shapes and sizes, squads going out on quests to fulfill the hankerings of the mob— beef ball noodles and lamb curry from Ramayani in Westwood; In-N-Out burgers and Popeyes fried chicken; spicy tofu stew and *galbi* from BCD Tofu House; banana cream pie from Marie Callender's. Some of their friends would stay over if it got too late. We'd emerge from the guest bedroom to find snoring bodies scattered on the sofa, or even piled in a platonic heap like a litter of baby hamsters, smelling of sleep, breathing as one.

In that environment, that emanation of easy hospitality and communitarian goodwill, you couldn't help but make friends and reconnect with old acquaintances. There were recognizable faces in abundance—former classmates and several children from families we knew. Ruby, Diana, and Jenny; Frank, Stenson, Lawrence, and Anton; Fat Chris, Handsome Chris, and Just Plain Chris; Nadia and Sweetie—they all ebbed and flowed through Ricky and Leonard's front door. And they were genuinely happy to see us, especially the girls: cheek kisses, little screeches of delight, and beratings about not keeping in touch assailed us every time one of them walked through the door and spied us in our state of social thaw. I don't think we realized how isolated our life at Berkeley was until then, and we experienced for the first time a pang of remorse for choosing academic prestige over the comfort of the close-knit network we knew we'd have found there in Southern California. I think Estella regretted it more keenly than I did. Though I too enjoyed our time at Ricky and Leonard's, I was ultimately glad at the prospect of heading back—to the cool green wilds of the north and the mothball-pungent space of the Essig; to frigid mornings spent gazing out the bay window of our rented house and sipping coffee, instant because we'd never had to make our own and we couldn't be bothered to learn.

I mentioned this to Estella on our last night there, or, more accurately, our last morning. (A bunch of us had just come back from a midnight showing of some action movie whose title I don't remember.) We were crawling into the bed in the guest room we were sharing, and I remarked how relieved I was that we didn't live in LA.

"Not," I added, "that it hasn't been fun."

Estella looked surprised. "Really? I kind of like it here. The Bay Area seems so boring by contrast."

"But wouldn't you get tired if we had to deal with this all the time? I thought you enjoyed the peace and quiet we have where we are."

"I do," she yawned. "But . . . I don't know. There's more to life than just studying and pinning insects."

"Like Leonard?" I asked. I meant for the question to sound pleasant and teasing, but it didn't. Perhaps I was too tired. His name caught in my throat like a fish bone, and my remark came out ragged and dry.

She was on her guard immediately. "Why do you say that?"

"He spends a lot of time talking to you."

"To us, you mean."

"But, really, he's interested in *you*."

"Well, are you interested in him?"

"No," I said with a sniff. "But I think he's bad news. I think you should stay away."

"Why? He's nice."

I coughed. "He *acts* nice."

"What are you talking about?" Estella was getting riled up now. I felt the blanket tighten around us, as if it too were agitated. "That's why he has so many friends. Because he's a nice guy."

I didn't say anything because now I was mad myself, and I knew the best way to irritate Estella was to remain silent.

"You're so annoying," she muttered. "Come on. Tell me, Doll. Why don't you think he's nice?"

I sighed long and loud for effect. "There are people who are genuinely nice and there are people who aren't—who are nice only because they want something. *Len*"—I sneered—"is not genuinely nice. You can see it in his eyes. You can see it in his expression when he strokes someone's ego, or expresses sympathy, or treats everyone to dinner, or lets someone use his stuff or borrow his car. Haven't you noticed how smug he gets? The satisfaction it gives him to have influence or power over people?"

I had one specific incident in mind, which I didn't mention because I hoped Estella would forget it. The day before, Leonard had insisted on taking us to the Hollywood Walk of Fame. I'd been standing a few paces away, and he had seized the opportunity to stand far too close to my sister.

"I'm so glad you're here," he'd said, gazing into her eyes, brushing the hair from her face with his fingers.

"Let me get this straight," Estella said, not mentioning the incident either. "There's something wrong with him because he wants other people to like him?" She sat up. "Guess what, Doll. That's what most people want."

"That's not true. Look at Ricky. He couldn't give a damn what other people think. He's just nice for the sake of being nice."

"So now your standard for niceness is *Ricky*? Ricky's not nice, Doll. He's just lazy."

All right, maybe Ricky wasn't the best example. And, in hindsight, the terms "nice" and "not nice" couldn't have been more inadequate in describing what Leonard was trying to be and what he actually was. But they were the best words I could come up with at the time. I see now, from the wisdom of my comatose state, what my younger self was attempting to articulate: Leonard's insatiable desire not just for mere approval but for unadulterated adoration; the swollen ego that relied on sacrificial offerings to maintain its hollow bloat.

But that was back then, and we had no idea what manner of creature we were up against—not I, whose blind instinct was to flee; nor Estella, who had fallen under its spell. We were two children squabbling over whether the doggie was a friendly doggie, not whether its breath would strip the flesh from our bones.

"I'm just watching out for you," I said coldly. "I don't want you to get hurt, that's all."

"You're jealous," she snapped.

At this, I let loose a derisive snort. "Fine, go out with him," I said. "See if I care. But when you realize what a jerk he is, don't come crying to me."

"Don't worry, I won't," came her retort. And we willed ourselves angrily to sleep.

Neither Estella nor I ever apologized to each other for our quarrel.

Such formalities were not the way of our family, and we were our family's children. Conflict, ill feelings, anger—dealing with them directly was unnecessary. We tended to leave that task to the eminently able hours and days, weeks and months, which gnawed at these hard matters as waves do at broken glass.

By the time we'd returned home to Jakarta, Estella and I had forgotten our midnight spat almost entirely. And not once during the vacation did the subject of Leonard come up again. I tried to believe that nothing more would come of Estella and Leonard's brief dalliance in LA.

The lack of communication between them stoked this hope. Those were the early nineties—before cheap international calling plans, before widespread mobile phone or internet usage even. And to my relief, Leonard, on vacation with his family in Switzerland and France, didn't bother with letters or postcards. When the end of our vacation rolled around and it was time to return to Berkeley, I was laughing at myself for worrying so unnecessarily.

As I now know, my relief was premature. While Estella, in Jakarta, was letting her newly sprung ardor cool, I'm fairly certain that Leonard was fanning his into a tremendous blaze, feeding it whole fir trees while skiing through the alpine powder snow, stoking its embers over dinners of buttered country loaves in French countryside châteaux. If anything, distance probably made Estella more desirable, leaving his imagination free to endow her with all the qualities of his ideal woman—a combination of magic mirror and genie, able to discern his true worth, able to fulfill the deepest yearnings of his heart. During our stay with him and Ricky, she had laughed at his bad jokes at all the right moments and said all the right things—at least, this was what he had perceived. And unlike the other girls in the crowd he mixed with, Estella possessed a certain intelligence and independence of mind, which he appreciated for all the wrong reasons. He wasn't interested in valuing someone else, but he liked the idea of someone worthwhile valuing him.

And so Leonard decided to set his sights on my sister. Since, at the time, he enjoyed winning people over, I'm sure he took special pleasure in wooing Estella to make her wholly his.

❖　❖　❖

The assault on Estella began in full force shortly after our second semester at Berkeley had started, and presumably immediately after Leonard had resumed his own classes. He began calling her all the time, and before I knew it, she and Leonard were talking for hours every night. Pyramids of roses and sunflowers, lilies and gladiolas greeted us on our doorstep when we returned from campus. Sometimes the arrangements came accompanied by chocolates, stuffed animals, or foil balloons.

Estella was flattered, and how easy it is to mistake being flattered for falling in love. Neither of us had ever had boyfriends in high school, unlike some of our classmates who dated without their parents knowing. We weren't bad-looking, but we were hardly beauties or the buxom type—the two kinds of girls at our high school who usually attracted advances from the opposite sex. I'm sure the reputation we'd acquired as nerdy entophiles didn't help, which was fine by us.

Leonard was the first guy who'd ever pursued Estella, and he did so with such aggression that she had no choice but to believe it was love. We had learned from the movies and our disappointed mother that love was the opposite of the watered-down stuff our father had to offer. Love was forceful and obsessive, extravagant and jealous. It never took no for an answer. Instead, it wore its object down until said object realized the right answer was yes. So when the first warning signs came, Estella merely thought them part and parcel of what should happen in a romance: Leonard grilling her about an outing with the BASA crowd and expressing his irritation that she'd spoken to other guys; his annoyance when she cut short their phone conversation because she had to go to class.

Once, he mentioned how pretty she looked with her hair down, then began asking how she was wearing it whenever they spoke (the wrong answer was "up"). The slightest hint that she wasn't paying close attention would spawn a suffocating cloud of sarcasm.

There is only so much room in a person's life, and none if someone else insists that he take up all of it. And though Estella tried to keep Leonard and me in separate compartments, my allotted space shrank until I found myself out in the cold.

Toward the end of our freshman year, their relationship reached the inevitable next stage: a series of back-to-back weekend visits, sometimes extending to the surrounding Thursdays and Fridays, Mondays and Tuesdays. Initially Leonard was the one who would fly in—he was over the idea of road trips by now. He stayed in the guest room at first, and then one night he didn't. Her class attendance dwindled. Her grades went into a nosedive.

Estella kept me updated whenever she had the chance. And what she was too embarrassed to tell me, my imagination filled in. I charted the progress of their relationship—its budding, its blossoming, its quick over-flowering into sweet decay—as if it were running through my own nerves, insinuating its way into the chambers of my own heart. Estella's soul could not be ripped from mine so easily—not yet. It is when a part of your body is being bruised, seared, sliced, that you are most alive to its existence. It was when Leonard was engaged in tearing Estella from me that I could sense her every tremor with an intensity that I could hardly bear.

Their first kiss. It happened during Leonard's second visit, after they went to Yoshi's in Oakland for a romantic night of sushi and jazz. Leonard insisted on driving (he always did) even though the car belonged to Estella and me, even though he'd had four sake cocktails in the space of two hours, even though it was pouring sheets. He turned the wrong way onto a one-way street, nearly hit an oncoming car, and swerved to a stop by the side of the road. The sound of the other car's horn, monotonic and urgent, rang in their ears. Estella didn't move, didn't speak, sat there trembling to the *rat-a-tat-tat* of the rain pelleting down so hard and fast on the roof and windshield that it felt like the whole world was being washed away. Then, without any warning, came Leonard's mouth. No lips. Only a mouth and its resident tongue, aroused and muscular and hot.

The first fumblings? The first strokings and squeezings? It is impossible to pinpoint their beginning; I can only imagine where and how: always at night, after dinner, after drinks, after a movie, after a concert—always after, when fatigue awakens lust and stirs it to languorous action in the plush, muffling seats of a theater, the recesses of our sofa, the back seat of our parked car, the carpet of Estella's room, then the yielding surface of Estella's bed.

The first sex. Probably not that first night he stayed in Estella's room, nor the second. Maybe the fourth or fifth, amid the dead of sleep. A rolling toward and a rolling on top. Hands slipping buttons free, sliding under elastic, rubbing gently, then more firmly. Sleepy half protestations giving way to sleepy submission.

The more Estella gave Leonard, the more he required, like a monstrous houseplant spilling out of its pot. I hoped against hope that the physical separation imposed by the summer break would slow him down. He spent most of the vacation period doing an internship his father had arranged for him at Goldman Sachs in New York. Estella and I split our time between Jakarta and an extended stay with our parents at Tante Margaret's then-husband's holiday home near Salzburg. But the commencement of our sophomore year only brought a fresh and frightening demand. Why, he asked, was it always he who had to come up to Berkeley to see Estella? Wasn't it only fair that she travel to LA equally often to see him? She flew down immediately for the sake of appeasing him, and continued her migrations from then on, alternating them with his fortnightly trips to the Bay Area.

Then: Why limit their visits just to weekends? He couldn't bear to be away from her, how could she take being apart from him? How could she be so loveless, so cold? Who needed to go to classes anyway? Alternating weekends turned into alternating weeks—six to eight days during which I had to endure Leonard's presence followed by six to eight lonely days in an empty house.

By this point, our parents knew about Leonard and Estella. Our mother was beyond ecstatic. Who wouldn't be to have a daughter in a serious relationship with a son from the Angsono family—*the* Angsono family? In those days the success of Leonard's family was at its peak. They were the owners of vast and lucrative holdings in timber, telecommunications, banking, real estate, and cigarettes (those were the main ones; they were a large family with countless fingers in countless pies). Perhaps most crucially, Leonard's father and uncles were on an amicable footing with high-ranking government and military officials, including President Suharto himself.

A marriage alliance with the Angsonos would benefit our fortunes. It would pave the way for joint ventures and favorable partnerships with Leonard's clan, and give us access by association to the powerful inhabitants of the sphere just above ours. Estella told Ma about Leonard once he'd started visiting on weekends (though she didn't mention that Leonard was staying with us, nor did Ma ever ask). Our mother immediately relayed the information to Opa, who responded with an approving nod. Ma then told our aunts and uncles, who greeted the news with delight.

But no one was more excited than Ma, and in all fairness, I don't think it was just because Leonard was an Angsono. The courtship gave her a chance to escape the flaccidity that was her marriage, to forget the colorless man that the love of her own life had morphed into. What was it that Tante Sandra had said all those years ago, about our mother living in Tante Margaret's shadow? I can't be sure of what she meant, but I'm inclined to think that she must have been referring to the whirlwind that was our aunt's Old World–trotting love life, which must have made our romance-starved mother positively grind her teeth in envy.

Our mother's self-absorption didn't mean she didn't love us—but it did affect how she expressed that love. Her views on what would serve us best were always tinted by what would serve her, and what she believed she would want if she were in our shoes. From our mother's point of view, Estella couldn't ask for a better catch: a scion of the Sono Jaya empire who showered his girlfriend with gifts and couldn't bear to have her out of his sight; who, for her birthday, booked out an entire French restaurant so they could dine alone and presented her at the night's end with seven tiny sky-blue boxes from Tiffany's—a pair of earrings for each day of the week.

Our mother practically fainted when Estella told her about it. "How romantic!" she gushed over the phone. "Your father never did anything like that. The nicest thing he gave me when we were dating was a dozen red roses. Oh, and a pearl necklace, but that's all. Len must be very serious about you, Stell."

He was. And what Estella didn't tell our mother (and what Leonard probably didn't tell his) was that his present also included a trip to New York and a suite at the Plaza for two. Even if she had, I doubt it would have made a difference. Our mother would have found a way to feign innocence about their impropriety. She was head over heels herself. Even more so when Tante Elise called to say hello and thus discreetly confirm that her son's interest in Estella was family-sanctioned. The two women began exchanging gifts: gourmet mooncakes in autumn; hotel-bakery Christmas treats in December; Japanese peaches, Ibérico ham, and jars of XO sauce just because.

From our father we heard not so much as a peep about the whole affair. "Everything all right?" he'd ask whenever our mother put him on the phone, and upon receiving an answer in the affirmative, he'd pass the phone back to her with a faint and receding "Good."

During the midyear break, Leonard's mother and ours organized a joint family dinner in Jakarta. The Angsonos insisted on hosting. Their cook used to be head chef at one of the five-star resorts in Nusa Dua, Bali. As if consciously conforming to stereotype, the mothers chatted amicably while the fathers ate in good-natured silence. Leonard held Estella's hand under the table. I felt queasy the whole night.

In the meantime, despite Leonard's lavish presents and gestures, his behavior continued to worsen. He demanded to know what she was doing at all times. Whenever she tried to get back on track with her studies, he accused her of neglecting him. Still, Estella made no attempt at flight. How could she? With every concern that sprang up, our mother did too, like a vigilant nursemaid, to lay it gently, maternally to rest. Leonard's obsession with always having Estella at his side, Ma explained, was a healthy jealousy, an indication of his complete devotion. "Would you rather he didn't care at all about where you went, who you were with?" Ma asked. Similarly, Leonard's rage over Estella getting her hair cut short into a bob without his permission signaled his knowledge of fashion and style: "Darling, you're so lucky. It's so rare to find a man who cares about such things. Your father wouldn't notice if I decided to cut off my head." Ma wasn't even fazed by Leonard's destruction of Estella's entomology textbook after Estella had dared to open it while they were watching TV. "I wish your father worried half as much about me overworking myself," Ma sighed.

Leonard detested Estella's interest in insects especially. He couldn't understand it, found it childish and unattractive, as unbecoming to a woman, he said, as a fondness for beer or too much makeup. ("I told you it wasn't ladylike to play with bugs," affirmed our mother.) I suspect that Leonard disliked Estella's affinity for bugs all the more because it linked her intimately with me, and he hated me. Yes, I would use that word "hate," for, as the sentiment grew, it became painfully obvious. Looking back, I'm impressed that he tried to disguise it for so long; I never saw a trace of such restraint ever again. When he first started visiting, he acknowledged my presence, though his lack of genuine interest was plain enough. Then he began to politely ignore me, which in a way I preferred because by that time I wasn't just wary; I was genuinely frightened. Our mother kept Estella aslumber, swaddling her in gossamer as if for a spider's snack, but the more I saw of Leonard and his effect on my sister, the more terrified I became. I did try to counter our mother's efforts—to rouse Estella and open her eyes—but Leonard must have got wind of it because he began to tell my sister he couldn't stand me at all. If the three of us were in the same room, he would fume and brood and make nasty quips. To him, I must have seemed the devil incarnate: whispering unfavorable things about him into Estella's ear, exhorting her to get back on track with her studies, encouraging her lurid fascination with disgusting creepy-crawlies, trying—oh, trying!—to tug her away from him, anything to get her away! He had no idea what a poor threat I actually was, how little influence I wielded, how successful he and our mother had been in binding her closer and closer to him.

❖   ❖   ❖

I still remember the night I knew it was all over for Estella. It was toward the end of our sophomore year, and one of the rare times when she and I were alone together. Leonard's ridiculousness had reached the point where he refused to let Estella do anything without him—not that she had that many other options. His constant demand for her undivided attention had strangled what little social life she'd had. But that night, Leonard had drunk a tad too much and fallen asleep on our sofa, his baby cheeks quivering with every snore, his slack body bathed in the light of the end credits from the Bruce Willis movie he'd been watching.

Estella had muted the television and crept to the kitchen, where I was studying, as usual.

"He's asleep," she'd explained, putting her finger to her lips. And she made us hot, sugary ginger drinks from sachets we'd purchased at an Asian grocery store.

Lowering herself into a chair, she shifted my microeconomics textbook toward her and began flipping through it.

"I'm taking this class, aren't I?" she asked.

"I suppose so," I said with a disconsolate shrug. "You know, the final exam is next week."

She sighed as she scanned one page after another. "I'm so behind, I have no idea what's going on."

I averted my eyes and shrugged again.

When I looked up, I saw that Estella was weeping—quietly, almost hastily, as if she were trying to get through it as quickly as possible. The table where we sat was next to the window, and she pressed her cheek flush against the cool of the glass. Tears slid across her face, following gravity's tilt.

"Oh, Stell," I whispered. "Can't you leave him?"

Slowly, she shook her head, rolling it against the glass back and forth as if she didn't have the energy to lift it even for a moment. And I began to cry too because I knew then how final it was, that I'd lost her for good. Impossible, I thought at the time, and even now, more than a decade later, I think the same thing. How did it happen so quickly? A mere year and a half, and my sister was no longer mine, or hers for that matter—so captive she couldn't make a break for it even though, deep down, she knew that she should.

"Gwendolyn. Help," she whispered.

"I tried," I sobbed back.

Tried, I said. Past tense. I had already admitted defeat.

"Why do you love him?" I asked, mad at her, at him, at myself. And when she didn't answer right away, I rephrased the question, voice vibrating with fury. "Look what he's done to you, Stell. And think about what he'll do later. This is only the start. How can you let this happen?"

She cast a weary glance in the direction of the doorway, beyond which Leonard dozed. "Because he loves me," she said finally. "He loves me so much. You can't take love like that for granted. You can't just throw it away."

A shiver ran through me. She didn't really believe that, did she?

"It's not real love, Stell. It can't be."

She was looking out at the garden now, and in the glass I saw a rueful smile flicker across her lips. "What choice do we have about the form love takes?"

As I lie here on life support, it's becoming crystal clear to me now—in a way it could never have been in the midst of it, in the thick of our youth. Yes, I see it illuminated and painful to look upon: that dogged faithfulness of Estella's, which, once implanted, would endure, despite the eventual absence of reciprocation, despite the future revelation of disturbing truths.

My sister, by the age of twenty, had been colonized—by Leonard now, but by our family long before. And it might not have turned out badly in the end if any of them had recognized that loyalty for the rare prize it was. Instead, they wound her love up and set it going without a second thought, never considering that it would tick on even if they forgot about her, like some lonely clock at the world's end with no one to tell the hours and minutes to.

"Doll," she murmured. "I'm sorry for how all this has turned out."

"Don't be stupid, Stell," I whimpered, partly scoffing, partly scared.

"No, Doll. Listen to me." Her voice was still low, but sharper, more urgent. "I'm sorry we can't be together anymore. Not really. Not in the way we always have been."

I shook my head, though I knew it was true. She leaned forward and gripped my hand. "I'll miss you, Doll."

"I'll miss you too," I echoed, sealing my surrender and hers.

How surreal it all seems now, and how dramatic, but could it have ever been anything else? When you're barely out of adolescence, life is pitched at an intensity you rarely experience again. That night, Leonard snored on for another two hours before suddenly snorting awake and calling for Estella. Until then, she sat with me and we read together, she comprehending what she could of consumer surplus, then of the insect vascular system.

That was the last real moment we shared as sisters before the marriage. The next day, Estella's awareness of doom had been submerged. She submitted to Leonard's fondlings absentmindedly; she took his temper tantrums in her stride. When summer vacation came around, the two mothers decided it was out of the question to separate Leonard and Estella for even a day. At the invitation of our family, Leonard joined us on a two-week cruise around Northern Europe. He strolled on the deck every sun-bathed evening, arm in arm with Estella and our mother. He joined our uncles and father for blackjack and baccarat every night in the ship's casino. Afterward, Estella stayed in Los Angeles for three weeks with the Angsonos, lunching and shopping with Leonard and his family on Rodeo Drive, accompanying Leonard's mother to galleries to select art for the house his parents had recently bought.

Once back in Jakarta, Leonard and Estella exchanged visits often, sometimes staying at each other's place for several days at a time (in separate bedrooms of course—whatever the families might have guessed about the extent of Leonard and Estella's premarital intimacy, they didn't want to encourage it). It was Leonard's last summer before graduation, and he really should have been doing another internship to prepare him for his entry into the family business. Even our cousin Ricky had been bundled off to do a stint at the not-yet-defunct Barings in Singapore. But Leonard was an only child, spoiled rotten by his mother and unchecked by his father, who, though not indulgent, left Leonard's rearing in the care of his wife. And so Leonard chose to wallow in idleness and made

Estella wallow there as well, reducing their lives to an interminable series of movie watchings, mall frequentings, swimming pool circlings, and lazy lunches and dinners.

Miraculously, Estella scraped by with straight Ds rather than flunking entirely. (I, on the other hand, got straight As thanks to all the free time I had.) The new school year began, and their relationship-by-commute resumed, but with one difference: Leonard proposed, a month after classes started. They were to be married after his graduation, in spring the following year. Naturally both sets of parents knew before Estella did. Naturally the proposal fulfilled all the requirements for "romantic": an enormous diamond ring from Cartier, selected by Leonard's mother; an expensive candlelit dinner at the French Laundry in the Napa Valley; Leonard down on one knee. Swept up in planning for the wedding, Estella neglected schoolwork completely, which wasn't a problem, since after the marriage, at Leonard's insistence, she would discontinue her studies altogether.

To my parents' credit, they put up resistance on this matter. Our father, bookish in his life before our mother, was the closest to outraged we'd ever seen. Our university-educated mother was indignant as well. It was a serious matter, so she took it up directly with Leonard's folks to see if they could reason with their son. But Tante Elise only offered profound apologies. There was no changing Leonard's mind, she said. And besides, perhaps he had a point. Estella attending Berkeley while Leonard was working in Jakarta would be disruptive at a time when they should be laying the foundation for the rest of their life together. She could resume her education in later years after the couple was firmly on their feet. Anyway (and this Leonard's mother said gently), it wasn't as if Estella was doing well in school. Didn't it make more sense for Estella to return to studying when she was more settled, when she wouldn't be distracted by the glorious tumult of young love? She herself had married Leonard's father straight out of high school, and she had no regrets. Our mother, I'm ashamed to say,

allowed herself to be bullied into agreement, and she in turn extracted resigned compliance from my father. The Angsono—Sulinado alliance was
on the verge of being complete, and it was too late to stand in its way.

❖   ❖   ❖

Estella and Leonard tied the knot in July 1993, in a midmorning ceremony
for close relatives and friends at Leonard's family's church—an enormous
three-spired cathedral in central Jakarta. A traditional Chinese tea ceremony was conducted for both families in the early evening, followed by
a dinner reception for a thousand guests—nothing in comparison to the
over-the-top weddings of this day and age, but more than respectable by
early-nineties standards.

The reception was held in one of the luxury hotels the Angsonos owned
shares in—I confess, I've forgotten which one. I was a wreck that night; I'd
been sleeping poorly for weeks and had barely eaten for days. I'm surprised
I can recall anything at all. But I do remember the ballroom was enormous,
with large glass doors that opened out onto a manicured garden through
which peacocks freely roamed. From my recollection of the heavy wooden
beams and gilt Javanese carvings that graced the ceilings, I infer the hotel
must have been one of the older ones in the city—a grand relic of the 1970s,
past its prime but imposing nevertheless.

Even when one spends so much time sifting through the past, certain
memories are bound to be more vivid than others. Two scenes from that
night stand out in my mind. The first, to my embarrassment, is a portrait
of self-indulgence: Me standing in the bathroom of a hotel room just after
the tea ceremony, crying myself completely dry so I will be bankrupt of
tears for the remainder of the night. My face is a mess and my eyes look
like they're hemorrhaging ink, but I'll wash up and ring the professional
makeup artist we're keeping on call for an emergency redo. In the meantime, the salt water running down my cheeks feels good. Refreshing, even

though my foundation is caked on so thick I'm surprised I can sense anything at all on the surface of my skin.

The second scene is more sinister, sparked by a bloodcurdling scream from the garden beyond the ballroom's glass doors. There's a flurry of activity: security guards and waitstaff flocking to the area, along with the bolder and more curious of the guests. When it's clear that whatever caused the kerfuffle isn't dangerous enough to warrant an evacuation, I surprise myself by trotting outside to take a look before anyone can stop me. It's by the footpath on the far side of the lawn, and not so much "it," but "they." Many pieces. Chunks of meat, slimy and bloody and plumaged in iridescent blue. The victim's tail feathers are strewn around and on top of the pile of flesh, as are the organs—a riot of violated beauty. To cap it all off, a very long, fine-looking feather has been skewered erect into the center of the heap, its gold-rimmed iris of indigo and turquoise gleaming in the dim garden lights like an incongruously merry eye, its delicate green hairs waving back and forth like a baby palm frond in the night breeze. In the distance are two running figures, looming closer, holding a plastic tarp stretched between them, as if the peacock is still alive and they're trying to bring it into captivity. Only as the tarp descends over the heap do I catch a glimpse of the message propped at its base, scrawled on cardboard in marker, or possibly blood.

POTONG ORANG CINA MASAK DI KUALI

The opening lines of that ubiquitous children's song about slaughtering a goose, but with "Chinaman" substituted for the bird to be chopped up and cooked in the pot.

Someone escorts me back into the ballroom.

I don't know if they ever caught the culprit. If I had to guess, it was probably a nobody nursing a grudge—a disgruntled low-level employee, perhaps, whose toe had been crushed by the great rolling wheels of one of our families' businesses. This was the kind of thing that would have been attended to without bothering the women of the families, or, beyond a certain point, the men. Our grandfather or one of our uncles might have politely asked a non-Chinese, *pribumi* acquaintance to "look into it"—perhaps a high-ranking officer in the Jakarta police force. Or if the Angsonos had handled it, they might have approached one of the army officials they knew.

Even if investigations met with success—a few nights in jail for the perpetrator, broken bones, a scar or two as a lasting reminder—the men in our families wouldn't have been informed of the gruesome details. They would have been assured it had been "seen to," and that would have been enough. People like us couldn't take these things to heart: Great wealth attracted enemies. Add "Chinese" to the equation and the resentment doubled—simple as that. All the more reason to get filthy rich: So you could rise above it. So you could earn respect and protection from the powerful. So you weren't at the mercy of others because of your slitty eyes and buckteeth.

Apart from my misery and the incident with the peacock, I suppose the wedding was a success. They got married, which was the main thing in theory. My sister looked gorgeous, but most brides do. And no one significant was slighted by any breaches in protocol, which, given the scale of the event, was no mean feat.

I regret not saying a proper good-bye to Estella. I meant to the morning after, once the madness had passed and people had stopped whisking her and Leonard here, there, and everywhere. But the wake-up call I ordered never came, or I was so tired and drunk I don't remember answering it, or else I thought I ordered one but didn't at all. Whatever happened, I rose and she was gone. With Leonard. For some reason, he'd got it into his head that the romantic thing to do was to embark on their honeymoon ASAP the next day. By the time I woke up, at the shamefully late hour of twelve, their plane was already winging its way to Italy. They were to spend three weeks there before heading to Japan. Leonard hadn't been able to decide between them, so they were heading to both.

A light was flashing on the phone by my bed. I had a message. Her voice sounded distant and crackly around the edges. "See you when we get back, Doll. We'll keep in touch, okay?"

WE'LL KEEP IN touch. As if I were a mere acquaintance, a minor friend. I would have been offended if I hadn't been so crushed.

I didn't realize at the time how forced my sister's nonchalance was—the effort she was making to commence married life in a state of joyous self-delusion. Smile and the rest will follow. It sounds like a tip from a self-help book on the power of remaining positive. Estella must have hoped that the same principle would apply.

I wonder, now, if she hadn't put up such a brave front in the months leading up to the marriage and immediately after, whether I would have behaved any differently. Let's say her message had been tearful and barely coherent—"Doll, I don't want to leave you" rather than "Keep in touch." Would I have made more of an attempt to shake off my self-pitying lethargy and fight for her in those initial years? To at least encourage her to stand up for herself against Leonard and her in-laws, since our family wouldn't?

I'd like to say I would have, but I don't think so. It's simply the excuse I fall back on as I lie here supine, trying to trace the sequence of events that turned my sister into a mass murderer. I tell myself she kept her unhappiness a secret, that she didn't reach out for help. But weren't the tears she had shed that night in our kitchen in Berkeley more than enough evidence that she was in desperate need of rescuing? Why did I let her push me away?

Truth be told, I blinded myself, as I would later with our mission to find Tante Sandra. Shouldn't I have known that something was terribly wrong the second Estella uttered that word—"redemption"—that night by the pool? And when she uttered it again as our car sped along the California highway?

We started off from the hotel at eleven the next morning, after braving the ghosts of that Matsuhisa dinner past. Not too early; we weren't gluttons for punishment. But not overly late; for all my skepticism, even I couldn't help but feel excited about the prospect of finding our aunt. Estella was in the driver's seat again. I played navigator, in my hands Map-Quest directions courtesy of the hotel concierge. Road maps were tucked into the glove compartment just in case. We'd barely made it to the interstate when I promptly fell asleep again. When I woke, it was to the rise and fall of truck song—the roar of engines escalating to a deafening pitch, the clatter and squeak of jostling bolts and rubber, and their diminishment into a peaceful swoosh of wind and air as we zoomed past. Like breathing, I thought, the workings of the world still illuminated by the clarity of sleep. The breathing of the open road. My eyes cracked open to the California winter sun, blinding and gray, to dusty hillocks dotted with stone and vegetation, green and also gray, to the sudden appearance, at our right, of rumbling wire flats housing feathered bundles, grizzle-eyed, gray as well.

"Chicken truck!" Estella called out gaily.

"How long did I sleep for?" I asked.

"Don't know. Not long. Maybe an hour? A little less?"

Estella driving without my company for an hour: This perturbed me, though I wasn't sure why. "Where are we?" I asked, sitting up, peering outside, as if it would help me get my bearings.

"About halfway there. How about lunch?"

Even as she was posing the question, she flipped the right turn signal on and we swooped off the freeway into the parking lot of a Taco Bell.

We ate our meal greedily, the more discerning palate for Mexican food we'd developed during our college days grown rusty from years of disuse in Indonesia. Within half an hour, we were back on the road, Estella again taking the wheel, despite me arguing that it was my turn.

She was aglow with it—the vitality that was becoming more evident with each passing day since she'd called me about Tante Sandra's photo. "Spunk," that was the American term for it. She steered with confidence, and her voice sounded almost brassy, with a sort of robust twang. It was as if she had unfurled herself, a banner fluttered open by a strong wind. I felt I could barely keep up.

An oncoming sign told us we'd reach Bakersfield in fifty miles.

"Hey, Stell," I said, breaking in on her happy chatter. She'd been keeping it going since lunch, speculating about our aunt's life (husband, children, house, hobbies?) and pointing out interesting billboards (ads for quaint specialty stores like the Preserves & Pickles Patch and Kast-Iron King). "I just want to say—I'm sorry."

She laughed, puzzled. "About what?"

"Oh, you know," I mumbled, suddenly feeling sheepish. "About not being there for you those first few years of your marriage. I know Ma and Ba didn't do anything, and neither did the rest of the family. But I should have known better. I should have—"

"Forget about it. It's not your fault." Her brow furrowed. "I was trying to be happy with Leonard, and given the way things were between the two of you . . . Well, I made my choice. It was a bad one. I never should have let him pull us apart."

"But I should have reached out, been more proactive . . ." I insisted again.

She shook her head briskly. "It wouldn't have done any good."

I opened my mouth once more to protest, but she cut me off. "It was beyond your help. The rest of the family might have had some influence—if they'd chosen to get involved. But not you. I would never have let you. I *couldn't*."

"What do you mean? Why was it beyond my help?" I asked.

She ignored my question and chuckled. "Never mind," she said. "Anyway, I'd only have burdened you. Stood in the way. You had your own life to live."

"Yeah, right," I scoffed. "All that life."

"Don't be so modest," she said, knitting her brow again. "You know I envied you. Everything you learned—about insects especially. You were able to keep taking entomology classes. You were able to continue working at the Essig—"

"I remember you saying there was more to life than all that." The remark spilled out before I could stop it.

"I did say that," she conceded with no trace of umbrage. "And I was right; there was more. It just wasn't as worth having as I thought."

She continued, grinning. "Anyway, it wasn't as if you didn't have more going on in your life than just studying and insects."

I stared blankly at her.

"Ray Chan?" she prompted, waggling her eyebrows.

I'd practically forgotten him. I supposed she had a point.

With her free arm, she leaned over and nudged me. "You guys had some fun, didn't you?"

It had all been far more innocuous than her tone suggested. Raymond— Ray for short. The engineering major with a buzz cut we'd met during freshman orientation at the BASA pizza party. One year above us, Chinese- American, and a native to the Bay Area, he'd gone out of his way to be friendly to Estella and me when we'd attended the BASA events. In one of our very first conversations with him, the three of us compared notes on stereotypes about the Chinese in our respective home countries.

"Stingy," I'd said.

"Here too," he'd replied.

"How about good at making money?" I asked.

He nodded. "Same as here. Partly because of the stinginess. And because we're all supposedly industrious."

"Exactly," I said. "People in Indonesia think that as well."

He laughed. "Not that there's nothing to back these stereotypes up. I mean, take my parents: I remember having a cold when I was a kid and being over at a white friend's place. His mother offered me a Kleenex and I kept trying to refuse. My mom always told us that tissues were way too expensive, so in our house we used toilet paper for everything. She used to say, 'If it's good enough for your ass, then it's good enough for your nose.'"

This made Estella and me smile.

"Same story with your family?" Ray asked us. "Toilet paper as tissues and bowl haircuts at home? Buying everything in giant economy packs because it's cheaper in the long run?"

Once again, my sister and I laughed, but we didn't answer the question. We'd long figured out that in egalitarian America, and in the socialist stronghold of Berkeley especially, being wealthy was more a cause for shame than pride.

"What about being rich?" I asked, steering the conversation both away from and closer to the truth. "Is that a Chinese stereotype here? In Indonesia, people think that the Chinese always have lots of money and that's all they care about."

Ray tilted his head and thought for a while. "Not re-e-eally. I mean, people are more likely to think of the Chinese running cheap takeout joints or doing laundry than as *rich*." He thought some more. "Do you mean 'rich' as in millionaire rich?"

"Um. Yes. And no . . ." said Estella, also trying to work out what "rich" meant in the Indonesian context. "A lot of the big businesses back home are owned by Chinese families. But people think that even the Chinese guy who owns the corner store is doing pretty well, comparatively speaking, I guess. Indonesia's a Third World country. Most people are pretty poor. So maybe 'rich' over there translates to 'middle class and above' over here?"

"You said yes just now," noted Ray, "when I asked if you meant millionaire rich. So the Chinese families who own big businesses back where you come from. They're millionaires?"

Estella gave a small nod. So much for avoiding the subject.

Ray chuckled. "Chinese millionaires. That definitely doesn't fit the stereotype here. Not yet, anyway. What about your family?" he joked. "Are you guys swimming in cash?"

Again, we let our laughter speak for itself and hoped for the best.

"And you said 'stingy,' " Ray said, trundling on. "So the Chinese millionaires are stingy too? They don't live in mansions and drive Rolls-Royces?"

"They do," I said evasively, but also trying to think through the contradictions myself. "Maybe it's a different kind of stingy?" I ventured. "I think you're thinking of it like frugal or thrifty. And that's what I meant too. But also, maybe, ungenerous? Spending it on oneself but not wanting to give any to others. Does that make sense?"

"Yeah, I guess," said Ray, trying to process this. Then he shrugged. "Then again, it's not like stereotypes are consistent."

"How about duplicity?" asked Estella. "And cunning? Are those associated with being Chinese here? They are back home."

Ray rubbed his chin. "Maybe they used to be. Stereotypes change. Shrewd, maybe. But downright duplicitous? I'm not sure."

"What about arrogant and snooty?" she continued.

"Hah! More like submissive and servile," said Ray with a hoot. He grinned. "Snooty, eh? And shady? And hella rich? Hey, Chinese-Indonesians sound pretty badass, if you ask me. Positively gangsta."

Not all our exchanges with Ray were so profound, though Estella and I had found such conversation refreshing. We'd never had friends who considered topics like racial stereotypes fodder for casual discussion. But when things got more serious between Estella and Leonard, I had to go to BASA events alone. And though I made a conscious effort at first, I gradually stopped attending altogether.

Estella stepped on the accelerator and shifted lanes in order to avoid the exhaust fumes from the ancient Oldsmobile ahead of us. "Didn't you guys meet up outside of BASA too?" she asked slyly.

I couldn't believe she remembered. I know I barely did. "Only once."

"A date, wasn't it?"

"Just lunch," I insisted, even as I recalled with some wistfulness what a perfect lunch it had been. It hadn't even been anywhere particularly special—some run-down café on Telegraph Avenue with wobbly, sticky-surfaced tables and a faint moldy smell emanating from the walls. But, as Estella put it, we'd had some fun. He'd been friendly and good-humored, and polite but not overly so. He'd found my fascination with insects "intriguing"—"Really. In a good way," he'd claimed. We'd parted with a handshake, but as our fingers had lingered in each other's, the silly parody of stiff formality had melted into a gesture of surprising warmth.

"We should do this again," he'd said.

We never did.

"What happened, anyway?" asked Estella. "Why didn't things go any further?"

"I don't know," I replied, even as I thought that maybe I did. Why ruin a perfect moment with what might come afterward? I used to wonder occasionally what might have happened if he and I had gone out again. It had always ended in a nightmarish vision, with Ray morphing into Leonard, his affability turning strained and his hand gripping too hard, his thin lips becoming fleshy and pressing themselves into mine.

"I don't mean to hurt you by bringing it up," said Estella, finally sensing my resistance and backing away. "I envied that part of your life, you know, even if things between you two didn't come to anything. Or maybe *because* they didn't come to anything. You can't spoil what you leave untouched."

"In that case, maybe we should turn around now," I observed, only half jokingly. "We should leave Tante Sandra alone. Whatever her reason for leaving, she's free of the family now. Why drag her back in?"

"Because she's the only member of our family we haven't managed to ruin." Estella spoke impatiently, as if the answer were obvious. "Maybe she'll rub off on us. If we have any shot at redemption, it has to lie with her."

I winced. "Could you *not* use that word?"

"What word? 'Redemption'?" Estella even rolled the *r* and flashed me a rakish grin.

"It's not funny," I insisted, disturbed by how many things Leonard was still tainting, even after his death. He was like a corpse decaying in a reservoir, its unwholesome juices seeping into the water.

"Sorry," she said. "I know it reminds you of him. But I can't come up with a better word."

Upon the invocation of Leonard's ghost, we sank into quietude. And it seemed that our minds drifted in the same haunts, for then Estella murmured with a thin smile the very words that were taking shape in my mind: " 'Everyone who does evil hates the light.' "

Those were Leonard's last words—the only ones he'd uttered in his final, feverish moments, sometimes in fragments and sometimes whole, sometimes in between the bouts of moaning and trembling and sudden paroxysms, sometimes in frantic repetitions like a mantra to ease him of his pain. Poor Leonard. Yes, even I could think "poor," for who couldn't pity him in the end?

Estella murmured something else: " 'And will not come into the light for fear their evil deeds will be exposed.' "

"What?" I asked, startled.

"That's the rest of the verse," Estella explained, checking her blind spot before shifting lanes. "I looked it up after he passed away. Since they were his dying words, I thought it was the least I could do. They're from the Bible."

Obviously. Leonard was always quoting the Bible in those days. We'd all thought he'd gone mad. I'd told him so once. "You're right, I am mad," he'd admitted. "I'm crazy for Christ." And how he had looked it, his grin awful in its breadth and height and toothiness, his pupils radiant with fanaticism—a stark contrast to the saggy crescents under his eyes, a by-product of his new habit of waking at five every morning to "commune with the Lord."

Estella continued. "I'm not saying we need to get religious like Leonard wanted us to. I just think we should stop hiding everything from each other, not to mention ourselves. Anyway, have some faith. She's Tante Sandra, remember? She's like—"

"Drops of dew." My response was immediate. And with its utterance came again the foolish conviction that retrieving our aunt would fix us all. That's right: *us*. Thanks to this quest of Estella's, the boundaries she and I had worked so hard to establish between me and the family were beginning to erode.

At that moment, our car reached the crest of a hill. The road and the land dropped away before us into a sun-bleached vista of gnarled trees and clumps of grass and some kind of crop in the distance—almonds? oranges?—planted in orderly rows, basking to the point of withering in a relentless, dazzling brilliance.

"What a gorgeous day!" exclaimed Estella.

I reached for my sunglasses.

It was early afternoon by the time we reached Bakersfield. We drove through what appeared to be the downtown district, past low-slung buildings in varieties of beige, their unremarkableness offset by the splendor of the Californian flora—spindly palms and dark, shaggy pines, carmine-tongued bushes and pale-barked trunks wreathed in brittle gold. The printed Map-Quest directions instructed us to turn onto a road lined with ranch-style houses and manicured lawns. We pulled into the driveway of number 2307.

"We're here," said Estella, sounding almost as if she couldn't believe it. She stepped out of the car.

"Let's hope she is too," I said, following her lead. The exterior of the house, the lawn, the mailbox were all emphatically neutral, providing no clues about who lived there or what they were like. No garden gnomes, no wind chimes, no children's toys, no bird feeder. In fact, the house showed so few signs of life that it might have been uninhabited. Estella looked as doubtful as I felt.

We climbed up the stairs to the front porch, rang the doorbell, and waited. A little while later, we rang it again. And one more time. We knocked. "Hello?" we called through the door. We walked into the yard and peered through the large front window, which was screened by curtains.

"Looks like she's out," said Estella.

"Or whoever it is who lives here. Or maybe it's empty."

"Great. Just great."

"Hello?" someone warbled suddenly from our right. "Are you looking for someone?" It was the next-door neighbor, an elderly woman wielding a pair of pruning shears. She was completely pink: her tracksuit a peppy fuchsia, her visor a cotton candy hue, her translucent skin a salmon fillet baked by the sun, the rims of her blue eyes a sensitive magenta. She peered uncertainly at us across the strip of concrete lane separating her property from where we stood.

I continued to scour the window for a gap in the curtains and let Estella speak with her. "Yes, I'm her niece," I heard Estella say, "assuming this is the right house. The woman who lives here is named Sandra, yes? Sandra—" She was clearly just about to add "Sulinado" but stopped. Who knew whether our aunt had kept her last name? Then again, who knew if she'd kept her first name either?

"Your aunt, you say?" the woman asked, as if by receiving further affirmation, she could ascertain whether Estella was telling the truth. I gave up looking through the window and watched the exchange from a distance.

"My mother's sister," explained Estella.

"Is Sandra expecting you, then?"

Estella threw me a glance before flashing the woman her best conspiratorial smile. "No, it's a surprise visit."

"Oh!" the woman exclaimed, suddenly tickled. My sister could be so charming when the occasion demanded it. "You came all the way from China, then?" the neighbor asked. "Sandra said all her relatives live abroad."

"So, this is the right address?" Estella asked excitedly, letting the mistake pass. Or maybe that's what our aunt had told her—that she was from China.

"Sure is," the woman said, evidently having decided we were trustworthy folk. "But she's away at the moment."

"What time will she be back?"

"What time?" The neighbor's face dissolved into confusion before she realized we didn't share her knowledge. "Why, she's back on Monday. She's gone away for the weekend. Asked me to keep an eye on things."

"Monday," I repeated. The day after tomorrow.

"What now?" Estella sighed, looking helplessly over at me.

"How long are you in town for?" the woman asked.

"We're staying in Los Angeles," I explained over Estella's shoulder. "And we're flying back tomorrow night."

The woman looked surprisingly crestfallen on our behalf. "Oh, I see," she said, shaking her head. "Seems an awful shame to come here all the way from China and not get to see her."

We thanked the neighbor and walked back to the car to discuss our next move.

"Doll, she's here!" squealed Estella. "Can you believe it? We're so close! I'll get my secretary to rebook us on a later flight."

The miracle of our circumstances suddenly dawned on me, making me dizzy. I placed a hand on the side of the car to steady myself.

"Yes, of course," I murmured, too dazed to say anything else. But Estella was already making the call. While she was doing that, I walked down the driveway and peered up the length of the street. Rectangles of grass, interrupted by the occasional picket fence, stretched as far as the eye could see. Tricycles and strollers idled on porches, and here and there the American flag fell gracefully from underneath an eave. As I listened to the lazy barks of bored golden retrievers and the docile roar of a distant lawnmower, I wondered how on earth Tante Sandra could have ended up here.

We'd brought the photos of our aunt with us—it had seemed the obvious thing to do, though it made no sense upon further reflection. What use would we put them to? Show them to strangers in the street and ask, "Have you seen this woman?" Shove them in Tante Sandra's face and cry, "It's you! We have proof, see?"

I took out the envelope and slid out the photo of her in London, which I'd mentally captioned, *Bell-bottomed and bohemian at Buckingham Palace.* Holding it up, I inserted Tante Sandra into the scene before me, standing her next to a coil of garden hose, reclining her in a freestanding hammock in someone's yard.

As if to protest the indignity, a memory flared like a struck match: the Tante Sandra of the photograph running at full tilt toward us through a wet expanse of paved stone, congregations of pigeons flying up on either side of her. She slowed to a trot as she approached us, pink-cheeked and triumphant. Her right hand clutched a brown paper bag. "Chestnut?" she asked and before we had time to answer, she cracked one between her palms and stripped away the leathery shell. "While they're hot," she explained. She broke the nutmeat in half and zoomed one of the pieces through the air in loop-the-loops. "Open wide! Here comes the plane!"

"Done," cried Estella, returning her phone to her purse. "Where to now?"

I blinked. "Where else? Back to the hotel."

She opened her mouth in an exaggerated yawn. "What? How boring."

"Do you have a better idea?"

"Let's go see the monarchs."

I stared at her. "You're insane."

"Come on," she pleaded. "Remember how much fun we had the last time? We have two days to kill! It's even the right time of year."

I put up a good fight. We hadn't brought any of our clothes or makeup or toiletries; we'd be paying for two hotel rooms at once, which seemed silly; we might not be able to find a hotel room at all. Inevitably, I lost. As I said, she was growing stronger, more vibrant, more forceful. And this change, I recognized, was good. I should encourage her, I thought.

Before we left, we asked the pink neighbor if she would be so good as not to tell our aunt we had dropped by. We would return and we wanted it to still be a surprise. The ready assent on her face suggested this was the most excitement she'd had all year.

We stopped at a mall on our way out of Bakersfield and bought enough clothes and toiletries to tide us over. I fell asleep in the car again. When I woke, we were gliding through the night and fog and the soft clementine glow of the streets of Carmel.

We'd stayed in Carmel the last time too, even though the prime grounds for monarch-peeping were twenty minutes' drive away on the peninsula's northern side. The city of Monterey might have been closer to the butterfly overwintering sites, but Carmel was less tacky and far more genteel—paved with cobblestones and populated by expensive restaurants and quaint stores advertising their presence via tastefully weathered wooden signs.

Guided purely by memory, we even managed to check ourselves into the same inn where we'd stayed eight years ago. We could have gone hotel hopping to find something more luxurious—with freestanding villas or an ocean view or a more extensive spa—but Estella was taken with the idea of staying at the exact same place. I was mystified by her desire to re-create the flight taken by our younger selves, but I tried to see things her way. Dining at Matsuhisa had been about conquering past trauma; perhaps she hoped this impromptu trip to see the monarchs would reignite the hope and optimism of the first one.

Our room, the receptionist informed us, was technically the honeymoon suite. There was nothing too obvious to declare it as such, thank God, but it did boast an enormous Jacuzzi in the bathroom, not to mention an oversized four-poster bed draped in dark velvet and silk. Also, the hotel directory on the vanity had been left open at a list of "couples' activities," which included a couple's massage, a lovebird brunch package, and champagne and strawberries in the evening.

"You must have stayed in a lot of these kinds of rooms with Leonard," I remarked, running a finger down one of the wooden bedposts. "Right after the wedding, I mean."

My sister smiled in a world-weary sort of way, as if to intimate that the answer was yes, but that she'd had her fill of them and everything else to do with romance.

"Still," she said, continuing what she hadn't uttered out loud, "if I had known what would come after, I would have locked myself in a honeymoon suite for good."

IT WAS DURING that first trip of ours to see the monarchs, back in 1996, that I'd finally learned the full truth about Estella's initial three years of marriage. She'd started recounting it to me after the ugly scene at Matsuhisa and the enervating drama with our mother in the car. And she'd continued filling me in on the gory details all through the long drive there and back.

Prior to that, I'd had some awareness that my sister must have been unhappy, but as I've said, several factors combined to conveniently justify my inaction. I was depressed; I was preoccupied with my studies during my last year at Berkeley; Estella rarely contacted me, in an attempt not to displease Leonard; and out of a twisted consideration for my welfare, she wanted to refrain from saddling me with her woes. The only other people who could have enlightened me about the extent of Estella's misery were our mother and father. And they were busy convincing themselves that she was happy and nothing was wrong.

The honeymoon really had been the best part of Estella's marriage, but not for the usual reasons. There were no torrents of passion, no heights of ecstasy; rather, it had an opiate effect—on both her and Leonard. Drugged by the wines and herb-scented earth of Tuscany, by Kyoto's fiery foliage and Tokyo's sapphire luminescence, Estella felt thoroughly serene. It was the equivalent of easing a lobster into a warm bath before heating the water by degrees. Under these conditions, Leonard was unusually tranquil as well, stupefied perhaps by the fact that a whole other person now belonged exclusively to him.

Once she and Leonard returned to Jakarta, the novelty of the opulence and decorum that characterized Angsono family life kept her stunned for a while longer—so I surmised. From her lips, I learned it was a world governed by a series of unspoken rules and implicit understandings, mystifying, but also enthralling to those who hadn't been raised in their midst or initiated into their ways. Estella was awed; our family—new money by their standards—had never placed much emphasis on the "proper" way of doing things, except in the areas of business and making money. Certainly, one bought furniture and clothes of a certain quality and mixed with people whom one might consider generally respectable, but beyond that one didn't give these matters too much thought.

And so months of married life passed before Estella's comprehension of her new situation ripened into fullest despair. It came slowly, as with any other fruit: a shedding of petals, a green swell blushing yellow, then brazen purple and red, sinking its twig earthward with the weight of its juice. But the gradualness of the revelation didn't make it any less cruel.

The most important difference between their family and ours, she noted, was that their married women didn't work. Our mother and aunts, including our aunts-in-law, all contributed to the family business in some capacity—if not overseeing new ventures or partnerships or consolidations, then keeping an existing wing of the business chugging along, or at the very least holding some high-ranking position in name only for advantageous tax or legal purposes. Even Oma, for all her domesticity, had been a titular member of several company boards. The Angsonos, in contrast, believed firmly that business was best left completely to their men, with the single women permitted to help in minor capacities only until they found suitable husbands. Sono Jaya, the Angsono family's conglomerate, was headed by Leonard's father, Om Albert, who was aided by his two younger brothers—Leonard's uncles. Leonard and his male cousins occupied all the topmost senior positions.

As Estella found out, patriarchy didn't mean that nothing was expected of her. Until the completion of their new house, which would be a short drive away from that of her in-laws, she and Leonard were to live in a luxury serviced apartment, which Estella was responsible for furnishing and decorating. My sister had done so quickly, using perfectly serviceable furniture that various members of our family had been keeping in storage or simply had lying around the house, her reasoning being that they would only be in the apartment for a year at most. But upon sharing this good news over dinner at Leonard's parents' house, where they were staying until that apartment was ready, an uneasy silence settled over the table.

Leonard broke it. "You used secondhand furniture for our apartment?"

Estella knew immediately she had made a mistake. "It's not 'secondhand,'" she reasoned. "It's my family's. There's nothing wrong with it. And I didn't want to be wasteful."

Tante Elise hastily stepped in. "My dear, why didn't you say you needed help finding furniture? We could have gone shopping together."

Before the wedding, said my sister, she might have apologized and assented, or tried to laugh it off pleasantly. But she told me a fighting desperation had risen within her—probably that impulse we all experience at critical moments in our lives, when we perceive that personal liberty and principles might be in danger of being swept away if we fail to take a stand at that very instant.

I remember musing, sadly, on how often that impulse to toe the line comes too late, welling up only when there is no longer sand under our feet and we find ourselves adrift with no land in sight.

"It's silly to waste money on new furniture if we're only going to be living in the apartment for a little while," Estella had maintained.

Leonard had replied, in that same overly reasonable, and therefore dangerous, voice, "Well, if you did your planning properly, the new furniture could be used in the new house as well."

Estella leaned back in despair. "Len, how can I plan that far ahead? I haven't even chosen the interior designer for the new house yet! And we can't just live in an empty apartment!"

Without a word, Leonard slammed his fork and spoon down and stomped out of the dining room. Om Albert, who absented himself from all domestic dramas, mentally if not physically, continued eating as if nothing had happened. Tante Elise slipped her hand over Estella's and smiled.

"Don't worry, Stell. We can go furniture shopping tomorrow. Money should be no object when it comes to creating a comfortable family home."

Estella said the next day she had called our mother for help. Ma was instantly indignant: How dare Leonard say our family's furniture wasn't good enough? How dare he call our sofas and beds "secondhand," as if they were no better than some stranger's musty, flea-infested rubbish? Ma hung up in a huff, saying she would have a word with Leonard's mother. Estella pleaded with her to be tactful, but as it turned out, she had nothing to fear. When Ma called Estella back a few hours later, her tone had changed entirely. Leonard's mother had explained the situation: Estella had misunderstood. Leonard hadn't meant any offense—he'd simply been encouraging Estella to consider the best solution for the long term.

Ma made no mention of the fact that while Estella and Leonard had been on their honeymoon, Opa had coaxed Leonard's father into investing in Tante Betty's ill-conceived cotton plantation project. Ma didn't need to. Leonard's father told Estella about it over dinner later that night, before his wife gently reminded him not to discuss work at home. Om Albert had brought the subject up innocently enough—the only two topics he enjoyed conversing on were business and golf. Deprived of the first and knowing his new daughter-in-law had never picked up a club, he then lapsed into his usual silence and left the talking to everyone else.

❖ ❖ ❖

My sister began to worry about what she had gotten herself into. During the courtship and engagement, she had known Leonard's mother as a pleasant woman with elegant manners and faultless taste. And Leonard had not provided any greater insight into her character, rarely speaking of her and giving almost no indication that he thought of her at all. Now that Estella had been welcomed into the family bosom, the full extent of her mother-in-law's power disclosed itself.

It was owing to Tante Elise that the pale green breakfast china was laid out every morning at 7:30 and that every member of the household, upon being seated, could expect a small crystal glass of freshly squeezed orange juice at the top-right corner of their place setting. It was also owing to her that lunch and dinner, when taken at home, were served on the dishware specially reserved for those meals, and that all family members present in the house at four in the afternoon were approached by Rina or one of the lesser maids and asked if they would care for tea or coffee and a little snack. Under Tante Elise's direction, the servants kept every room and its objects in immaculate order. If you moved a cushion from one armchair to another, ten minutes later the cushion would return itself to its original place. If you rearranged the coffee table books, or the candles, or the photos on the shelves, when you next entered the room, they too would be restored to their original places, with an extra luster to boot, as if they'd been wiped with a clean rag, which they probably had. There was even an order to be found in the bathrooms: pajamas and dressing gowns were refolded every morning and placed on the ottoman by the bathtub or shower, except every third day, when they were re-placed with fresh ones; all towels were changed every second day; all toi-letries left out on countertops were arranged on mirrored trays in order of height.

("Frankly, I'm not surprised," I said upon learning about the Angsonos' enchanted self-rearranging house. "Your mother-in-law does act like she has an entire banyan tree up her ass.")

My sister said the stifling orderliness extended even to the behavior of the family members themselves. Every weekday, Om Albert and Leonard, farewelled by their wives in the foyer, left for the office in their chauffeured black SUV at 9:30 a.m. Dinner was always served at 7:30 p.m. on the dot. The whole extended family gathered every Sunday at a restaurant in the Grand Hyatt for lunch. There were also guidelines for proper conduct and good living that were regarded as plain common sense: One dressed before coming down to breakfast. One showered before dinner. For good health, one ate a piece of fruit at least once a day. One always wore slippers in the house, but removed them before entering the bedrooms. There were thousands of other things, impossible to count, every convenience and comfort and ritual so discreet and regular that, in sum, they functioned like a well-paved road—indiscernible when maintained and jarring when disrupted.

Of all this, Leonard's mother was the overseer, herself as discreet as any part of the great apparatus whose cogs she ordered polished and oiled. She was not its master, nor its inventor. As the sweet, pliant, and capable wife of the eldest son, she had simply inherited the responsibility of its running and become so fluent in it, so absorbed, that although her slender manicured hand seemed to gesture its continuance, *it* was doing the gesturing. It operated her.

Under her guidance, Estella learned what was "necessary," what was "good," what was "suitable." Tante Elise's tutelage also helped her to better understand Leonard's outbursts, which had become more and more frequent since their honeymoon. The tantrums he used to have in California, while not excusable, had at least been comprehensible—triggered by jealousy, or fear of Estella's waning affections. In Jakarta, his temper spiked seemingly for no reason at all. Several times, when they were still staying in his parents' home, Estella had simply entered a room only to have Leonard sulk or storm out in disgust. Things worsened once they moved into the serviced apartment, which Leonard's mother had helped her decorate exquisitely. Leonard hurled a plate of fruit across the room against the wall.

Leonard emptied the closets of all his clothes and flung them onto the floor. Leonard left abruptly in the middle of dinner and didn't return until three in the morning, piss-drunk.

Estella's pleas for an explanation would go unheeded or else would receive a cryptic reply. "You're my *wife*; learn to act like it." "Can't you do anything right?" "Where were you raised, in a village?" Or else, a sneer. In these moments, Leonard's mother seemed a godsend, an angel sent down from heaven. Estella would call her and explain what had happened, down to the minutest detail. And like a doctor making a diagnosis, Leonard's mother would ask a few specific questions and then discover the root of the problem. The maid had not cut the strawberries into halves. All button-down shirts should be hung, never folded. Soup served at dinner had to be almost boiling hot.

It bewildered her, she told me. Leonard had never had these kinds of expectations in college. If anything, both in his apartment with Ricky and at her place in Berkeley, his attitude toward all things domestic had tended toward the easygoing, if not the downright slovenly. He hadn't much cared when he ate. He had never been too particular about whether beds were made or kitchens were spotless. In fact, the thought had crossed Estella's mind once or twice that she was rather lucky that he wasn't fussier. But this all changed when they began their life together in Jakarta, and the unreasonableness of Leonard's new behavior was something that even his mother couldn't deny. Together, Tante Elise and Estella came up with a likely explanation: Leonard was now married and settled; accordingly, whether conscious of it or not, he expected a life of the same quality that he'd enjoyed growing up. That was his mother's word: "quality." To her, there was nothing subjective or arbitrary about the laws by which their world was governed: They simply reflected life as it should be, at its best.

Stress was the other probable cause of Leonard's moodiness—so conjectured his mother one afternoon at the Shangri-La. She had taken Estella to high tea to celebrate selecting the "right" marble flooring for the new house.

"Adjusting to working life must be very hard on him, poor thing," Tante Elise had sighed before she'd bitten, teeth first to preserve her lipstick, into a jam-and-clotted-cream-topped scone. "Leonard's father is determined to be strict with him, to make sure he can run the business properly. He is the eldest son, after all. But you and I, Stell. We must take care of them. Make sure they can at least relax at home. We have to reward them for working so hard. It's the least we can do as wives."

I'd never thought of our family as particularly progressive, but next to the Angsonos, we were practically radical feminists.

My sister had given up hope of our family intervening by then. Plans were in the pipeline for a partnership between Sono Jaya and Sulinado Group that would combine the Angsonos' dominance in the kretek cigarette market and our family's holdings in tobacco and cloves. It was a match made in heaven, even if the union between Estella and Leonard was just the reverse.

Yet my sister still found herself believing that she was reasonably happy. Marriage into the Angsono family had shot her into the stratosphere of the highest of high society. Our family was certainly wealthy, but not nearly as sickeningly rich as the Angsonos, or as long-established, or as philanthropic or social. As the wife of the heir apparent to the Angsono family fortune and enterprise, Estella now received daily invitations to charity balls and fund-raisers, innumerable ladies' lunches, weddings and birthday parties, anniversary celebrations, and dinners by the dozen. It was her responsibility to discern which ones were important and which ones were unnecessary; which functions she could attend alone and which ones required Leonard's presence as well; which invitations she could decline with a simple handwritten card or an apologetic phone call and which ones required not only written regrets but accompanying gifts—

costly floral arrangements, a wicker basket of imported treats, a bottle of good champagne.

As her social obligations grew, so did her wardrobe. Leonard's mother overheard someone at a lunch remarking snidely that she'd seen Estella in the same evening dress at least three times. Hours later, Estella received a considerate phone call from her mother-in-law suggesting they spend the next few weeks shopping. You'd think it would be every woman's dream, being asked to buy new clothes on her husband's credit card, no expense spared. But it was the dream of a poorer woman. Estella's wardrobe was already enviable by most standards, and this multiday shopping excursion had the air of a forced expedition, fueled by a grim determination to succeed.

It was one of the awkward times in the fashion year when the boutiques hadn't yet received new stock and all that remained were tired leftovers. In the company of her mother-in-law, who was still smarting from the wound of that overheard comment, shopping became a joyless gorging. Upon entering a store, Tante Elise would march over to the first rack she encountered, pick out a dozen items, and the shop assistants, like sharks sensing blood, would join in the frenzy.

My sister recounted to me how this continued until late afternoon, with a break for lunch. And it resumed the next day, and the day after. Clothes, shoes, bags, watches, jewelry, scarves—they left no category of item unpurchased. Estella's new acquisitions were impossible to count and, upon arriving home, were ferreted away by the maids for unpacking, tag removal, dry cleaning, and storage in closets, drawers, and cupboards with the rest of her existing wardrobe. It was as if they had never been new, so she was even deprived of the elation she might have felt at the sheer volume of her purchases—not that it would have afforded her much. Estella felt somehow sick to her stomach about the whole affair. She couldn't put her finger on why. It had something to do with condescension—and with excess, and with so-called propriety. But as Estella had nobody to articulate these feelings to or with, they remained unformed and, thus, unfounded.

◆　◆　◆

Estella and I had always relied on each other, and so had never cultivated any deep friendships with schoolmates, or even our own cousins. The result was that she and I had people we could laugh and chat with, but no confidante apart from one another to whom we could pour out genuine sorrow or woe. Severed from each other, she drifted, as did I, in helpless isolation. Listening to Estella triggered memories of my own loneliness during that period.

I'd felt the loss of my sister most acutely during my late nights in the Essig. Technically, volunteers were only allowed in the collections during official hours. But I'd become such a fixture that I could stay as late as I liked, as long as I cleaned up after myself.

The museum always had more specimens than they could process, from faculty collecting trips and the occasional donation from a member of the general public. The storage fridges and freezers were always crammed: innumerable vials of insects jumbled together in ethyl alcohol solution, and containers of moth and butterfly carcasses, wings carefully folded and pressed flat. There they waited, with a patience only natural to the dead, for someone with the spare time to liberate them from storage, skewer them with a pin, and spread their legs, antennae, and wings in the name of humankind's insatiable quest to catalogue nature's treasures.

As I sat hunched over my mounting board, painstakingly manipulating tarsal segments into place with the aid of insect pins, or squinting through a stereomicroscope lens while gluing a staphylinid's teeny abdomen onto a tiny triangular card, I would find myself thinking of Estella. We had developed our fascination for insects together, and it made sense that I would feel her absence most strongly when surrounded by the creatures that we loved.

The Essig functioned as a sort of chrysalis for me. If I were a pupa in midmetamorphosis, a soupy mess of organic matter in flux, then the Essig served as the hard-shelled covering that provided me with some semblance of structure, that prevented me from leaking out into a primordial puddle. Absorbed in the pleasurable monotony of adjusting antennae and teasing out little limbs, of printing out specimen data in a minute font and scrutinizing dipteran halteres, I missed Estella terribly—and enjoyed missing her because the loneliness gave me a faint idea of what it would have been like if she were there.

Years before, when the cancer was nearly done sucking all the life out of Oma, Estella and I had snuck into her bedroom and found her old housedresses. We'd burrowed our nostrils into them, trying to recapture her scent—the rose and talc and burnt butter of bygone days, not the antiseptic and urine and decay that she reeked of at the end. In the same way, in the feverish late-night pinning of insects, did I catch a whiff of my sister and thus glut myself on what I'd lost.

If only I had known how much Estella was suffering as well—that she too was lonely, deserted by Leonard, who, despite his continued possessiveness, spent less and less time with her. His weekdays he passed at the office, at business lunches and dinners, and, of course, on the road, visiting factories, making calls, and dozing in the dark-tinted, air-conditioned interior of a shiny black luxury car, a patient driver guiding them through the ever-sluggish and ever-worsening traffic of the city. Leonard's newfound interest in golf took up a good portion of his weekends. At meals with his parents or extended family, he was attentive enough, but dining alone with Estella, he barely spoke. And yet he would throw a tantrum if she was unavailable when he sought her out, if she'd made other plans when he had decided on the spur of the moment to eat at home.

Furthermore, perhaps under the influence of his mother's opinions, or the cookie-cutter notions of feminine beauty and style that so saturated Jakarta high society, Leonard began to find fault with Estella's appearance. (When my sister revealed this to me, I could barely contain my rage.) After social functions, he would compare her to other women. Couldn't she do her hair properly, so she looked elegant like Rita Salindo or glamorous like Jerry Santo's latest actress girlfriend? Couldn't she do her makeup so she looked as pretty as everyone else? Shouldn't she hire a personal trainer to keep her in shape? Her face was getting fat, he complained, and she was getting chubby around the waist. To be honest, he stated, it was beginning to disgust him. Look at Coco Winardi—two kids and yet what a figure! It wasn't like Estella didn't have the time, and it wasn't like they didn't have the money. The least she could do was have the decency not to let herself go.

This, added to Leonard's mother's close attention to her wardrobe, left my sister bewildered. She acknowledged that she had gained a bit of weight, but it wasn't as if she couldn't fit into her clothes. She had never been fashionable, never worn much makeup, but she had never thought of herself as frumpy or unkempt. Then again, never before had her appearance been subject to this kind of scrutiny. Our mother, too absorbed in augmenting and preserving her own beauty, had always left our fashion and upkeep to us. And now, here was Estella's husband saying that she should consider eyelash extensions, and her mother-in-law asking her politely (always politely) whether that was the same red silk blouse that Estella had worn just last week, or whether it merely looked very similar.

And it wasn't as though Leonard was tending to his appearance or watching his figure. My sister watched him drink heavily in the evenings and suspected that he drank heavily at his "business dinners" too, which she suspected were not always business and not always just dinner. This she gathered from the remarks he and his friends would make during get-

togethers that included their wives. The comments were seemingly harm-
less ones, but nonetheless, they'd set all the men giggling.

If any of the wives asked what was so funny, she'd receive only snig-
gers in response.

"Boys will be boys," another wife would usually say with a good-
natured shake of her head. And life would roll on: the "boys" growing red
and sweaty from liquor and cigars, the wives exchanging gossip drenched
in so much honey one almost forgot it was gossip at all.

At these gatherings, the women would exchange stories about their children, who were often playing together in an adjoining room under the su-
pervision of several nannies. To make sure Estella felt included—for they
were very considerate and took pains to bring her into the conversation—
they would ask when she and Leonard were planning to have children.
They would teasingly share tips for enhancing her fertility, and his. Herbal
concoctions you could get from this Chinese sinshe or that Javanese bomo.
Foods to eat and not to eat. Sex positions that would help the sperm reach
the egg more easily. All of them agreed that it was best to lie flat for half an
hour after intercourse so that gravity would work in favor of conception.

Estella would nod and titter with the rest and, over time, began to contemplate taking their advice. She had begun to yearn for a child, and not just
because her mother-in-law had begun inquiring tactfully about when she
and Leonard were thinking of having children. A child would love her un-
conditionally. A child would cherish the affection that Leonard now seemed
to scorn. A child would be a worthy endeavor—a true and meaningful labor
to compensate for the reduction of her life to this glittering hollowness
through which she moved each day as if in a mirrored labyrinth.

◆   ◆   ◆

The child didn't come. They had sex often enough—thoughtlessly and
drowsily, before bed or in the middle of the night or in the early morning—

and still, nothing. Estella kept her misery and anxiety to herself. She had become afraid to discuss anything with Leonard for fear of setting him off. It was only when Leonard entered the bathroom afterward and found her lying on her back in the bathtub with her feet propped up against the wall that he realized she wanted to get pregnant, then turned as furious as she'd feared.

He wasn't angry because he didn't want kids; in fact, he'd assumed that a baby would come along as a matter of course. But here was his wife exhibiting clear doubts about his virility. As if he needed gravity's help! They fought. As always, the conflict remained unresolved, adding another notch to the history scored by each new quarrel, each new fit of rage from Leonard or bout of sullen muteness from Estella. Indignant that his manhood had been called into question, he began actively trying to impregnate her. He never explicitly said so, but it was obvious: Sex became resentful and driven—a mad repeated motion to thrust into being something beyond their control. Months passed. He demanded she get her fertility checked, which she did, to discover that there was nothing obviously wrong with her except that she should try to relax. Too much stress could affect these things.

Estella said Leonard had snorted when she'd reported back from the doctor. "Yes, because your life is *so* full of pressure," he'd said. "So much work to do."

For the sake of maintaining peace, she hadn't responded, but such silences, which had so long been her refuge, had also long ceased to demonstrate submission. Instead, they sprawled defiantly in the spaces allotted to them, eyeing him with contempt. The obvious suggestion about what Leonard should do, now that she'd seen a doctor, remained unvoiced. It was out of the question that she should bring it up, and out of character for him to do so.

And so Leonard did not get his own fertility checked (or, at least, he never told her if he did). And they kept on as if nothing had happened, except that Estella abandoned hope of conceiving and Leonard furiously continued to hope even as he furiously denied ever hoping at all.

❖　❖　❖

The months passed. They celebrated their second wedding anniversary (if "celebrated" was the right word). The new house, behind schedule, was finally ready. They moved in, all her furniture and art purchases leaving it still too barren for two.

It was at this point that Leonard began to enter what Estella and I would later refer to as his "muscle period." The house was equipped with a full gym: cardio equipment, weight machines, dumbbells, floor-to-ceiling mirrors, medicine balls—the works. Estella used it for an hour twice a week during sessions with her personal trainer. Then one day, out of the blue, Leonard hired a personal trainer of his own—a beefy, amiable man in his thirties who used to be on the national weight lifting team. Estella began to wonder if Leonard's trainer actually lived in the house without her knowledge: He was in the gym almost every day, early in the morning and late at night, alert and smiling, ready to oversee Leonard's bulking up.

This new phase brought Estella relief, she said. Weight lifting distracted Leonard from her supposed shortcomings and flaws in a way that work and alcohol never had. And the physical distance they were able to keep from each other in the new house helped as well. For the first time since the start of their relationship, Estella had some room to breathe.

She began collecting again, just like when we were children, but this time, because of Leonard, in secret. She wandered the house with tweezers and a jar, pouncing on insects before the servants did. A bright blue wasp rendered docile by impending death. The stout body of a death's-head moth, broken in two. The cerulean wing of a swallowtail, torn. She arranged them artistically in a glass-topped jewelry case along with a sachet of mothballs, which she refreshed regularly. The case was kept in her dressing room, in a drawer with her scarves—a place as safe from Leonard's eyes as any. Not that he bothered to rifle through her possessions anymore, as jealousy had spurred him to do when they were at college.

Just as my activities at the Essig reminded me of Estella, her collecting made her think of me, she said. And she would recall our conversation in our kitchen in Berkeley on our last real night together, what I'd warned her about Leonard getting worse, and that question I'd asked: *Can't you leave him?*

But the answer was still no. Even more so than before. Not merely because the two families were now entwined in business, or because Leonard's family was Catholic and would never sanction a divorce. Nor was it apathy, or because divorce was still generally frowned upon—Tante Margaret was living proof that one could split up and continue to circulate in society, even if she did have to put up with being the subject of gossip for a few months each time. The real reason, however implausible, was that Estella still loved Leonard.

At least, that's what she had the audacity to call that faded remnant: "love." If you ask me, it was contagion. He had grown on her, and it was irrelevant whether she still had any affection for him or not. People nowadays speak easily of cutting ties: with parents who behave badly and friends who rub them the wrong way, with lovers who fail to satisfy and spouses they have come to despise. But my sister revealed herself to be a helpless traditionalist, unable to shatter what circumstance had wrought. If I'd been her, I would have clawed and scrabbled and bit like a cornered rat—at Leonard, at my family and his. But no matter how bitter she became, even once she found out about Leonard's affair and our parents' knowledge of it, that contagion inside of her still held her back, arresting her movements, refusing to let her go.

She was a fool not to have suspected. After all, it wasn't as if unfaithful husbands were rare in our world—our opa a case in point. I suppose it is the sort of thing you think could happen to everyone but yourself. Add to that Ma and Ba's complicity, though, and perhaps her shock was more excusable.

She made the discovery when Leonard was away on business in New York. Like the obedient daughter she was, she took the opportunity to ask our parents if they wanted company for dinner; I'd long since graduated and had been living at home for about two years by that point. But for some reason I was out of town that night. Ma and Ba were delighted to have her over. They rarely saw her anymore. Being an Angsono was practically a full-time job and our family had ceded her willingly. Ma asked a lot of things about the new house. Ba brought out three German Rieslings, just for comparison's sake. The atmosphere around the table bordered on convivial, and my sister felt almost content. As bad as things were with Leonard, as stifled as she felt by her in-laws, at least she had our parents, who really did care, despite their shortcomings.

After dinner, Estella hung out with Ba in his wine cellar as he pottered around unpacking new acquisitions. It seemed to satisfy what remained of his inner intellectual—the sorting of his wines by provenance and year, grape and blend. Sitting there on a stack of unopened crates, listening to Ba's inebriated prattle about this wine and that, Estella had the sensation of listening to a lullaby. So the cut, when inflicted, came all the more as a surprise.

"These aren't drinking well at all this year," said Ba, cradling a bottle of Médoc. He squinted closely at the label. "Not drinking well at all," he repeated mournfully, as was his habit when he was very, very drunk.

"But they are saying it will reach its prime in five years, maybe eight," he continued. "Would you like a case, Stell? I'll give you ten. The least I can do. I know you're unhappy. Very unhappy. The least I can do, my darling. I feel it's our fault, you know. Even though your mother said it isn't." He shook his head and replaced the bottle. "But I told her . . . I told her yes, it is. Yes, it is."

To this day, I remember my sister's vivid reconstruction of that fateful night in Ba's cellar. How deeply it had affected her! To the point where every detail had apparently etched itself into her brain. And her telling of it seemed to transfer the scars to me: I found myself re-creating the scene in my own mind, as if I had been there.

After offering to compensate my sister for her unhappiness in immature Médoc, our father seemed to forget she was there at all, falling into the underworld of his own thoughts. He shuffled away into another aisle, and Estella listened to the trail of disembodied words, interrupted now and then by the clink of glass against glass or the soft thunk of a bottle being shelved.

The words kept flowing. "I told her it's our fault, and she asked me, didn't we think of nothing but Estella's happiness? Didn't we act out of love—out of what would be best for her? And they were so in love too, the two young people. The Angsono boy especially. Such a good match between families. Such a good, prosperous match." The voice paused, as if its speaker were taking time to peer around and think. "Compare it to our marriage. What did I bring to it? Nothing. Nothing. It's true. One has to be frank about these things. I brought nothing. And it wasn't enough. Wasn't enough. Poor Sarah. Poor me . . ."

The voice paused again, this time as if it had lost its way. Then it stumbled back on track. "Another woman is a serious matter, I said to Sarah. And she agreed with me: Yes, but what good would it do to tell Estella? To make her unhappy? And I said, she is already unhappy. But Sarah insisted: What was the point? If you ask me, I think it's an insult to our family. An insult! How dare he! But what good would it do to tell? Make it all worse. Too late now. Nothing to be done. Didn't we act out of love?" From the darkness, there was silence. Then a plaintive echo. "Out of love," it sighed, leaden in the cold air.

The terrible truth of these last words hounded Estella as she burst out of the cellar. She ran through the house and out the front entrance into her car.

The driver awoke with a start.

"Home, ma'am?" he asked.

"Yes," said Estella.

As they sped down roads made clear by the lateness of the night, she wept over the fact that there was no sanctuary anywhere.

ONLY NOW, WHEN I'm interrupted, do I realize how far I've burrowed. I'm dragged out by the legs from Estella's story as I learned it on our first monarch-viewing trip, and from the reenactment of that trip during our mission to find our aunt, into the present, this bed, this comatose solitude, by a woman's voice. I have a visitor, but I don't know who it is, and she can't know me all that well either. She's just whispered to the nurse, "Are you sure this is her?"

I hear the nurse answer in the affirmative before walking briskly away.

Whoever this person is, she seems nervous. There's a long silence before she speaks. And when she does say something, she does so with a wobble, like a novice cyclist who's just started pedaling.

"I'm not sure if you can hear me. But I want to apologize."

I'm intrigued. I wish I could tell her to go on. Thankfully, she does so without my encouragement.

"I know what I did with Leonard was very wrong. I wasn't thinking clearly. At first I was worried about keeping my job—he was my boss, after all. But then, I guess, I began to like how he showed so much interest in me. It wasn't as if I was anyone important . . ."

Revelation dawns. It's Leonard's mistress. Her voice, already timid, lowers to a whisper. It's almost as if she's worried about someone eavesdropping.

"But that's no excuse. Please forgive me. I had no idea it would lead to this."

Lead to what, I wonder, before the second revelation hits: She thinks she's responsible for Estella murdering us all. And since I'm the only one who is still around, she's come to confess to me.

Leonard's mistress begins to cry. "I didn't mean for your family and his to . . ." She breaks down completely and stops trying to speak at all.

There, there, I want to tell her. *It's not your fault. I mean it. As if you could ever hope to be so significant.* Obviously I can't, so I stew motionless and silent until she finally decides to take her leave. To my relief, she makes no attempt at any physical plea for forgiveness—hand-grasping, or the like. Her departing words get straight to the point: "Again, please forgive me. And don't haunt me. Please tell the spirits of your family and Leonard's family to forgive me as well."

Of course there's an ulterior motive, the superstitious little fool. I've a good mind to will myself to die just so I can rattle her windows and flick her light switches on and off.

Her visitation has its own ghostliness about it, though, and it spurs me back into my memories in search of the actual motive behind Estella's deed. The more I dwell on it, the more I'm positive that it had nothing to do with Leonard's mistress, though I can't quite explain why.

I crawl back into the tunnels of the past—through Estella's quest to redeem our family and into the wounds reopened in its course, into the thick of our first flight up the California coast to see the monarchs. I was so sure we could escape for good, from Leonard, from his family, from ours. We were together again. Nothing could stop us.

Could I have been any more naive?

Estella and I had devised the plan together lying in bed after the incident at Matsuhisa. We'd been dying to see the monarch butterflies overwintering in Monterey County ever since we'd heard about them during our first month at the Essig. One of the curatorial assistants had mentioned it in passing, and when we asked him about it, he'd explained: Every autumn, the monarch butterflies in the northern US and Canada undertook a mass migration to warmer climes down south. Monarchs east of the Rocky

Mountains traveled to Florida and Mexico. Monarchs west of the Rockies congregated in groves on the California coast.

"It's quite a spectacle," he'd said, almost dreamily. "Huge clusters of them everywhere. You should go sometime, if you can."

Now the chance had come and we seized it. Drunk on rediscovered sisterhood, we packed a suitcase and sped off before dawn. We borrowed Om Albert's car—a silver Beemer—and left a considerate note: *Gone on vacation. Back in a few days.* No other details. They'd see us when they saw us. We turned off our mobile phones.

I remember the thrill of having her back, of her being mine again and not *his*. It almost frightened me, the intensity of my emotions, my attachment to her. And over the course of the long car ride, as she unfolded the events of the last few years in the same way she unfolded the faded maps of California we discovered in the glove compartment, my elation rose and peaked. We had defeated Leonard. We had overcome. Good had triumphed over evil at long last. Estella and I even speculated about our post-Leonard future. I'd acquired plenty of hands-on knowledge and experience working for the family, which would put us in a good position to start our own company.

"I don't know anything," Estella sighed. "I'm useless. I know how to call the interior designer, how to train new servants, and how to balance a social calendar. That's about it."

"Don't worry," I said. "You'll get the hang of it. We'll do this together. And I don't mind doing the heavy lifting for the first few years."

The vision shimmered before us like a mirage. We mused on possible business ideas: Something boring but stable? Something cutting-edge and creative? Commodities? Food and beverage? Light industry? Estella would jolt upright in the passenger seat at intervals, energized by random ideas. Cereal! And then, half an hour later—desalination technology! At the passing of a sign advertising accommodation—a hotel chain! At a pit stop just off the freeway—self-driving cars! The ideas got progressively and deliberately more ridiculous, veering into genetic modification—boneless chickens and odorless durians, shell-less prawns and stingless bees, and insects as tame pets.

"Insects as clothing!" she exclaimed, and we spun images of insect-leather jackets and six-legged hats before casting them away in gales of laughter as I veered us into the parking lot of a seasonal outdoor market.

CHRISTMAS VILLAGE! the signs proclaimed. They also promised SANTA CLAUS!, RUDOLPH!, and AWARD-WINNING CHRISTMAS ORNAMENTS!

"I guess there are awards for everything," I remarked.

Once we were back in the car, a newly acquired crocheted angel dangling from the rear-view mirror, our talk took a turn for the serious, partly due to Estella's contemplative caffeine-and-sugar-induced transcendent state. In the course of half an hour she'd downed a triple-shot peppermint mocha and a large spiced apple cider. She was now nursing a Styrofoam cup of luke-warm eggnog between the blue alpine-patterned mittens I'd insisted she buy.

"Do you think Ma really meant what she said last night in the car?" she murmured, staring wide-eyed into the distance. "That she and Ba let all this happen," she chose her words carefully, "because they love me?"

"Of course she meant it." I sneered. "But it doesn't make it right."

As if fueling her meditative powers, she took another sip of the sweet eggy brew. "Ba said the same thing back in the wine cellar, when he accidentally spilled the beans—that they did it out of love."

"Did what?"

She squinted, trying to recall Ba's drunken ramblings from several months back. "All of it, I suppose: encouraging Leonard and me to get married; not telling me he was having an affair."

I shrugged. "Love sucks," I said, not knowing what else to say.

"She's a junior-level accountant," Estella said. "His mistress."

"At Sono Jaya?"

She snorted. "Where else? Screwing an employee, how unimaginative can you get?"

"At least she's not the maid?" I ventured.

"You know, he wasn't even sorry when I confronted him."

Estella went on to recount how she'd restrained herself for a while, not letting on that she knew anything, even after Leonard had returned from the supposed business trip in New York. (Who knew what was true anymore?)

He'd been back a week when she decided to confront him, but she needed more conclusive evidence. When she was sure he was asleep, she'd snuck out of bed and searched the drawers in his dressing room and study. Nothing. Then, when she'd turned in desperation to rifling through his briefcase, she discovered the diary that he kept for *her*.

It was one of those free weekly planners that insurance companies give to clients every year. It was filled with Post-its, playful in tone, and, puzzlingly, written in English. Perhaps their author had wanted to demonstrate her worldliness and sophistication—though the English was ungrammatical enough that it had the opposite effect. Or maybe their author had thought using a foreign language would render the notes more difficult to comprehend if a coworker happened to catch a glimpse. They were exactly the kind of notes one would expect a mistress to write:

Want to exercising later?
I can't work. I think of you.
Love you so much.
I wearing what you buy me. See you tonight.

Estella went to the bathroom and threw up. Then she stuffed the corner of a towel in her mouth and screamed. Then she sat on the cold marble of the bathroom floor, thinking what a waste her life had been and how perhaps she should slit her wrists with the pair of nail scissors by the sink. He'd be sorry then, even if she only succeeded in bleeding all over the bathroom. Reason prevailed: No, he wouldn't be sorry at all. He'd just get mad at her for making a mess.

She hated him, she told herself, cramming the towel into her mouth again. The problem was, she knew she didn't—not completely, not yet. Exhausted, she crept back into bed and lay next to him, red-eyed and plotting for the remainder of the night. Eventually, the hum of the air-conditioner and the sound of Leonard's somnolent shiftings and grunts gave way to the songs of morning—the chatter of birds, the calls to prayer from the mosques, followed by the *tok tok tok* of the food vendors' sticks and the honking of cars, all barely audible through the heavy curtains and windows but deafening to her ears.

Then Leonard's alarm clock rang and she could carry out the plan she'd spent hours conceiving. The problem was, her plan had some flaws, though she couldn't see them at first. It relied too much on him responding in a certain way—just so. She was like someone new at playing chess, seeing and anticipating only one possible move in response to each of hers.

She would reveal only a little at first: what our father had accidentally let slip. Leonard would deny it. Then she would disclose that she'd found the incriminating evidence. His face would pale.

"How could you do this to me?" she would ask. Her fury would be pure and resplendent. For once, he would cower before her.

"Oh my God. Stell, I never meant for you to find out," he would say. "It meant nothing. I'll break it off right away."

"You piece of shit," she would say. How long she had yearned to say those words out loud. Because he was. A piece of shit.

He'd be shaking by now. "Please, Stell. Forgive me. I'm so sorry. Give me another chance."

"I'm leaving you," she'd respond coldly. "I want a divorce."

Leonard would get up from his chair, the napkin on his lap dropping to the floor. "No, Stell. Please don't leave."

"Why shouldn't I?"

He'd approach her cautiously. He'd be crying, tears streaming down his face. "Because I love you. I'm so sorry. I don't know what I was thinking. I shouldn't have . . ."

It would then be her turn to cry. "It's not just this, Leonard. It's everything. You treat me so badly."

"I know. I know. But I love you, I swear. Please don't leave me. I'll change."

Her spine would straighten. "I have to think about it."

He would get down on his knees and hug her calves. "Please don't leave."

"I need time to think, Len." She would extricate herself and walk out. And after that, the imagined scene went black. The curtain fell. She didn't know what she would decide. Would she leave him, or accept his apology and give him a chance to reform himself?

That was how it was all supposed to play out. And by the time she had mustered up enough energy to get out of bed, descend the stairs, and confront him during his breakfast, it had taken on the quality of fact foretold.

So it rattled her when he called her a crazy bitch without even glancing up from his newspaper.

She pressed on, revealing she'd found the notes. Her voice was trembling, faltering. Her tears came too early.

"How could you do this to me?" she asked.

He drained his coffee and calmly wiped the corners of his mouth, as if he hadn't heard her. He pushed out his chair and rose to his feet.

She repeated her question. His gaze was lizard-like and indifferent, with a modicum of what appeared to be revulsion.

"What happened to the woman I fell in love with?" he asked. But the question wasn't directed at her. It was as if she were an inanimate object and he were speaking out loud to himself.

He walked out. Too late she picked up the coffee cup and hurled it after him. It shattered against the doorframe. This made her feel somewhat better, so she did the same with the saucer and the shallow bowl of chili sauce and the plate with the little heap of unfinished fried rice on it.

She never got to tell him he was a piece of shit.

He came home very late that night, long after dinner, close to two in the morning. He turned on the bedroom light, and she scrabbled awake. She'd spent all day crying in bed like some moron in a soap opera, among mounds of sodden, crumpled tissues.

"You're a mess," he observed. She couldn't deny this. She hadn't bathed. Her hair was matted. Her face was puffed up with grief.

"Can you blame me?" she said bitterly.

He jerked his head in the direction of the open suitcase at the foot of the bed. A pile of clothes and undergarments sat inside, trying to look ready for immediate departure, doing an unconvincing job.

"Are you going to your parents' place?" he asked.

Miserably, she shook her head. She'd called Ma earlier to tell her what had happened and to ask if she could stay with them. Ma had told her to try to work things out first before doing anything rash.

He sat down on the corner of the bed. "Don't worry. I'm not going to leave you."

The nerve. The indignity. But she had no energy left.

"Stell, you really need to pull yourself together."

It was worse than drowning. Worse than burning.

He rose and headed to the bathroom.

"I didn't want this," he said, undoing his shirt buttons. "I thought our life together would be different."

The bathroom door clicked shut. She heard the shower running. She considered going to our parents' anyway. It wasn't as if they'd turn her away once she was there, but she felt so tired.

Then she crawled over to her side of the bed and fell asleep; all she wanted was blankness—the effortless passing of the hours, the absence of consciousness.

At this juncture in her story, Estella removed her mittens, pried the lid off her eggnog, confirmed that none was left, and sighed.

I repeated Leonard's words, incredulous: "'What happened to the woman I fell in love with?' What the hell did he mean by that?"

Estella smashed the empty cup between her palms and rivulets of cream trickled down her wrists. She flung the remains into the back seat and licked her hands clean, the left one first, then the right, like a cat. "Same thing as 'I thought our life together would be different,' I suppose."

Only years later would we find out what he actually meant.

We had driven up to see the monarchs, supposedly, but I'll admit that they didn't make much of an impression on me. I was too fixated on Estella, and my memories are primarily of the effect they had on her—how happy she was, how entranced; the gasp that escaped her when she spotted the first sleepy cluster, dozens of wings folded at rest on a drooping eucalyptus branch; the brightness in her eyes as she watched the livelier ones flit about in the cold sunshine. The sight of my sister's pleasure only heightened the excitement I'd been feeling since the start of our journey. Watching her was like watching a hungry child devouring a sundae, face aglow and smeared with chocolate sauce, chin dripping melted ice cream.

We only stayed two nights in the end, returning to LA as giddy and giggly as schoolgirls who'd just come back from playing truant. Leonard, either too proud to show he cared or actually indifferent, treated us with an aloof disdain. Our mother gave us a good scolding, but seemed relieved that we weren't dead or kidnapped or raped, as she had feared. Our father was mostly amused and asked if we'd had a good time.

Leonard's father seemed to have barely registered our absence, but it was clear that Leonard's mother regarded our shenanigans as something incredibly shameful: as if Estella had run off with another man. When we walked through the Angsonos' front door and our mother rushed at us, showering us with furious embraces and kisses, Leonard's mother had stood there motionless, scarlet as a slab of barbecued pork. She refused to speak to either of us for days, and when conversation resumed, it was decidedly frigid, even more distant than usual—the manner of a respectable woman interacting with someone whom she considered morally debased.

❖   ❖   ❖

"It's not fair," I said to Estella a few nights later in our room—it had become our room ever since the dinner at Matsuhisa. Leonard had given no sign that this arrangement bothered him in the least. "*Her* son does the philandering and manhandling, and she acts as if you're the culprit."

Estella laughed. "Yes, she should be ashamed of herself, shouldn't she?" It pleased me to see that she had grown bold, brash even. She wore her indignation like an emerald choker, her shoulders thrown back, her neck long and haughty.

"Why don't you ask for a divorce?" I asked.

She laughed again: a delicious ripple that sent shivers down my spine. "Maybe. Can't be bothered right now, though. We'll see once we're back in Jakarta."

It was like watching a freshly hatched butterfly spreading its wings for the first time. It was beautiful. And even better, we seemed to be of one mind. It was as if I were inhabiting her body, her soul, experiencing her newfound courage firsthand.

I was foolish to think Estella could keep it up once we returned to the old routines—to the structures that had so long prevented her from being herself. A few days later, both families flew back to Jakarta. We passed through customs with our long caravan of luggage-laden carts and porters trailing behind, and emerged into the muggy, smoggy air of the capital. A few minutes later, the Angsonos' three cars pulled up—one for Leonard's parents, one for Leonard and Estella, and a minivan for the suitcases and boxes of all their newly acquired goods. My parents' two cars (similarly allocated) pulled up behind. It was time to part ways.

I hugged her fiercely.

"Don't forget," I whispered. "We'll start something new. You don't need him."

She didn't reciprocate, but she let me hold her. And when I released her, she smiled.

At the time, her placidity reassured me. I took it to mean she was confident, assured. Of course this was the end of her and Leonard, her demeanor seemed to say. Of course she would get a divorce. Of course we'd start a business together. Of course, of course . . .

I was wrong. I thought she was serene when in reality she was resigned. Or perhaps the improbability of actual escape had only begun to impress itself on her as we were waiting for our cars. The complete hopelessness of the entire situation probably struck her later, as she glided through the wrought iron gates of their property, designed by the architect that Leonard's mother had hired. Can I blame her for being daunted anew by the loveless mansion that she was supposed to call home? Who wouldn't have lost their nerve upon being confronted by the foyer—the great marble staircase and its swan-themed balustrades; the urns and statues and draperies, brawny in their elegance, selected and strategically placed to impress and impose?

She could no more escape her life than she could escape her own skin, or so it must have seemed. How enmeshed she was in it. And, if she were honest with herself, how embedded Leonard was in her. Like climbing ivy, Leonard had grown on her in the most insidious way. He had set down his roots during their college years, and the only way he could be dislodged now was for her to rip out her heart.

Meanwhile, I rode off with Ma and Ba, gestating the embryonic brain-child that would become Bagatelle. As I gazed off into the horizon of our sparkling future together, Estella's and mine, I hadn't the faintest inkling that she had already jumped ship.

◆　◆　◆

The fundamental concepts of Bagatelle took firm hold of my mind in the months that followed our return from the US. Whenever I chattered excitedly about them to Estella, her response would be, "Great!" She was a wonderful sounding board. She asked insightful questions and encouraged me to think everything through. Yet all she would give me was an evasive "We'll see" whenever I asked her for a pledge of involvement. Then some apologetic excuse would follow about the social obligations she had to get out of the way, or the errands that needed doing, or the household affairs she had to manage.

The monarch-viewing trip had reconnected us, and though we weren't nearly as close as we had been in the pre-Leonard past, I was high with excitement. It took me several weeks to realize that Estella was never coming on board. Back then, I didn't know that this was a deliberate decision—and the method she had settled on as her only viable way out. If she couldn't save herself, then she would live vicariously through me. At the time, I thought she had given up, but now her logic seems all too clear. To attempt to actually change her life would only drive home the fact that she couldn't. Much better to conjure wild dreams of freedom, to bask in imagined success, than to batter herself against the bars and find they would not break.

As far as her married life was concerned, things pretty much picked up where they left off. Leonard continued seeing his mistress (at least this was what Estella assumed; neither of them brought it up). He would come home late several times a week, and go out of town supposedly on business at least once a month. He kept up his rigorous bodybuilding routine. They still had sex, though Estella found the idea of sharing her husband repulsive. But as always, Leonard seemed to require little to nothing from her in their physical relations; mere acquiescence was enough.

It would take the monetary crisis to really change anything. And in the Angsono family's case, it changed a great deal.

EIGHT YEARS LATER and here we are again, I thought as Estella and I stood next to each other, squinting up into the trees. We kept our hands in our pockets and our backs hunched against the cold. It was almost noon, but the sun still hadn't broken through the clouds and the sea fog tinted everything a gentle gray.

"We're not going to see any monarchs at this rate," my sister complained.

"Maybe we should come back in an hour or two," I suggested.

As if on cue, the clouds parted and the sun cast a spotlight on a high branch overhead. We saw them then: a cluster of brown triangles hanging heavy from the lobe of a eucalyptus tree, made conspicuous by the warm light that set the monarchs' wings opening and shutting at intervals like a colony of winking, disembodied eyes.

The minutes passed and the sun grew even stronger, rolling back the fog and flooding the grove with light. More clusters revealed themselves, flashing orange. Here and there, individuals took flight and began dancing in the air, a few even fluttering downward like animated autumn leaves.

Estella came to life too, her eyes brightening, her face bursting into a brilliant beam. And I felt unnerved all of a sudden by how much that scene resembled the one so many years prior. Sure, our mission was different this time: not escape, but the retrieval of our long-lost aunt. Still, hadn't we stood there, in more or less the same spot, on that first trip? Hadn't my sister looked just as ecstatic? What cosmic logic had guided us to that same place, like the hands of a clock returning to the same numbers on different days? Was it the same invisible force that herded those poor butterflies up and down an entire continent every year?

"They look distressed," I observed. The day was definitely warming up now, and it was as if the heat had set the monarchs in motion without their consent. I couldn't help but contrast their agitation with the peaceful dormancy of my bagatelles and wonder if they might have been better off in a state of rest.

Estella merely laughed. "They look free, if you ask me," she said as one alighted just above her left ear. "It's from the Majesty collection," she said, pointing, then sucking in her cheeks to mimic a fashion-model pout.

I played along. "No, dahlink," I said with a frown. "Ze balance is all wrong. It should be just above ze eyes. To give an air of meestery."

With an outstretched finger, I brushed the monarch's furry chest in an attempt to prod it into place. It flitted away.

"No touching the butterflies!" someone yelled.

It was one of the park volunteers, a pudgy, bearded man clad in a ratty white T-shirt and a dark green fleece vest.

"No touching!" he cried again, before issuing a slow explanation that made clear his uncertainty about our English-comprehension skills. "Your fingers are oily. The oils damage their wings."

He was talking about human fingers in general, not just mine, but I still couldn't help but be irritated by his choice of phrase.

I stared him down coldly. "Thanks, I know how to handle lepidopterans. It's my line of work."

My English was faintly accented—that couldn't be helped—but the imperiousness of my tone was enough to startle him. He recovered and shook his head. "No exceptions, miss," he insisted, though more politely than before. As he tottered away, I was reminded of what Ray Chan had told us about folks here thinking that Chinese people were submissive. And I couldn't help but wonder what Ray was doing now.

"Let's go to the aquarium," Estella suggested, tugging me back into the present. "We didn't get around to it last time."

We got into the car and drove ten minutes east to the town of Monterey. Truth be told, I felt relieved that we were diverging from our previous itinerary. After last night and this morning, I'd started to fear that Estella would insist on replicating our first trip entirely. Somehow I knew I would have found that difficult to refuse.

I tried to lose myself in the dark climate-controlled corridors of the aquarium, among the snoozing, bulb-snouted octopuses; among the jelly-fish pulsing like gelatinous disembodied hearts and the towering forests of silky green kelp. Sitting on the carpeted platform steps in front of the floor-to-ceiling tanks, we gazed into deep blue voids at the swirling schools of silver, the broad-sided tuna and sleek-winged skates slicing through the water like knives. But my mind refused to wander sufficiently. No matter how hard I stared at each exhibit's depths, there was always a trace of our present situation reflected dimly in the glass.

I used to have nightmares about Tante Sandra, right after we'd learned that she had died. I would see her body tangled in seaweed, kissed by tiny colorful fish passing her in long trains, like people paying their respects at a wake. I'd see her free-floating and decaying, flecks of her flying into aque-ous space, what was left bobbing on undersea currents, drifting through the ocean to who-knew-where.

As Estella and I passed through the aquarium, I imagined our aunt in the same scenes, but alive, holding her breath, incubating in that shadowy otherworld, waiting to come back from the dead, waiting to wash up on American soil, gasping for breath and born again, ready to start a new life unencumbered by the family, by us.

We reached a tank containing a great white shark. I read the sign. It was the first and only one worldwide to be on exhibit for such a long period of time. Apparently, great whites didn't do very well in captivity as a rule. It glided through the water, its eyes cold black marbles, its nostrils perma-nently flared, its teeth perpetually on display.

Suddenly it struck me. "Oma lied to us about Tante Sandra that whole time," I murmured.

Estella stared. "You're only processing that *now*?"

"But why?" I asked, ignoring her incredulity.

She shrugged. "Tante Sandra probably told her to keep it a secret. The whole point of running away is to not be found."

Impeccable logic. Still, I found myself bothered by the fact that Oma had lied so thoroughly and for so long—about Tante Sandra, about the cancer too. It frightened me to think that our grandmother might have had hidden depths.

The shark made another pass in front of the crowd, and a little girl to our right buried her face in her mother's skirt.

"Hey, how do you feel about finding someplace to eat?" Estella asked suddenly. "It's almost three."

My stomach growled by way of response. We'd eaten breakfast just before leaving the hotel, but it was hardly enough to tide us over until dinner.

What more was there to uncover? I wondered, casting a last glance over my shoulder at the shark in the tank. If we couldn't trust Oma, who could we trust? What else was still submerged in our family's seabed? What rotting carcasses of ships? What skeletons nibbled clean?

"It's a nice day," said Estella as we exited the aquarium. "Why don't we eat somewhere outside?"

Nontouristy dining options simply didn't exist on the waterfront. We ended up at a restaurant where the walls were plastered with life preservers, oars, and photos of men posing with their caught fish. The wooden rafters were draped with nets and plastic lobsters on strings. The tables were covered in red-and-white-checkered oilcloth.

The crab cakes were too salty to eat, but the mussels and cioppino we ordered to share were decent enough. From the canopy-covered area on the pier where we sat, we could see the afternoon sun glisten on the water.

The waves lapped against the posts below, and the sloshing sound they made forced me to relax.

The lunch rush was long over, but a family of four occupied the table next to us: a wife and husband and two young boys who bowed their heads when their food arrived. The father prayed on their collective behalf, and from his accent I could tell he was American, though the exact ethnicity—Chinese, Korean, Vietnamese, Japanese?—was much more difficult to place. Because their eyes were closed, Estella and I stared unabashed, and I saw a yearning sort of look creep into my sister's gaze. The parents were trim and clean-cut, the mother wearing a pastel-pink polo shirt and khaki pants, the father in the same outfit but with a blue top. The boys—aged around eight or nine and five or six, respectively—were dressed in matching clothes as well: red-and-white-striped T-shirts and blue jeans. They clasped their small hands and squeezed their eyes shut in exaggerated imitation of their parents.

The perfect family, I thought sardonically, even as I knew Estella was thinking a more earnest version of the same thing, contemplating her life as it might have been, if she'd had kids, if things with Leonard had turned out differently, if she had wound up with somebody else.

As the father's words winged their way up to heaven, his eyebrows flexed and his forehead crinkled, as if his face were being sculpted by a dexterous invisible hand into ripples and arches. It reminded me of how Leonard had looked when I'd once stumbled across him in prayer. I'd opened the door to his study and found him kneeling on a purple velvet cushion, hands raised and palms upturned, oblivious to my bursting in. I'd never seen him look so vulnerable. As his lips moved, myriad expressions flickered across his face—ecstasy and pain, entreaty and satisfaction, worry, sorrow, effort, exhortation, pleading, resignation, peace. I should have left the room immediately, but I was spellbound and he hadn't heard me come in. I couldn't catch most of what he was saying, but at intervals he would break into a babble that sounded like "shibola-la-la" or "elia zerubabayel"—"speaking in tongues," I learned this was called. Or he would inhale deeply and on the exhale utter "Jeeee-zus, Jeeeee-zus," like he was wheezing. There would sometimes be a word in between: "Jeeeee-zus. Lord Jeeeeee-zus. Jeeeezus. Precious Jeeee-zus."

"In Jesus's name, amen," the father concluded. The family's eyes flew open and they began to tuck into their food.

Estella and I ate in silence for a while. And she sounded almost mournful when she opened her mouth to speak. "Sometimes I wonder how Leonard would have turned out if only he hadn't died."

"You think religion would have actually made him good?" I asked.

She shrugged. "Who knows? But I'll say this at least." She cracked a crab leg in two. "He was the most bearable toward the very end."

❖   ❖   ❖

Leonard's discovery of Jesus was neither spontaneous nor singular. Many of our set converted from Buddhism or were "born again" at around the same time. If the Krismon brought the entire country to its knees, it also sent a good number of Chinese scrambling for salvation in Christ.

The Krismon was what we called it in Indonesia—shorthand for monetary crisis, "*krisis moneter.*" Bloomberg, Reuters, and the other global news services termed it the Asian financial crisis, or sometimes the more lurid "Asian contagion."

Thailand triggered it. Following the decision to uncouple the baht from the US dollar, the currency's value fell by 25 percent. Other currencies in and around Southeast Asia followed suit, including the Indonesian rupiah, the combustion of which was perhaps the most spectacular of all. It revealed that our astonishing growth was being fueled by massive amounts of private short-term foreign debt. Panicked big-business owners, *pribumi* and Chinese alike, began pulling out of the rupiah, which sent it plunging even further. Defaults were rampant and bankruptcies widespread. Banks liquidated, jobs vanished, food prices soared.

And as always in Indonesia, the Chinese were blamed. We, the unassimilated traitors. We, the heathen parasites on decent Muslim *pribumi* society. We merciless merchants, we hoarders of riches, abandoning the nation's sinking currency like the perfidious rats we were, and tripling the prices of rice and cooking oil to squeeze a profit out of these dry times.

Never mind that the wealthy *pribumi* businessmen were divesting themselves of their native currency as well, or that all shopkeepers, regardless of ethnic origins, were forced to raise their prices. Anti-Chinese suspicion and resentment had been simmering in the national psyche for decades. Searching for scapegoats, high-profile politicians and army officials began denouncing us in public. In towns and cities outside the capital, Chinese-owned shops were vandalized, stoned, and torched. The water was coming to the boil.

The most well-connected of us predicted the events of May 1998 several months before they actually arrived. Chinese blood might have denied us power in politics and the military, but money did ensure we had favorable connections with those in the know. A minister here, a general there, let drop an enigmatic warning of bad things to come for our kind. Word spread, rustling through us like wind through a rice paddy, and to whatever extent we could, we prepared ourselves for flight. Condominiums, apartments, and houses were set up in Singapore and Hong Kong—the regional strongholds of our people—and valuables were stashed away. Long-term visas and permanent residencies were applied for via agents. We might not have been able to stop the train, but at least we had our ears pressed flat against the tracks.

The rumblings grew louder as mass discontent rose. For more than thirty years Suharto had relied on economic growth and prosperity to buttress his corrupt authoritarian regime. Now that the Krismon had swept away the foundations, his power crumbled. The opposition he'd attempted to censor, exile, and kill came out of hiding and reared its head. Protesters clamored on university campuses for the president to step down.

Then May rolled around. The violence that broke out in the city of Medan was the precursor. Clashes between student demonstrators and armed security forces somehow morphed into the looting and burning of Chinese-owned stores. The same would happen in Jakarta on a grander, bloodier scale. The police and military opened fire on unarmed students at a protest at Trisakti University. Chaos erupted. Cars and buildings were set alight, with special attention paid to our businesses and homes. Our men were beaten, our women raped.

"Our businesses and homes," I have the gall to say. "Our men, our women." As if any of our affluent set shared in their fate. While China-town was burning, along with anyone unlucky enough to be trapped by the flames, those of us who'd had the means to purchase foreknowledge and plane tickets were already abroad, watching the footage on CNN and BBC.

Leonard's parents invited all of us Sulinados to take refuge with them in their family's Singapore mansion. Opa had already purchased a house there, but it wasn't quite ready to live in, and the same went for the luxury condo my parents had bought. So in the end, most of us did end up sheltering with the Angsonos. It was very spacious—more a compound than a house, with several guest villas behind the main structure. And though no one said it, I think the members of both clans felt that there was something to be said for communally weathering out the storm. It was comforting to huddle together on sofas as we watched the riots rage on big-screen TVs. Perhaps having company distracted us from the guilt we felt not only at being able to escape, but at feeling lucky about having done so—not to mention the knowledge that niggled at us, deep down, that the wrath being meted out on those small-time shopkeepers was meant for the filthy rich like us. We were all Chinese supposedly, of one race, of one blood, of one yellowy hue. But in truth, we were divided into two very different creatures: Our breed had wings and theirs didn't. And now, with the onset of bad weather, we had flapped away and left the wingless to be trampled underfoot.

We and the majority of the other wealthy Chinese families continued to wait out the next several months abroad. We made cautious trips back to Jakarta as necessary to tend to business, but remained on our guard, keeping one foot in and one out. Only when political stability of a sort had been restored did we inch our lives back into the country, but never quite as fully as before. We kept the overseas real estate and assets, along with the foreign residencies and citizenships. It was the only sensible thing to do.

The rest of the country rejoiced in this new era—the termination of the despotic Suharto regime and the onset of democracy and reform. For them, violence had been a necessary price: the pain of a woman birthing freedom, squeezing its enormous head out from between her thighs. For us Chinese, the unrest of 1998 had driven home the fact that we were aliens in a hostile land.

The financial crisis and the May riots: I think they were what prompted so many of our set to zealously embrace the Christian faith—or, rather, a type of Christianity that I'd certainly never encountered on the rare occasions my family had gone to church. This souped-up, rebranded version came with live bands playing loud music and pastors in designer suits. It came with stages instead of altars and mood lighting instead of stained glass. The singing alone could take an hour, the lyrics displayed on giant screens above the musicians' heads. I had to admit, the sermons were far more compelling than any I'd slept through in the past. Listening to them was like listening to a life coach, but with God thrown into the mix. Topics included how to unlock your fullest potential by giving your life to Jesus, and how to effectively receive the spiritual and material blessings that your heavenly father was itching to shower you with.

Who knew that following Christ came with so many great perks? Accordingly, people took comprehensive notes and highlighted relevant passages in the Bibles they brought with them. When they sang, they stretched out their hands, grateful for all God would provide. And when praying, they babbled in the same way I would hear Leonard do later, when he too joined the flocks of the saved.

I gleaned my observations from the two services Estella and I were invited to attend. The first invitation was extended by our cousin Christopher, which should have raised suspicions from the start. Chris was much older than us, and we'd never been that close as kids, but it turned out he'd promised God he'd bring each of his cousins to church at least once.

The other invitation came from our friend Nikki, whom we'd barely seen since Candy's baby shower, when she'd shown off her new eyelids. We bumped into her at a charity luncheon. In her usual brash, frank way, she invited us to her church's Easter Sunday service, providing we had nothing better to do. We didn't. As I've said, our family were nominal Christians by and large. Besides, our mother had always taught us that Christmas and Easter were the worst days to go to church; the crowds were unbearable, and one had to take the trouble of arriving early in order to get a seat at all. Ma had been right. Estella and I showed up five minutes before the service, and the auditorium was already a zoo. Luckily, Nikki had saved us seats. We exchanged cheek kisses. Her eyes looked as large and natural as ever.

No spiritual change of heart from Estella or me came of either invitation, apart from an unwillingness to attend any more services if we could help it. Each time, we could sense our hosts glancing at us every now and then, gauging our reaction every step of the way. Chris awkwardly asked us afterward if we wanted to go out for lunch with him and his wife. We declined, pleading another nonexistent engagement. Nikki was shrewder: She'd locked us in beforehand for an Easter champagne brunch at the Hotel Mulia that did actually end up being fun. She must have been embarrassed about trying to evangelize us, for it seemed as if she were trying to avoid speaking about the service or the sermon altogether. Instead, she flitted gaily from topic to topic: what the rest of our friends from high school were doing these days; the guy she was dating; how things were going with Estella and Leonard. ("Oh, you know, marriage" was my sister's standard evasive response, which she always delivered with an equally evasive smile.)

As the stack of oyster shells piled up on Nikki's plate, she told us that if her boyfriend proposed, she was going to get a boob job: "Two presents in one: for me and for him." This set all three of us laughing, until Nikki suddenly stopped and looked sad.

"Jarvis is a good catch," she said, still speaking about her boyfriend. "The most respectable guy *I've* ever dated, at least. My parents couldn't be happier—they keep reminding me I'm almost thirty. But he keeps commenting about how small my boobs are. What do you think? I mean, I've always liked them . . . till now."

It was the most disconsolate I'd ever seen Nikki. I raised my glass of Bollinger and motioned for Estella to raise hers.

"I've always envied your boobs," I said solemnly, maintaining my poker face until the three of us once again broke into guffaws.

"You know," she said after our second round of laughter had died down, "I think that's why I've decided to follow Jesus." The phrase "Follow Jesus," which would have sounded artificial coming from anyone else, rang surprisingly true on her cupid-bow lips. She continued, "Jesus couldn't give a flying fuck about my boobs."

That brunch with Nikki happened a little less than a year after the riots. The economy was much weakened, but at least it was still limping along. The interim president, Habibie, had declined to run for a full term. Within months the country would have yet another president, which seemed surreal. What we didn't know was that we'd have two more over the span of the next five years.

Still, the most important thing, financially speaking, was that families like ours were out of the danger zone. Though Indonesia's economic outlook was shaky, the worst was clearly over. Our fortunes had been diminished considerably, but they were more or less intact. Building them up again would only be a matter of competence and time.

Unfortunately, it was that first quality—competence—that would prove problematic for the Angsono clan. It wouldn't have been an issue if Leonard's father hadn't unexpectedly died of a stroke in early 1999. (He was stuck in a severe traffic jam when it happened; by the time the car made it to a hospital it was too late.) Albert Angsono had been a formidable businessman indeed. Leonard's great-grandfather and grandfather had laid the foundations for the family's wealth, but under Om Albert's stewardship their riches had skyrocketed. Leonard may have been the eldest and only son, but he was nowhere near the financial visionary his father was. His two uncles and their sons were far more able, but longstanding Angsono family tradition demanded it be Leonard who take the reins.

Our family was also undergoing a personal crisis, though not death (not yet). While we were cooling our heels in Singapore, we took advantage of the high-quality medical facilities and arranged a raft of overdue checkups for Opa. He was diagnosed with Alzheimer's. Despite Tante Betty's grumblings, Om Benny was named the head of Sulinado Group.

So began a new era, for both us and the Angsonos. However, though we Sulinados, like most other Chinese-Indonesian tycoon families, would be able to run in place until the economy began to genuinely recover in 2001, under Leonard's inept leadership, the Angsonos somehow managed to sink even further than they already had. Sono Jaya had survived the Krismon, but needed major surgery if it was going to bounce back. Leonard insisted on taking the lead and butchered it beyond repair.

Exactly what made Leonard act the way he did was difficult to say. I'm not sure if he knew himself. Perhaps he was crazed with grief. Om Albert and Leonard had never been particularly close, but nevertheless, they were father and son. Most certainly, there was pride involved—Leonard must have always known on some level that he was a disappointment to his father. Where Angsono the elder had been disciplined, focused, and shrewd, Angsono the younger was spoiled, lazy, and not very bright. Perhaps Leonard saw this as an opportunity to prove himself a worthy heir to his late father's leadership.

Whatever the case, he eschewed his uncles' and cousins' frantic counsel and proceeded, with determination, to run the family empire into the ground. One couldn't even call it an execution—this was no clean shot to the heart, no quick severing of the head. Just a frenzy of mad stabs, protracted and horrifying to watch: the poorly timed selling of various branches of the conglomerate; a string of ill-judged acquisitions and mergers; imprudent attempts to dispute debts and deny corruption charges via expensive and time-consuming court battles.

During this period, Leonard abandoned tending to the flesh. He simply didn't have the time for personal-training sessions anymore. He needed to prioritize, he said. The fact that he was at home every night, albeit in his study or pacing the house making phone calls, suggested that he was also neglecting his mistress—at least for now. Oddly enough, Estella was privy to his business affairs more than ever before, if only because he began mumbling about them at dinner. Worry possessed him, eating from his lips in mutterings and rants at breakfast as well, and right before bed, and finally in his fitful sleep in between snorts and starts. Yet Sono Jaya's performance on the whole continued to decline, and all Leonard received in return for his anxiety and effort was loss after loss.

Without the bodybuilding, all his muscle turned to flab. He couldn't sleep. He developed excruciating back and neck pain that frequent massages and acupuncture couldn't cure. He was a wreck. I couldn't blame Estella for being secretly pleased.

Another woman might have been distressed at the erosion of her husband's fortune and, by association, hers. But Estella hadn't married Leonard for his money; she'd been deluded enough to think him madly in love with her, and helpless enough to form an attachment that simply wouldn't go away. Leonard was now suffering in a manner akin to how he had made her suffer, and she exulted in his being forced to draw close and share in the orbit of her pain.

She took a perverse pride during this period in ensuring that her conduct and bearing as a wife were faultless. In this respect, more than five years under her mother-in-law's tutelage had served her well. She dressed and groomed herself impeccably, and met her domestic and social obligations without flaw. She even fielded Leonard's occasional complaints about everyday extravagances with equanimity, though they caught her by surprise. Before this, he'd never given the cost of comfort any thought: not the expense of ordering new parts for their German plumbing system, or the price of a private eight-course dinner party for fourteen prepared by Jakarta's top sushi chef. It had never occurred to him to consider whether upholstering the seats in the new BMW with Hermès—not generic "Italian"—leather was really necessary, or whether it was even prudent to buy a new BMW at all. Most of the time, though, he was unable to bring himself to live below the standard of what he had been taught was the "right" way to live, and so he simply tried to get on with his lavish life. "Penny smart, dollar foolish," he'd say—a phrase in English he'd picked up in college but modified unwittingly. The few times he did give into an irrational urge to cut corners—for example, when he sold his luxury yacht—he felt unutterably ashamed, unspeakably debased.

Our family's financial ascension would only begin a year later, but the Angsonos' abrupt descent led us to change our relationship with them. Where the association of our name with theirs had once opened doors, in this new era of zealous reform, it now put us at risk of being labeled corrupt cronies of the old establishment. Our business dealings with the Angsonos had become more liability than asset: Leonard's bad judgment, not to mention his newfound resolve not to "let anyone get the better of him," made him a dangerous business partner indeed. Pragmatically and pitilessly, Om Benny set about disentangling Sulinado Group from Sono Jaya.

The Angsonos' misfortune also affected how our parents treated Estella's situation, whether they were aware of this change or not. Previously, they'd looked the other way at Leonard's treatment of Estella, not to mention the annexation of her from our family into theirs. Now Ma asserted the rights she and Ba had as her mother and father. They invited her out for meals much more frequently. And Estella was bold enough to accept, even when it conflicted with plans with her mother-in-law or the extended Angsono family. Leonard, of course, was always invited by our parents as well, but he felt acutely what this signified: a loss of face, a lessening of respect, a subtle shift in the balance of power. So he refused to come along, even when it meant he would be dining alone. It was just as well that he was absent: These days, our mother was much freer in criticizing Leonard and his family. Where she never did so before, she gave vent viciously now: the nerve of Leonard in treating her daughter like a two-bit concubine; the airs his family had always put on, and how they deserved everything that was happening to them. Our father—always quietly indignant on Estella's behalf—couldn't have looked more cheerful during these bouts of rage. He would happily siphon glass after glass, basking in the righteous fury of his wife.

It was around this time that our mother suggested Estella leave her life of leisured entrapment and regain some independence.

"How do you feel about running Mutiara?" she asked one night after dinner. The maids had just cleared the table and brought in dessert: some very fine Harum Manis mangoes and a fluffy Japanese cheesecake sent by Om Gerry Sukamto's ever-thoughtful wife, Lilly. Ma would have never dared to make such a proposal before, but now she didn't feel she had to respect the Angsonos' outdated notions about married women not working.

I was there too, though I'd moved into my own place a few months earlier (not long after Sono Jaya and Leonard began to fray—perhaps it was my unconscious way of celebrating).

"Mutiara? The silk factory?" Estella asked. "The one that Om Jan was running?" She speared a mango slice and ignored the cheesecake. Lately, she had begun taking better care of herself, watching what she ate, being more diligent with her personal-training sessions. She was nourishing the sense of self-worth that her husband and in-laws had starved.

Our mother nodded. "I've been trying to find a replacement since he passed away last week. The position is yours if you're interested."

"Sure, why not?" said Estella instantly. And I felt a swell of mingled disappointment and hope: disappointment because Estella had agreed so quickly to running Mutiara, but had been so cagey about helping me start Bagatelle; hope because if she'd said yes to Ma, there still might be a chance she'd say yes to me. Not that the plans for Bagatelle had progressed much since the trip to Monterey. Thanks to the Krismon and the instability that followed it, I'd put further conceptualization on hold. The waters were still too murky to make solid plans for starting a new business, especially as the fashion industry was so high risk. That was my excuse; undeniably it was a good one. But if I were honest with myself, I hadn't resumed working on Bagatelle in earnest because Estella, though supportive, had been noncommittal. My timing must have been off, I thought as Ma clapped her hands in delight at Estella's ready assent. I must have requested too much of my sister too soon. Our trip to Monterey had prompted her to wear her circumstances with more dignity, but the diminishment of the Angsonos and her husband had strengthened her even more. I made up my mind to bring up Bagatelle again when she and I were alone.

After dinner, when Ba had disappeared into the wine cellar and Ma had retired to bed, Estella and I drifted up to her old room; it was more or less unchanged. Since returning from Berkeley, I'd rarely ventured in. It evoked too many happy memories of Estella. They would have smothered me if I stayed too long in their midst.

The walls were still pink. The dream catcher still dangled above the bed. The same framed poster of a pile of sleeping kittens hung above the enormous desk. Her old stuffed animals, dolls, books, and high school trophies sat expectantly on the shelves as if awaiting her return.

Estella pulled out the desk's bottommost drawer.

"Where are our collections?" she said with a frown. "Did they throw them out?" It seemed to strike her only then how long she had been away. She hadn't so much as peeked into that drawer since before her marriage. Practically all of its contents had been removed: the exoskeletons in assorted glass jars, poorly spread butterflies pinned into a Gucci handbag box, an envelope of detached butterfly and wasp wings. All that remained was our dismantled ant farm and an empty sachet that once had contained mothballs, long since evaporated into thin air.

"I bet Ma asked the maids to get rid of them," she sighed, shutting the drawer again. "Ma always hated our insects."

I made my move. "There could be other insects. You're doing Bagatelle with me, aren't you?" I tried to sound playful and nonchalant, though I could barely hear myself speak over the beating of my heart.

She smiled. Then those two infuriating words: "We'll see."

I burst into tears.

"You agreed to Mutiara!" I cried. "Why not to Bagatelle?"

Gently, she placed her hands on my shoulders and sat me down on the edge of the bed. "Doll, it's a great idea. I mean it. Just go ahead without me. I can help you without getting involved."

"It won't be the same!" I hiccuped. "Don't you see? It's our chance to be together again. It'll be like it was before."

She shook her head. "Gwendolyn," she said, her voice like a vanishing morning moon. "It will never be like it was before." She put her hands on mine. "Promise you'll go ahead with Bagatelle without me."

"Why? What's the point?" I mumbled.

"I'll be so proud of you," she said, not answering me. With the heel of her hand she wiped away my tears. "Promise me," she insisted.

I was silent a long time before I nodded. Then we rose together and left the room.

At the time I didn't understand why Estella wanted to remain on the sidelines, cheering me on. But the hindsight from my hospital bed grows ever sharper as I dive toward memory's bottom, groping for precious clues that will put everything into place. I'm convinced of it now: that Estella regarded Bagatelle as a soap bubble—apt to burst if she dared touch it; that she saw me as her avatar, forging a path to freedom in her stead. She contented herself with what she considered attainable: namely, Mutiara. She was officially installed as its CEO before the month was out.

Leonard was furious, as was his mother, but their anger was impotent. Any power over our family they'd once possessed had disappeared. Our mother gave Estella records of the company's fundamentals, as well as access to all relevant documents. The operations manager gave her a tour of the factory and the office, which was on site. They cleared out our dead relative's desk and hired a new secretary for Estella. And just like that, my sister was transformed from a lady of leisure into a working woman.

Well, kind of. As I've mentioned, Mutiara was hardly an exciting business to oversee. It ran more or less by itself, and it didn't run so much as plod. It was a shabby affair to boot: a stunted brick of a building crumbling at the corners like old toast. Estella had the entire office refurbished— ordered the walls repainted and new carpeting put in, replaced the air-conditioning units and installed brighter lights. But there were only so many improvements she could make.

The offices were located one level above the factory floor, which was as dingy as one might expect. The ceiling was low and the space a tad too small for so many large machines. Thanks to an ill-conceived cost-cutting measure, the electricity on the first floor had been wired to ensure that the lighting was permanently dim. As a result, the work being done seemed even more sinister than it was.

The cocoons arrived in crates from China, dead, each inhabitant steamed in its own wrappings before it could complete its passage to winged adulthood. A musty stench swept across the floor when they opened the boxes and lingered throughout the production process: the boiling of the cocoons to loosen the filaments, the unraveling of them onto wheels, then the reeling of them into skeins—a third of which Mutiara sold to other manufacturing companies in Indonesia and the remaining two-thirds of which Mutiara retained for its own use. It took Estella a while to get accustomed to the smell. She swore it permeated even the office air-conditioning units, steeping her and the other employees in putrescence.

It wasn't ideal, but Mutiara would be a welcome refuge once Leonard's unraveling began in earnest. We thought he'd hit rock bottom, but he hadn't found Jesus yet.

In the meantime, I remained faithful to my promise to Estella, spending all my spare time working on my plans for Bagatelle. Up to that point, I had envisioned it as jewelry made from dead butterflies, beetles, wasps, et cetera, with their bodies and wings hardened somehow—enameled, perhaps. But the idea of keeping them alive occurred to me after Estella told me about the cocoons. If only there were some way to preserve them, but keep them alive. Even better, to control their movements—to transform them from insects into exquisite animated dolls . . .

As Estella embarked on the newest stage of her life, I set about preparing for mine. While she redecorated Mutiara's office, I converted my apartment into the habitat I'd always dreamed of: oak and walnut paneling, chocolate leather and green velvet, accents of brass and gold. "Very masculine," my interior decorator said with a laugh when I told her what I wanted. Whatever. I was going to start my new life on my own terms.

I didn't draw the parallels at the time, but I see them now: Estella, me, and Leonard at the start of the new millennium, each of us undergoing our respective metamorphoses. Estella's transformation was recent but anticlimactic. Mine was imminent and promising. Poor Leonard's was, ultimately, fatal.

Still, as Estella would say four years later, on that pier in Monterey, on our second jaunt to see the monarchs, on our quest to find our aunt: Leonard was the most bearable toward the end—at least to her. To the rest of us, he was insufferable. And though his pathetic end state gave me some satisfaction, I resented that it made my sister feel more sympathy for him than she should have.

I WOULD NEVER have imagined that Estella and I would be able to laugh together about that last, hyperreligious phase of Leonard's life. Yet there we were, eating hot fudge sundaes by the Californian seaside, doing exactly that. The vacation atmosphere of Monterey must have been infectious: a sunny, salt-air boardwalk beachiness despite the late autumn chill. After lunch, we'd strolled farther down the waterfront to partake in some window-shopping, flicking through racks of discounted souvenir T-shirts and running our hands through barrels of saltwater taffy.

"Dessert?" Estella had asked, pointing to an old-fashioned ice-cream parlor next to a store called Swell Seaside Shells.

"We just ate," I said, amused.

"It'll be our dinner," she said. Dragging me in by the wrist, past the *Please Wait to Be Seated* sign, she plunked us down at a window-side table overlooking the beach.

She took the lead on reminiscing about Leonard's late-blooming religiosity, as she had with everything else on this trip.

"Remember when he got born again?" she asked, sucking a glob of hot fudge off the back of her spoon.

"How could I forget?" I said, half wincing, half chuckling. "You called to tell me at, what, three in the morning?"

She laughed. "I panicked. I didn't know what else to do."

I couldn't blame her. Unlike an actual birth, Leonard's spiritual rebirth had come without warning. An old high school chum of his—Kelvin Chandra—had invited Leonard to an evening event organized by his church. A "miracle healing service," they called it. Kelvin had promised it would help with his neck and back pain, and Leonard had thought it was worth a shot. It cured him, Leonard would later claim, of his physical ailment as well as what he often termed "the hole in his soul."

He had come home at one in the morning after going out for late-night coffee with Kelvin when the event finally finished. His friend helped him process everything that had happened: the strangers praying over him, his experience of fainting, the vision he'd had of a man in radiant robes performing surgery on his heart.

"I think he's having a mental breakdown," Estella had whispered over her mobile phone, from her bathroom. "He came into the room, woke me up, and began crying nonstop. He was begging for me to forgive him, swearing God's changed him for the better."

"Good for him," I'd yawned. "I'm going back to bed."

"Doll, this is serious! He was acting like a lunatic. He wouldn't leave me alone. The only reason I'm talking to you now is because he finally passed out."

He'd kept repeating his pleas for forgiveness, but she'd just stared back in disbelief. And when he'd tried to take her in his arms, she'd pushed him away. Then he'd begun howling about how he deserved it, before curling up at the foot of their bed and whimpering himself to sleep like a dog.

I almost choked on my ice cream now that I recalled the details in full. "You were convinced he'd joined a cult!" I laughed.

After that, the anecdotes flowed freely, each one seeming, for some reason, more hilarious than the last.

She remembered him getting some famous pastor from the UK to cleanse their house of evil spirits. The man's name was Eli Elizer, or something like that—an authority on spiritual warfare who was doing a speaking tour of Asia. He went from room to room, bellowing and anointing all the doorframes with special oil.

I recalled how Leonard began accepting the invitations to dinner at our parents' place—and how they begged Estella not to bring him anymore once his intentions to convert them became plain.

Estella recalled his baptism, which had taken place in a private swimming pool, at the house of a fellow church member. There were five people being dunked that day and Leonard was one of them—the fourth in line, to be precise. My parents and I were in attendance, more out of curiosity than anything else. Tante Elise was there too, only to see with her own two eyes if her worst fears were true. Just days before, she'd consulted a Catholic priest, who had confirmed that her son was committing a grave error in getting rebaptized.

"Remember his testimony?" Estella asked.

I did. It had stood out from the others, though it too had been delivered in a nervous stammer and had gone on for an excessive amount of time. I remembered it because, despite the bad delivery, Leonard had been shockingly honest. He spoke about how terribly he had treated his wife, and even admitted that he'd kept a mistress. (He'd got rid of her a few days after his conversion—Leonard had made the announcement to Estella after coming home from work.) He listed all his past sins: the drinking, the sudden outbursts of temper, his selfishness, his pride. And he praised the Lord for how He had transformed him and was changing him still. Tante Elise turned red, then turned tail, fleeing the scene as soon as her embarrassment of a son emerged from the pool.

The most amazing thing of all was that Leonard wasn't lying. He really had been behaving better. I learned this from Estella, who called me often in those days in an attempt to make sense of Leonard's surprising about-face.

After more than seven years of marriage, Estella had grown accustomed to the snide remarks, the criticisms of her appearance and mannerisms, the brooding silences that had become such integral parts of their interactions. In that last stage of his life, he instead began inquiring about her day. Or asking her opinion on something related to business. Or telling her funny stories, although religion hadn't improved his comedic abilities.

At first, Estella kept a wary distance. Then she began trying to provoke him, as if she couldn't bear the suspense of having Leonard's inner brute concealed for so long. She introduced lapses in her domestic management that she knew he normally wouldn't stand: meals served late, and tepid; towels infrequently replaced; business shirts folded, not hung. The maids carried out her wishes with incredulity, then promptly made themselves scarce. Leonard didn't seem to notice with all that God on the brain. Estella had even begun talking about Mutiara whenever she could, to remind him that she had deliberately gone against his and his family's wishes. He'd responded by showing interest, asking questions, nodding and smiling.

"I swear, Doll," said Estella, dragging her maraschino cherry through the soupy mess left in her sundae bowl. "I thought aliens had abducted him and replaced him with someone else."

I laughed. "Then maybe he's still alive, flying around in a spaceship somewhere."

The comment was designed to make her laugh too, but instead she sighed. In our irreverence, I'd forgotten that she'd actually loved him, and I'd taken the jokes one step too far.

"I remember," she murmured, "when I realized what religion was doing to him."

Out of compassion, I adopted a gentler tone. "I do too. Remember? I was there."

Ever since finding Jesus, Leonard had been relentless about trying to get Estella to accompany him to church. Estella had held out as best she could, but it was like being under siege. Five months after Leonard's baptism, she finally caved. She agreed to go with him, and she insisted I come too.

I did of course. (Could I ever refuse Estella? Even when I put up a fight, I always eventually gave in.) It was the same church that had hosted the event where Leonard was saved. They had no building of their own, so the congregation met in the ballroom of a luxury hotel, and it disoriented me to see the familiar backdrop of weddings, anniversaries, and birthdays now serving as the venue for a religious service. The setup was similar to that of the Easter service we attended with Nikki: chairs arranged in rows, facing the front, and a stage platform flanked by two projector screens displaying religious song lyrics.

A band headed by a man singing and strumming a guitar led the congregation in song—tunes alternately upbeat and ballad-ish, catchy but odd once you realized what they, and you, were singing about: "blood" and "lamb," "power" and "blessing," "lifting up" things and declaring God "worthy." The man sometimes closed his eyes and raised his hands, as did the people around us. At the end of the fourth song, the drummer stopped, but the keyboardist continued to play a stream of notes that had no beginning and no end, that floated the listening ear down quiet streams as the guitarist stopped singing and began to pray. He was addressing God directly, that much was clear, but he seemed to be doing so as if it were part of a show, a display, for the audience as well as the Holy Trinity upstairs. "Lord Jesus . . ." he intoned frequently (the same elongated "Jee-zus" of Leonard's prayers). The guitarist pleaded with Him to open hearts and touch lives and bring comfort and peace. Then he prayed for someone named Pastor Mathias—that he be anointed by the Lord that morning and that he wield God's truth like a double-edged sword.

Gradually, the guitarist's words faded, overtaken by a thundering voice, also praying to God. I squinted one eye open. Pastor Mathias himself had mounted the stage. He was Chinese, swarthy and pockmarked, and he looked more like a construction worker than a man of God. But he wore a well-tailored black suit and a maroon collared shirt, and in his right hand he hefted a black leather-bound Bible as a sign of his authority. Estella had one eye open too, but it was trained on Leonard.

Like I've said, Leonard wasn't unique in embracing Christianity. Thanks to the recent economic and political turmoil, it had become all the rage—especially the kind claiming that material prosperity was an outcome of following Jesus. But where this brand of Christianity made most of its adherents sleeker and glossier, Leonard seemed . . . more pathetic, somehow. Diminished. Reduced.

The sermon began. We both saw the same thing: Leonard rapt, hanging on to the pastor's every word, following along in his own Bible, eagerly highlighting passages. More than that, we saw the hollows in his cheeks, the dark circles around his eyes. His face, once baby-cheeked and fleshy, had acquired a wild, ascetic look.

The contrast between the sermon going on in front of us and Leonard's appearance couldn't have been starker. Pastor Mathias was speaking of the prosperity that God wanted to lavish upon His children. This message was on par with what we often heard recent Christian converts in our set say: how their God was a god of abundance; how spiritual *and* material riches were to be found in Christ. The whole economy had started to pick up by that point, along with everyone's fortunes, but a Christian belonging to this school of thought was more likely to attribute the turnaround to divine favor. Only Leonard seemed to be the exception, both in health and circumstance. Everyone else was on the rise, but it seemed God could only do so much with a man so lacking in talent. Being born again improved Leonard's business abilities not a jot, though to his family's relief, it made him more accommodating, more willing to heed his uncles' and cousins' advice. Sono Jaya stopped leaking money, but as long as Leonard was in charge, the chances of the family's conglomerate actually recovering from its losses looked dismal.

What Estella and I perceived in Leonard that Sunday only seemed to confirm this. We saw how weak he'd become, how toothless with spiritual enlightenment. Certainly, he'd been on the decline before that, but he'd retained his surliness, had put up a fight. With one foot in the kingdom of heaven, he seemed to be wasting away without minding at all.

Leonard's downfall didn't just appear out of nowhere. Rather, it came as the termination of a long, straight road. You can see it well before you reach it, and there are signs to alert you so you're not too surprised. Even so, I don't think either my sister or I foresaw exactly how Leonard's end would come or what form it would take, or that it would mean total, physical destruction.

We surveyed the melted remains, admitted defeat, and paid the bill. It was getting dark.

"Let's go back to the hotel room," Estella suggested. "We can order a bottle of wine from room service."

"Sounds good to me," I said.

We made our way to the car. As Estella steered us back to Carmel, I couldn't help but dwell further on those final months of my brother-in-law's life. Instead of taking the highway, my sister opted for a roundabout scenic route that hugged the coast so we could take full advantage of those precious last rays of sun. Set against the dimming backdrop of the rugged coastline, with its long stretches of brush and shaggy wind-slanted trees, the events that led up to Leonard's death took on a gothic hue as I turned over in my mind all that I had learned from Estella.

It had started harmlessly enough: a question one morning at breakfast before he and Estella left for work.

"Doesn't it ever trouble you?" he asked Estella.

"Does what ever trouble me?" Estella asked back.

"You know, how we made our money. How we still make it, despite all the government talk about cracking down on corruption."

"I'm not sure you can call what you've been doing 'making money' "— that's what I would have said if I were in her place, anyway.

Estella was more tactful, as always. "Which country do you think we're living in, Len?" she asked. "This is just how business operates here."

"But doesn't it make you feel . . . *sinful?*"

Estella tried not to cringe. "What choice do we have?" she asked, trying to sound lighthearted. But Leonard refused to be anything but serious.

"'You are a chosen people,'" he intoned, staring into his bowl of chicken congee, as if the mysterious words he muttered were written inside. "'A royal priesthood, a holy nation, God's special possession. That you may declare the great deeds of Him who called you out of darkness into his wonderful light.'"

My sister's response was only natural: "What?"

"First Peter, chapter two, verse nine. God commands us to shun sin's darkness and live in the light."

"I should get going," said Estella uneasily. "We're expecting a shipment for the new factory lab."

Leonard continued to stare trancelike into his breakfast. "You do know how the Halim family got the exclusive government contract for Mutiara in the first place."

"Of course I do," Estella sighed. "It's how everyone gets government contracts—including Sono Jaya, in case you forgot."

In response to this parry, Leonard gave a melancholy nod. "I know," he murmured before falling silent again.

Not knowing what else to do, Estella left for work. She called me from the car, and we tried to make sense of the conversation together.

"I don't get it," she said.

I stated the obvious. "Religion."

"Is it?" she asked. "Then why aren't the other fanatical Christians we know acting the same way? No one else looks like they're crazy, or dying. No one else seems to be worried about how 'sinful' doing business in this country is. Everybody but Leonard is happy to look the other way."

"Maybe we just don't know about it," I said, racking my brain for the other gung-ho Christians of our acquaintance. "Maybe Martin Yulianto is actually withering away underneath all that flab. Maybe our cousin Chris didn't really transfer seven hundred thousand US dollars into the offshore bank account he owns under a different name."

I couldn't keep it up. I broke into a chuckle.

"It's not funny, Doll," said Estella. "You aren't married to him."

"True. Thank God."

"Har-har. Thanks for all the help," she quipped. I could tell she wasn't really mad, but I apologized anyway.

"Have a good day at work," I added.

"I'll try."

I really didn't take my brother-in-law's guilt too seriously. After all, Leonard was a creature of change. How many identities had he picked up and thrown aside since meeting my sister? Amiable jokester, jealous boyfriend, ill-tempered drunkard, womanizing muscle-head. And now: holier-than-thou religious fundamentalist. Surely, this phase too would pass. Besides, other, worthier matters required my attention. I'd obtained the start-up capital from the family for Bagatelle. I'd rented office space, hired top-notch scientists from Europe to start experimenting, and assembled a team of designers, marketing experts, and legal staff. At long last, my life was taking off, and Leonard wasn't going to stop me. Estella was right, I wasn't married to him, yet thanks to what he'd done to my sister, he'd managed to guzzle up a great deal of my youth. Estella continued to keep me updated, though. And Leonard continued, inexplicably, to obsess about the sin on which our luxurious life was built.

The Bible verses he quoted took on a definite theme: repentance, turning from evil, becoming pure. He seemed to dread going into the office, instead spending extra time doing his early-morning devotionals and often leaving only after Estella had departed for Mutiara. Or at least she assumed he went to work. He was often back at home before she was that she began to wonder. The only evidence that he had left the house at all were his shoes, discarded and idling at the bottom of the great staircase banister, toes pointed into the house interior rather than toward the front door, which was how the maid would lay them out in the mornings. For all Estella knew, Leonard simply changed the direction of his footwear and stayed at home. It wouldn't have surprised her.

He even began to experience spells of paralysis. He would be sitting in the bedroom slotting in a cuff link, or at a dinner party swirling a glass of wine, when revelation would arrest him. He would stop and stare at the $4,000 Cartier cuff links his fingers had been fiddling with and the plush ivory carpet and the white French linen on the bed. Or he would gaze slack-jawed at the hothouse peonies in the table centerpiece or the plate of untouched foie gras being cleared away by a waiter. He was surrounded by opulence, by a world made possible through unrighteousness. And this knowledge ate away at him from the inside out. Perhaps it was only natural that he set about trying to shatter this world into pieces. He began by pleading with others to open their eyes too.

According to my sister, he'd even brought the matter up with his uncle, Om Paulus. "Wouldn't it be wonderful if we could live with clear consciences?" he'd asked the man at one of the Angsono Sunday lunches at the Grand Hyatt. The weekly family tradition was still going strong, even if Sono Jaya wasn't.

I'd learned about the debacle from my sister, who'd called me immediately afterward, while the entire awful exchange was piping hot in her mind. They'd been dining on dim sum in the hotel's Chinese restaurant, and Om Paulus had just bitten into a steamed dumpling. He'd coughed and swallowed before turning a cold eye on his nephew.

"My conscience *is* clear, Len," he growled. "If yours isn't, then that's your problem, not mine."

"So it doesn't bother you that we defaulted on so many of our loans during the Krismon?"

"A lot of companies defaulted, Len. We didn't have the money."

"Sure we didn't," Leonard said.

Leonard's other, younger uncle, Om Marcus, shushed him angrily from where he was sitting. The lazy Susan in the center of the table stopped moving. Except for the kids, who were at their own table, the whole family was all ears.

"What are you getting at, Len?" asked Om Paulus in a dangerously low voice.

Tante Elise tried to intervene, though her standing among the Angsonos had taken a tumble when Om Albert died and her son began ruining the family. "No business talk on Sundays!" she sang out desperately before turning to Leonard and pleading, "Don't bring this up now."

"Why not?" he asked. "Shouldn't we face the facts about where we get all the money to live like this?"

"Well, it certainly doesn't come from you," Om Marcus thundered. "Since your father died, your stupidity has been draining us dry."

Om Marcus's eldest—Leonard's cousin—chimed in. "It's a good thing Om Albert lived long enough to oversee the debt restructuring. If you'd been in charge, we'd be completely bankrupt by now. You'll never be a tenth of the man he was," he spat. "Or even a hundredth. You're worthless!"

All hell proceeded to break loose. They were lucky they were in one of the restaurant's private rooms. Even the children started paying attention at that point.

"Tante Estella, what's going on?" asked one of Leonard's nieces, tugging on my sister's sleeve.

"Nothing," Estella replied unconvincingly, just as Om Paulus barked, "Now you listen here, Len!"

Leonard's uncle continued, "This family's had it up to here with you and your newfound piety. If you want to be religious, fine, but don't be a pain in the ass. We've already lost a bundle thanks to you, and I'll be damned if I'm going to let you take away what's left!"

"No business talk on Sundays," implored Tante Elise again, feebly.

Om Paulus turned on her. "Shut up, Elise. The only reason we're talking 'business' is because your son's an imbecile."

Tante Elise began to cry.

"What did Om Leonard do?" the same niece asked my sister.

"Nothing," Estella replied again, no more convincingly than before. Meanwhile, Leonard, stunned by his family's hostility, had sat in silence for the rest of the meal.

Even that didn't stop Leonard, I mused as the very last traces of light disappeared and our car was swallowed up by night. The road was winding past golf courses, resorts, and private estates now. The only illumination came from our car's headlights and the footlights of elegant hedge-bordered signs informing us what we were driving past: Cypress Point Golf Club, Pebble Beach Golf Links, Casa Palmero, the Mariposa Ranch.

It had become increasingly clear that Leonard was preparing to do something rash. But no one had any idea what it would entail until he'd mentioned it to my sister. They were in the car on the way to Barry Sutiodjo's parents' fiftieth wedding anniversary. Estella was fidgeting absentmindedly with her brooch when Leonard suddenly said, "Maybe we should come clean about it all."

"Huh?" she said, not sure what he was talking about.

"About our sins. Sono Jaya and Sulinado Group should go public about them. You know, confess."

This was enough explanation for Estella to know roughly what he had in mind. The pin in her fingers slipped and drew blood.

"Len, you can't be serious!" she cried.

"Why not?"

My sister stared at him, which he apparently took as a sign he should keep going. "I've been praying about it and God has shown me the way. I can do an interview with one of the newspapers. Herry owns one. He could make sure it's done well. That we're put in a good light."

"A good light . . ." repeated Estella, resting her forehead in one weary hand.

Still not noticing anything was wrong, Leonard waved his hands around with the enthusiasm of a madman. "It's a shrewd move, when you think about it. All the politicians and the media are talking about clamping down on corruption. They're trying to dig up dirt on everyone and it'll only get worse. But if we expose ourselves of our own accord, it could work in our favor. We could be an example! We could pave the way!"

"Pave the way to what?" Estella practically screamed. "What planet are you living on? You think people will congratulate us? Hold us up as model citizens? Throw us a parade?"

"What's the worst that could happen?" he asked.

Estella wanted to slap him. "Oh, I don't know . . . *prison*? Frozen assets? The government—which is still corrupt, by the way—helping themselves to everything we own?"

Leonard was taken aback, and a little sliver of his old stubborn self stole back into him. He clenched his jaw, bore his eyes into the back of the driver's head, and refused to respond.

Estella attacked once more. "If you think a public confession of what everyone has been doing for decades is going to 'work in our favor,' then you're a fool. The government will use us as a scapegoat, proclaim they've done something about corruption, and go back to business as usual."

At that point, her voice broke. She sobbed out the last of what she had to say. "Are you really *that* selfish? You'd not only drag your family down, but mine as well? You'd sacrifice not just yourself, but all of us?"

Without any warning, Leonard's shoulders began to shake and he covered his face with his hands. "But how else can we flee from sin, Stell? How else can we live in the light?"

The fact that such an exchange happened at all bore testament to what an entirely different person Leonard had become. Gone was the time when Leonard was the dominant one, a petty tyrant expecting my sister to comply with his every unspoken whim. In those last days, Leonard started treating my sister with some consideration, as a partner or an equal to be considered and consulted. He also developed a troubling overreliance on obtaining her approval, even if it was about a decision he'd already made. She felt like a nurse taking care of an invalid. Mostly she humored him. Occasionally, to make him happy, she accompanied him to church. But Leonard's plan to expose both Sono Jaya and Sulinado Group was potentially far too disastrous to dismiss. Estella told me and our parents, and our parents told my mother's siblings. Needless to say, Om Benny was furious. Albert Angsono's incompetent son was determined to sink our family with them.

Om Benny immediately contacted Leonard's uncles. They planned a joint intervention, to take place after that week's Angsono lunch in one of the hotel conference rooms. Leonard's uncles and male cousins would be there, along with Om Benny and Ma. It would be an attempt to reason with him, to give him one last chance.

Leonard's account of the meeting, Estella told me later, was incoherent. She was barely able to piece together what had happened. If it had only been rage—fury—that had made her husband gibber like an ape, there would have been no cause for worry. But it was the fact he gibbered about, of all things, the room's lack of windows that unnerved her most.

"It was impossible to breathe," he told my sister. "Who designs a room like that?" And when my sister was about to point out that most hotel function rooms don't have natural light, the futility of it all suddenly struck her, the meaninglessness of any effort to shake him awake. So she just lis-

tened to his ranting about the room's blindness—comparing it to both our families' blindness to the truth—and how all he could do while they were "talking and talking" at him was to drown them out with prayer, asking God to give him strength to do the right thing and not to be tempted into giving in to sin.

When Estella finally interrupted him to ask what they had wanted from him (even though she knew; our mother had told her about it prior to the intervention taking place), he looked disoriented, derailed, as if he didn't know. My sister was shocked: Had he really not registered anything they had said? He then quoted that verse from the Bible—his future last words, the ones that he would murmur again and again under his dying breath: "'Everyone who does evil hates the light and will not come into the light for fear that their evil deeds will be exposed.'"

After Estella related Leonard's account to me, I called Ma to ask her how it went.

"Badly," she informed me, point-blank. "Very badly. I don't think he's going to change his mind."

To hear her tell it, Leonard's uncles and cousins, herself and Om Benny had practically been on their knees.

"We begged him not to go through with it. We told him to think of his late father, of his grandfather, and how going to the media would destroy everything they'd worked so hard for. We asked him to consider how many lives it would affect—to think of his nephews and nieces too. The poor children," Ma lamented, the drama queen in her taking over. "It's not fair to drag them into all of this."

I cut Ma off. "But he's not actually going to go through with it, is he?"

Ma was silent for a while. "It looks like he is. He left us, you know, before we were done. Ran out of the room like a lunatic. Said that he has an interview scheduled for Thursday next week and that there's nothing we can do to stop him."

At this piece of news, I almost dropped the phone. "What are you going to do?" I asked.

Another pause from Ma. "After Leonard left, your uncle and I stayed to discuss the problem with Leonard's relatives. We came up with an idea."

◆　◆　◆

The flames flickering in our hotel room's fireplace looked uniform and sterile—the inevitable result, I supposed, of them being powered by gas jets instead of burning wood. We were halfway through the bottle of Napa Valley red Estella had ordered through room service—a 1995 Opus One. Not too bad. Estella lounged on the sofa, glass in hand, staring into space. I prodded the fake logs with the iron poker that had been provided for decorative purposes.

"I'm glad I found out at the very end what Leonard meant," Estella said suddenly.

"What Leonard meant?" I repeated.

Estella nodded. "When I confronted him about his mistress. 'What happened to the woman I fell in love with?'—that's what he said, remember? He explained it at our last dinner together.

"That dinner . . ." she continued, wide-eyed. And I realized it wasn't space she'd been staring into, but the past. "Why didn't he tell me before then?" she mused before chuckling. "He always had bad timing. Remember when we first met him? That joke about eating at Chez Panisse every night of the week?

"Anyway," she continued, refilling our glasses, "I suppose I should be grateful. I couldn't have asked for a better way to remember him. Though it would have made things so much easier if he'd just acted crazy and unreasonable.

"But everything about that night was unexpected. He was ravenous too—the hungriest I'd seen him in a long time. Probably because he was so

excited. He kept talking about how confident he was that the interview would go well, even though it wasn't for Herry's newspaper. I told you Herry refused to run it, didn't I, Doll? He was a better friend than Leonard deserved.

"Anyway, do you know what the worst part was about that dinner? Leonard kept talking about how blessed he was to have me by his side. How thankful he was that I'd stuck with him, despite everything he'd done. How happy he was that I was being so supportive about the interview despite our families being against it, despite me trying to talk him out of it at first. And get this: He took my hand and told me how much he loved me. Can you believe it? I think the last time I heard him say anything like that was on our honeymoon. Of course he'd choose to tell me he loved me on that night of all nights . . ."

My sister gave a bark of a laugh and threw her head back against the cushions of the sofa. "Can you *believe* it," she said again, more softly, before picking up the story where she had left off.

"That's when I couldn't help myself. I said, 'I thought I wasn't the woman you fell in love with.' He looked confused. I reminded him that was what he'd once said. Then he turned all flustered and contrite. He said he was sorry for how selfish he was back when we'd started dating. He explained it wasn't me he'd fallen in love with, but rather an impossible ideal—a woman who would know exactly what he was thinking and feeling at all times, who could anticipate his every want and need. Even when it became clear that I wasn't her, instead of coming to terms with it, he'd just tried his best to make me conform. He'd thought everything would fall into place after we got married. Obviously, he couldn't have been more wrong.

"Hearing him talk, you'd think I'd actively deceived him. That I'd tricked him into marriage. As if." My sister's expression softened. "Still, call me stupid, but that night for the first time ever, it felt like there could be hope for him and me—for us being happy together someday; for picking up the pieces, throwing them away and starting again.

"I know, Doll, I know," she said hastily, anticipating my outcry. "He was infuriating by the end: getting all religious, trying to ruin his family and ours. But that dinner did remind me that I loved him. And for the first time in more than a decade together, he was actually trying to communicate, to be honest, to be kind. He was pathetic, yes, but could you blame me for finding it a little bit endearing? Like an old dog with no bite left in him . . ."

She let the words trail off as she contemplated her glass.

"By that time, it was too late of course," she remarked with a peculiar smile. "He must have been on his third or fourth helping of stew. To be honest, I was surprised he hadn't keeled over yet, but I suppose it would have been suspicious if he'd dropped dead mid-dinner. In a way it's lucky it took a few hours for him to die." That strange smile again. "Well, if 'lucky' really is the best word."

I recalled the panic that the situation's urgency had created, forcing the two families to take measures they'd otherwise have considered unthinkable. Leonard, who'd lost all instincts for survival, had made the mistake of telling them when his interview with the newspaper would take place. Faced with a deadline of mere days, the families had no choice but to take drastic steps. Though they could have easily hired someone to do it, the risk of indiscretion would have been far too great.

Better to keep it in the family. Better to entrust it to one of our own.

You'd think it would have been an impossible task, getting Estella to terminate the life of her husband. It certainly hadn't been easy to convince her—she was, rightfully, horrified—but our family had prevailed in the end. As I mentioned, our family had urgency in their favor, which they used to their fullest advantage. And they had persuasive strength in numbers: After the abortive meeting with Leonard, Om Benny and Ma had called an emergency family conference.

The late-night meeting had taken place at Opa's house, even though

Opa himself was long past the point of participation. New Oma, ignorant of the exact reason for the gathering (and ignorant in general), kept Opa company upstairs as his heirs held a conference below. Om Benny and Ma had summoned their siblings, but none of the spouses were in attendance, or any of us children. It was a delicate matter, and I suppose they had to draw the line somewhere for the sake of secrecy. Estella wouldn't have been there either if she hadn't been vital to their plan.

She had told me about it afterward over the phone. They had sat around the glass-and-chrome table that served as a replacement for the carved wooden slab of Oma's time. My sister figured out pretty quickly that some sort of prior agreement had been reached. The conference was being held solely for her benefit—to convince her to act on the family's behalf. And they deployed every possible tactic in order to win her over. It was the only way, they pleaded, and she, as his wife, knew it. Reason hadn't worked, begging hadn't worked, and time was running out fast. Leonard would be the ruin of not one but two families—and more, depending on how much that reporter could trick him into confessing.

Our mother was the most relentless because she could be: Hadn't Leonard done enough to destroy Estella's life? Would she let him continue in this way? Would she allow him to ruin her relatives? He was danger-ous and had to be stopped; even Leonard's uncles agreed. His own family! What did it say about the man—that his own flesh and blood felt he simply had to go? It would be a kindness, anyway, to put Leonard out of his mis-ery. The man was obviously not right in the head.

Estella made a valiant attempt to resist—she did love him, even if she was barely conscious of it anymore. But her love had been starved and abused for so many years that it didn't stand a chance. And she'd always been susceptible to our family's influence; they'd played a hand in bring-ing, then keeping, her and Leonard together. Now they were trying their hardest to turn her against him. Perhaps their success was inevitable.

After an hour and a half of pleading, she stopped saying no, resorting to silence instead. The meeting ended at two in the morning with a final entreaty to my sister to sleep on it and let them know her decision later that day. She called my mother in the afternoon.

Her answer was yes.

In Estella's defense, there's something very abstract about agreeing to murder someone that makes its reality difficult to register, especially if there won't be any blood or physical struggle involved. That is, until you see your handiwork in action: the dilation of the pupils, the slackening of the jaw, the exhalation of the life force like a deflating balloon.

The wine was all gone now, and Estella and I lay sprawled side by side on the couch. All our talk about Leonard seemed to have stirred up something foul—a miasma that settled over us, that made it difficult to think. Through barely open eyes we watched the unnatural flames in the fireplace dance.

"It only hit him after dinner," murmured Estella. "In the shower. His legs gave way. He called for help. I wrapped him in a bathrobe. He was shivering all over. I dragged him to our bed with the help of the maids. 'It must be food poisoning,' I told him. Strictly speaking, it was true. Then he asked me to call an ambulance. To call a doctor. I stroked his forehead and said they were already on the way.

"It took forever for him to die, Doll. At least, that's how it felt. It was torture to watch, but I think *listening* to him go was even worse. That Bible verse—the one about evildoers not wanting to come into the light. He kept muttering it over and over, sometimes all of it, sometimes just parts. It couldn't have been coincidence, Doll. He must have known we were responsible. It was awful. I even lay down beside him and tried to calm him. I told him I loved him, which at least was true, though I know you've never believed me. I told him help would be there soon. I told him everything would be okay."

She sighed. "I know what's done is done, Doll, but every now and then I can't help but wonder: What if I hadn't done it? What if he were still alive?"

"Oh, Stell," I said, my voice tumbling out as a drowsy mumble, "don't think like that. It was kinder for him that you did it. If you hadn't agreed, the family would have just hired some thug."

"Yeah," she said, "I guess you're right. That's what you said at the time. When I called you after the family meeting to ask you for advice."

"I did say that . . ." I acknowledged faintly, recalling what else I'd said. A lot of it rehashed the arguments the family had already put forth: about Leonard leaving them no alternative, about having to act quickly, about him being too unstable to stop. I also remembered how much energy I had put into persuading her to poison the man who had been the bane of her existence, and mine. Vengeance. I'd thirsted for it all those years, and at long last the opportunity to carry it out was being extended to me, handle first. Or, rather, to my sister. So I'd whispered in her ear and closed her fingers around it, and lo and behold, she had struck.

For all our talk of "us" and "them," for all our condemnation, we were our family's children. Was it surprising—that a rotting tree had yielded rotten fruit?

When Estella spoke, it was as if she had read my mind. "Tante Sandra wasn't rotten, though," she murmured, "not like the rest of us. She would never have let us kill Leonard. Oh, Doll, I'm so glad we've found her. She'll set us straight."

She closed her eyes and settled herself farther into the cushions. I did the same.

The fire burned on.

❖   ❖   ❖

The next morning, we woke up later than intended, so we paid a late-checkout fee to avoid having to get ready in a rush. Then we drove up to the grove to see the monarchs one last time.

It was early afternoon by the time we got there, and the sun streamed down in warm waves, setting off flurries of motion as its light rolled across the trees. A freckle-faced ranger in plaits was giving a short informational talk about the monarchs. She was surrounded by attentive tourists nodding their heads and snapping photos.

"Why do you think the monarchs huddle together in clusters?" the ranger asked. "Would anyone like to take a guess?"

"Because they're lonely?" a chubby boy in red fleece ventured. Everyone laughed.

"Good answer," chuckled the ranger. "I'm sure they enjoy the company, but it's mainly because clustering keeps them warm. When they're packed together like that, it protects them from the wind and the cold."

"But what about the ones on the inside?" the boy asked. "The ones covered up by the others?"

The ranger smiled. "Believe it or not, they're just fine. It's actually warm under all those wings."

"We should get going," whispered Estella. "So we have enough time to talk with Tante Sandra before we drive back to LA."

I bid the butterflies a silent farewell and raced to catch up with my sister. She was already in the driver's seat. The engine was purring and ready to go.

SURELY I HAVE the answer now. Why did my sister kill us? To avenge Leonard's death. Acting purely out of self-interest, we slaughtered him for trying to do the right thing. I can stop delving now. I can leave my memories alone. *Let me burrow backward*, I beg myself. *Let me return from the past.* But I know I'm lying to myself about solving the mystery. There's more to it, I can tell. The gaps are too glaring. Why the late-blooming obsession with redeeming the family if she was just planning to murder us? Why the seemingly genuine desire to find our aunt if she actually didn't care about our redemption? And why take the lives of not just our family and her former in-laws, but also so many of our friends?

I don't want to go any further; fear has sprung up alongside curiosity. I think I do know the answer deep down somewhere, and that I won't like what I find. But here's the problem: It's like asking someone not to think about elephants. What else comes stomping through one's head, especially if there's nothing to serve as a distraction? Especially if the alternative is a silent hospital ward and a world that's given you up for dead? Where do I have to go besides my memories? Even if I resist them, here they are, pulling me in like quicksand. How can I possibly stop now, on the cusp of discovering our long-lost aunt? The woman who was supposed to be the antidote to our evil, capable of saving us from what we had become?

Estella should have known better. Her quest for redemption was clearly doomed from the start. Our family was too far gone—Estella and me included. Nobody could salvage us, least of all Tante Sandra.

It was stupid of us to track her down. We dug up the body of someone we'd lost more than twenty years prior and expected to find her as fresh and whole as she had been in life. Everything was wrong from the moment the door swung open.

She was still lovely. That was the unnerving thing. She was lovelier in person than the desert photo unearthed by Estella had suggested, even though it hadn't lied about the purple blotch that marred our aunt's décolletage. She had aged more than her older sisters—our mother and two other aunts—but her weathered features gave her a natural beauty that surpassed their pale perfection. They were porcelain figurines never taken out of the box, but she—she was a mountain, a tree, made handsomer and more rugged by exposure to the elements.

At least, that's how she appeared at first glance. The longer I stared, the more her loveliness began to resemble the molt shell of a cicada—a brittle, translucent sheath that should have been cast off a long time ago to make way for new growth. The seconds continued to pass, us staring at her, her staring back. And it seemed to me that the soul encased within her had moldered, and now the old skin was nothing more than a shroud.

It must have been my imagination—if everyone else saw what I was seeing, they would have run away screaming. I shook my head vigorously, and my vision resolved, consolidating the shell and its contents into a single coherence: the aunt of our memories, now in her midforties, nothing more.

Tante Sandra spoke first. "Rose said you came by on the weekend."

We gathered that Rose was the pink neighbor's name. She must have been too excited to keep our secret. Our aunt looked us up and down. "You're all grown up," she observed.

"Everyone thinks you're dead," Estella blurted.

"Yes," our aunt replied coldly, "that was the idea."

She eyed us again, as if trying to decide whether to slam the door in our faces or invite us in. Finally, wearily, she motioned for us to enter, turning her back on us before we had even stepped across the threshold.

The plastic shoe rack next to the front door was a jumble of sneakers, sandals, and practical low-heeled pumps. On the wall opposite was a rickety rattan console piled high with leaflets, sale catalogues, and ripped envelopes. In front of the hall closet stood a small rolling suitcase, black and durable, plastic handle still extended.

"Sorry I missed you the first time," said Tante Sandra, not sounding very sorry at all. "I was away on business. I just got back."

"What kind of business?" asked my sister.

"A conference. For people in the food and beverage industry. I own a restaurant and a convenience store."

We tried to suppress our surprise, but our aunt seemed to detect it nonetheless. She glanced over at the suitcase, as if contemplating flight once more.

"I'll get us some coffee," she declared abruptly, stalking down a corridor leading into the heart of the house. We took off our shoes and followed.

The place had an undeniably retro feel, with its walls textured in wood and plaster and brick. A fluffy sienna shag blanketed the floors—in a soothing way, as if telling the house not to cry. Estella and I sat down on the cream-colored sofa that bordered the sunken fireplace of gray and brown stone. I noticed the complete absence of any photos, or any decorative item suggesting good taste. A crystal swan occupied the mantel, flanked by a statue of a big-eyed, snub-nosed boy fishing in a boat, and a framed cross-stitched cloth declaring desperately *Home is where the heart is* in valentine red and baby pink. Similar thrift-store-type items had been placed here and there: a snow globe gone dry, salt and pepper shakers doing the hula, a bunny figurine.

Our aunt eventually emerged from the kitchen with a tray of refreshments: mugs of instant coffee, a melamine plate of sand-colored sandwich cookies, and a heap of powdered creamer and sugar packets, the kind you sometimes saw people squirreling away in food courts and cafés.

"How did you find me?" she asked, sitting down heavily. I noticed, for the first time, the heft around her belly and thighs.

Estella took the letters and photographs out of her purse. She handed Tante Sandra the picture of her in the desert. "You disappeared in 1981, but the date in the corner reads 1984," she explained. She gave our aunt the second letter. "And you gave Oma this address."

Estella's voice sounded how I felt—profoundly uncertain, but trying to pretend everything was okay. We knew we were supposed to be feeling happy, but Tante Sandra certainly didn't seem thrilled we had come.

Our aunt smiled grimly as she examined the photo and letter, the way a chess player might when acknowledging the soundness of an opponent's move. "How long have you had these?" she asked.

"I found them last week," said Estella. "They were among Oma's things."

At that moment, the same thought occurred to my sister and me. Tante Sandra anticipated us before we could speak: "Don't worry, I know she's dead. She wrote me a letter. Said she didn't have long to live. Cancer, right?"

We nodded.

"Was she in a lot of pain at the end?"

We nodded again. She nodded too—in a somber and respectful way. But there was also something perfunctory about the gesture, and she didn't seem too distressed at this piece of information.

"Does the rest of the family know?" she asked. Seeing our confusion, she added, "About you finding me, I mean. Of course they know about your oma."

"No," I answered. "We weren't sure ourselves whether we really had found you . . . until now."

"Are you going to tell them?" she asked.

Estella and I were quiet. That had been the original plan, but now we weren't so sure.

"Don't," our aunt said curtly. "Don't tell them. It may not make a difference now, but what's the point? I'm not going back. Life here suits me well."

Is that what you think? was my ungracious thought.

Our aunt picked up a cookie and bit into it. Though she swiped at her lips with the back of her hand, crumbs clung stubbornly to the corners of her mouth.

There were so many questions Estella and I wanted to ask, about why she faked her own death, about her life since, about the mark on her neck. Now her hostility, unspoken but plain, made our words run dry. We sat there, fidgeting, uncomfortable, at a loss for what to say.

"It's been a long time," she remarked, breaking the silence for us. "You and your cousins were just kids when I left. How are you? Do you work? Are you married? Any children?"

As with her question about Oma dying a painful death, her curiosity about our lives had a distinctly cursory air.

"I work for the family," said Estella, picking a question and answering it.

"I used to, but I have my own business now," I was about to say. But our aunt cut me off with a laugh—a pretty, girlish giggle I remembered well. Unlike its owner, it hadn't changed a bit. Drops of dew, I thought, suddenly overwhelmed by what our aunt once was, and was not anymore.

She extracted a little more information about us, then moved on to ask about the rest of the family, inquiring after everyone in turn in a grazing sort of way. We answered in the same fashion. No, we weren't married. Estella's husband was dead. (Food poisoning. Tragic.) No, no kids. All the cousins were fine. Our parents were okay. So were all our uncles and aunts.

We told her about Opa's Alzheimer's, mentioning that New Oma was taking good care of him. Then, because she looked puzzled, we told her about Opa remarrying. She assimilated this information quickly, then sighed.

"I guess I shouldn't be surprised," she said in a flat voice. "Nothing should surprise me anymore."

There was a brief pause.

"Has your uncle Peter come out?" she asked.

"He lives with a 'good friend,' " I answered.

"How's your aunt Margaret?"

"On her third aristocrat," said Estella.

Estella chiming in like that startled me a little. She usually left the snide quips to me, but she'd grown more assertive over the course of this trip. My sister followed this remark with a question of her own.

"Why did you leave?" she asked our aunt.

"It's a long story," came the reply.

"We have time," my sister assured her, resting her mug of lukewarm coffee in her lap.

Our aunt scrutinized us, deliberating.

"How much do you know?" she asked finally.

"Nothing," said Estella.

Our aunt chuckled. "At least your oma could be trusted with that," she murmured. "Well, you have come a long way," she continued in a louder voice. "And I suppose finding me deserves some sort of reward."

"Reward" wasn't the right word, but Estella and I had no way of realizing that until after.

❖   ❖   ❖

He'd said his name was John, and our aunt had taken him at his word. It was what he'd chosen to call himself in Australia because he'd liked having a fresh identity to go with that new stage of his life. And it was almost the truth; all the Aussies called him "Johnno" anyway, which bore a striking resemblance to his real name. But looking back on it, she might have been spared a great deal of heartache if she'd known he was actually Jono.

They were both students at the University of Melbourne—and Asian, which had been enough reason for her to ask if the seat next to him was taken. When, upon the conclusion of the lecture, she discovered they were both from Indonesia, Jakarta no less, the name "John" made everything fall pleasingly into place—especially when coupled with his appearance, so deceptively Chinese it bordered on racial caricature (slanted eyes, yellowish skin, even a bit of buck about the teeth). She wasn't on the lookout for potential differences between them, not in that foreign land, so close to home geographically but populated with Caucasians and sheep. And so her assumption was that he was like her: of the same ethnicity, most likely of Protestant or Catholic background, and from a family either Westernized or with aspirations thereto. If he'd used his real name, "Jono," it might have raised a red flag—that he was likely Javanese (i.e., *pribumi*), thus probably Muslim, and therefore from a wholly different world. But instead he'd claimed he was John. He was shy and sweet, and they got along right from the start.

The tone in which Tante Sandra related these events had a sandpapery texture to it, almost as if she were trying, in the telling, to smooth the splinters and sharp edges of the past. Yet it also laid bare the rawness of the wounds, giving us a glimpse of the Tante Sandra of our memories, vulnerable and tender, beneath the scars.

"Oh, there were warning signs," she said, shaking her head. "He barely spoke around my friends. And once he tagged along for a dinner at a Chinese restaurant and didn't eat anything but soy sauce and white rice. I used to invite him to join us for all sorts of activities: bowling, picnics, parties, visits to the beach, the zoo. He always said he had to study, or sometimes he said he was sick."

It was only when he finally told her about his true identity that the strange behavior made sense: He was afraid her friends would sniff him out if he said too much; every dish they'd ordered at the restaurant had pork in it; he worked part-time to make ends meet and rarely had the cash or the time for the kinds of excursions she and her friends liked to take.

He had been right to worry that her friends would expose him, though really they had merely created the conditions for him to expose himself. It had been someone's surprise birthday party and she'd persuaded him to come along. The majority of guests had gone home, but the remainder chatted idly in the host's living room as someone strummed a guitar. Her friends were various nationalities of ethnic Chinese: two others from Indonesia, but the rest from English-speaking Singapore, Malaysia, and Hong Kong. They started talking about exams—one of the Malaysians had boasted that he had better things to do than study, like sleep.

The other Chinese-Indonesian girl laughed and called him as lazy as a *bumiputra*—the Malaysian equivalent of Indonesia's *pribumi* and Singapore's ethnic Malays. The Chinese-Malaysian guy scowled. "That's not funny," he said with a glower, which only made one of the Chinese-Singaporeans tease him even more: "Be careful, if your face gets any blacker, you'll really look like one of them."

Meanwhile, Jono turned red and went very still. Sandra laughed along with the rest of them and only noticed something amiss when he stood up abruptly and stammered that he should get home. He ran out and Sandra followed, catching up only after he'd made it a good way down the street.

"That's when it came out," our aunt told us, "that he wasn't actually Chinese."

They ducked into someone's garden and sat on the grass behind a tall hedge to talk about it. In their earnest, youthful minds the matter seemed far too important to leave for another time. She learned that he was Javanese and Muslim, and he was poor. By her standards, at least. His father worked as a low-level manager at a margarine factory. The fact that John was attending university in another country was beyond anything his family had imagined possible, but the death of a moderately well-to-do relative had resulted in a windfall for his father. John had convinced his father that sending him to Australia to get an engineering degree would be a good investment. Australia wasn't charging university fees at the time, not even for international students. He worked like mad on his English-language skills, then enrolled in a program that placed him in a public high school in Melbourne so he could take the qualifying exams to gain entrance into one of the universities. The money was enough to pay for English lessons, various fees, and a one-way plane ticket, with a little left for initial living expenses, but once he was on the ground, he would have to find some sort of part-time work. And that was how he came to be there, he concluded, defensively. Then she asked the burning question she'd been saving for when he was done: So he really didn't have any Chinese blood at all in him?

He admitted it then: A great-great-grandmother from his mother's side was reportedly Chinese. The looks had skipped everyone in his extended family except him, where they'd banded together to make his childhood a living hell. How they'd teased him about it—everyone, from his classmates to his cousins. His nickname was Cina—China—and the jokes never got old:

Hey, Cina, don't be stingy. Lend me some cash.

Hey, Cina, watch where you're going. Or can't you see with those slitty eyes?

Go back home, Cina. Indonesia's through with communism.

John laughed bitterly as he spat out the remarks, each one evidently seared into his memory like a cattle brand. He'd never told anyone before, but the jokes were why he'd made such an effort to leave.

"That's when I should have walked away," muttered our aunt. "That's when I should have figured out that something wasn't right."

But she hadn't. She was stupid and young and idealistic back then. And there was something magic about the setting that dazzled her, made her heedless of the danger of their situation. There they were, in a stranger's garden, a little after midnight, whispering together about profound things like racism, poverty, and childhood trauma. The cool dark was redolent with the scent of eucalyptus, and the low hoots of the tawny frogmouths overhead lent the moment a wild and wondrous touch. Instead of walking away, she kissed him. Just a hasty peck on the lips. He looked stunned for a few seconds, but then he broke into a bashful smile.

They were an unlikely pair, the rich Chinese girl and the misunderstood *pribumi* boy from the other side of the tracks, but they'd connected with each other, and wasn't that what mattered? If only she'd known she'd misread him, that experiencing discrimination hadn't given him empathy for her race, but the exact opposite—a budding resentment toward her kind for causing him trouble through no fault of his own.

Still, as long as they stayed in Melbourne, everything was fine. She stopped expecting him to spend time with her other pals, and they hung out alone instead, studying together in the library, strolling along the Yarra River, treating themselves (in keeping with his budget) to shakes and sandwiches at their favorite milk bar.

"Fantasy land," remarked our aunt. Estella and I nodded, recalling our own college days—or our freshman year, at least. Entomology, each other, and solitude. The enchantment cast by university life apparently transcended time and space.

John's summons back to reality was unnecessarily cruel. His father was hit by a bus. The news came by telegram. He borrowed money from Sandra to pay for the plane ticket, and he never came back.

They wrote letters to each other at first (Tante Sandra didn't go into details about the content), but as the months went by, he wrote less frequently until he stopped writing at all. It was understandable, she told herself. He had a lot to handle. He had to support his mother and younger siblings. His father's supervisor had kindly let him have his father's old job at the margarine factory, but then his mother came down with a mysterious lung infection and there were doctors' bills to pay and medicines to buy.

She knew it was unreasonable to demand more attention from him, especially since their relationship had barely begun when he'd had to leave. She hadn't told her parents about him, and now she wasn't sure if she had anything to tell. She planned to visit him when she was in Jakarta, but she didn't get there until over six months had passed—she'd already planned a trip to New Zealand with her friends for the upcoming break, and the long break after that had been promised to our family. (That trip to London, where the photo of her at Buckingham Palace had been taken, where she'd plowed through pigeons and offered us hot chestnuts.)

When she met John again, in Jakarta, she was a term into her third and final year. He greeted her stiffly, as if there had never been any romance between them, or even friendship. Not only that, but the toxicity she'd overlooked on that magical night had already begun eating away at him. Months, that was all it had taken, triggered by the steady shower of unfortunate events that hadn't stopped pitter-pattering on his head since his father's untimely death. He told her all about it when they met at the coffee shop around the corner from where he worked—at a different job from when he'd last written. He'd been let go from his previous position. The margarine company had been bought out by a Chinese-owned conglomerate. They'd enacted a massive restructuring, which resulted in him being made redundant, and it had taken him some time to find employment elsewhere. To pay for his mother's medical treatment and keep up with the rent, he'd resorted to borrowing money from a loan shark. Even though he had a job now—as a foreman in a mosquito-repellent factory—it paid less than the previous one, and that made it hard to keep up with repayments.

He spoke calmly enough about it—or, rather, he spoke softly and low, avoiding eye contact as he stirred the coffee in his glass mug, bringing the sugary black grounds swirling to the top. In her naivete, she reacted dramatically: "That's terrible! How can I help?"—something like that. It was a mistake. He sank his head between his shoulders, muttering that he was sorry for mentioning it, he wasn't asking for help. He would manage just fine.

"You could find another job with better pay," she suggested. She immediately felt stupid for proposing something so obvious.

Sure enough, he responded with a sneer: Yes, that had occurred to him. But it had taken so long to find this job he thought it would be better to stay put. The last thing he could afford was another interruption to his pay. He was about to say something else, but seemed to think better of it. He closed his mouth. After a few seconds, he opened it again and said it anyway: He suspected it had taken him so long to get hired because the interviewers thought he was Chinese. It was hard to ignore how he looked.

He could apply to Chinese employers, she proposed awkwardly after a silence that lasted too long.

He'd tried, he replied in all seriousness. But they always figured out quickly that he wasn't one of them. The shift would be subtle but always detectable—a fading warmth, a stiffening smile, a slight shrinking inward like that of a fearful snail.

He made a feeble joke about Sandra being the only one he'd been able to fool. Then he looked at his watch and said he should get back to work. As an afterthought, he asked her what she had planned for the rest of the day. She said she didn't know, though that was a lie. She was going to the beauty salon with her mother, to get their hair done for Vera Sukamto's wedding reception that night. But she felt that to tell him the truth would make a mockery of the hardship he was suffering.

He asked when she was going back to Melbourne. In a week, she said, before asking tentatively if he'd ever be able to resume his studies there. He shook his head. No, it had been selfish of him to force his father into squandering all that money on an overseas degree. If only his family had that money now. He looked at his watch again. They wished each other the best and parted.

"And guess what?" said our middle-aged aunt, her voice full of scorn for her younger self. "Even after that, I didn't get the hint. Would you believe I still wrote to him from Melbourne, even though he never replied? Would you believe I suggested we meet again the next time I was back?"

"Why?" I couldn't help but ask.

"Who knows," she answered, taking the last cookie on the plate even though Estella and I hadn't eaten a single one. As she bit into it, she frowned. "Maybe it was too hard to let go of what we had. What I thought we had, at least. And once I was back at university, our differences seemed so small again: So what if he wasn't Chinese, so what if I was rich? It didn't seem right to abandon the relationship, at least not without a fight."

At the end of this reflection, she appeared for a split second like the naive Sandra of the tale we were listening to. Then the Tante Sandra of the present reasserted herself.

She and John met three more times after that, the next two meetings occurring on visits home during her final term in Melbourne. Both times they met in the same coffee shop, and against the unchanging backdrop the alterations in him seemed more pronounced. It was like seeing a cliff collapse, she told us. Each time, a new chunk had fallen off. The second time he told her to stop calling him John. Going by a different name had been stupid and pretentious, he said.

He told her that his mother's lungs stayed in bad shape no matter what the doctors prescribed, but he'd found extra employment to help the family scrape by. The work was beneath him—washing dishes three nights a week at an upscale seafood restaurant. But he couldn't be picky. Every bit helped.

Lots of Chinese customers, needless to say, he added offhandedly. Her people did well for themselves. Her family included.

Our aunt could have sworn she saw a thin smile cross his face; then it vanished. He explained: He'd read a newspaper article about synthetic textile manufacturing. It had mentioned Sulinado Group, its founder-patriarch, and the five children who helped run it. He'd remembered she had five older siblings and put two and two together.

She didn't think it mattered, she said, feeling guilty all the same. The omission wasn't deliberate; it had just never come up. He supposed, in a quiet voice, that it didn't matter—at least not in Australia, not back then and there.

He rose to his feet to go. She stood as well and bade him good-bye.

They met for the third time after the end of her final term, once she had returned to Jakarta for good. To her shock, he was the one who proposed it, in a letter. The letter came as a surprise too, congratulating her preemptively on finishing her degree. It was hardly warm, but it was civil, and in it he mentioned they should meet once she was back.

Their last meeting had left such a sour taste in her mouth that she'd sworn off trying to maintain their bizarre and estranged relationship. He obviously couldn't stand her anymore, and the way he talked about the Chinese made her squirm. Yet after reading the letter, she found herself relenting. Maybe his hostility had all been in her mind. So what if he'd mentioned that finding work had been difficult because he looked Chinese? And so what if he'd faced discrimination when trying his luck with Chinese employers? That was the reality of life in Indonesia, and she'd simply never felt it because she was rich.

So what if he'd found out her father was Irwan Sulinado, the rising textile tycoon? It was true, and arguably she was at fault for not mentioning it sooner, thus making him think she had something to hide. It was probably true too that a lot of the patrons of the restaurant where he worked were Chinese. Even if the implication was that a lot of Chinese had money to spare, that was undeniable as well: Her people *had* made good in Indonesia. In short, John—or, rather, Jono—had simply been stating the facts. She was the one who'd been sheltered from them all her life.

She decided to write back telling him when her flight home was and saying that she'd like very much to meet.

"By the time we met at that coffee shop again, I was convinced that I'd been the one in the wrong." As our aunt said this, she shook her head at her younger self's idiocy. "Foolish, I know. But can you blame me for trying to believe the best of him after all he'd been through? His father's death, his mother's illness, having to pull out of university and scramble for a job? And let's not forget his little brother and sister. He had to support them too, make sure they weren't forced to drop out of high school to find work. Going through all of that would be enough to make anyone bitter. He'd lashed out. He couldn't help himself. I thought I should give him another chance."

Estella and I stared silently into our mugs. I felt suddenly ashamed of our presence there, our prying open of the life of this woman we'd presumed to know and love, whom in actual fact we had never really known at all.

Of course the meeting with Jono had been awful—made worse because she'd hoped for the best. He'd lost so much weight he was barely recognizable; there was nothing left of his face except those cartoonish buckteeth and slitty eyes.

Things weren't going well, he admitted, averting his gaze. But he was happy she'd made time to meet him. He offered his congratulations again and asked her what she was planning to do next. She was about to tell him, but he cut her off: She'd work for Sulinado Group, of course; her father probably had a high-ranking position ready and waiting for her. As with the observations he'd made previously about the Chinese, it wasn't so much what he said as how he said it, and how it came out of nowhere before disappearing into thin air, leaving her wondering if she'd misunderstood.

That pretty much summed up Jono's behavior: sustained attempts at being pleasant interspersed with flashes of bitterness. "Attempts" because the strain showed after a while. Gone was the tendency to dwell on his own unfortunate affairs. When she asked him how things were, he answered succinctly and moved on, obviously thinking hard about questions to ask her and then trying to look interested in the answers she gave. It wasn't like him at all, not even when they were in Melbourne, when he'd been spare with words in general but always genuine when he did have something to say. The contrast between that and this desperate geniality couldn't be starker. And then there were those occasional jabs, blurted before he could stop himself: one about how nice it must be not to have to worry about finances; one about how she probably didn't have many other *pribumi* friends; one about how making money seemed to come naturally to "her kind"; one about how, thanks to his appearance, he experienced all the drawbacks of being Chinese without any of the perks.

She was completely drained at the end of it. And then he dealt the final blow. He finally stopped talking and looked down at his hands, which were fidgeting in his lap. He coughed. He had a favor to ask—one he felt he could only request of a true friend like Sandra. He'd mentioned at the start that things weren't going well. The truth was, he was still having trouble paying off his debts. The loan shark who'd lent him money was charging interest rates that were through the roof. He'd tried his best to keep up, but, slowly and steadily, he'd fallen further and further behind.

That's terrible, she said. She was so sorry. She meant it, but at the same time she felt her stomach caving in.

She waited for it. It came: He needed to borrow some money from her. Not much—not to her, given who her father was. He winced after he said these words; he hadn't meant to sound so mean. He tried to recover as best he could, but the result was a blend of sullenness and mortification. He didn't know where else to turn, he said. And he wouldn't ask if it weren't for his mother and siblings. He named the sum and added that it included the plane fare he'd borrowed from her more than a year ago.

He was right: It wasn't an enormous sum at all. She'd bought handbags that cost more without so much as a second thought. She also realized that she'd forgotten entirely about the money for the plane ticket; it might as well have been loose change that she'd misplaced. Still, her insides crum-bled away entirely. They had laughed together once, whispered in each other's ears, kissed and held each other's hands. Now, nothing remained. Worse than nothing: a creditor and debtor.

Of course she'd help, she said, forcing a smile. She would get the money from her parents. It was no trouble at all. He mumbled his gratitude, unable to look her in the eye, and they arranged to meet in a few days so she could give him the cash.

The conversation left quite an impression on her. She looked so pale and shaken when she got home that her mother—our oma—insisted she take to bed. That was the problem with living abroad for too long, opined Oma. Your stomach forgot how to digest the food at home. Tante Sandra didn't mind the enforced rest. She welcomed it, in fact. It allowed her to take refuge in endless sleep. As the baby of the family, she was the only one of our uncles and aunts still living in our grandparents' house. Oma was pleased to have an excuse to be maternal: to stand over the stove mak-ing plain congee and herbal soup; to sit by her child's bedside stroking her brow and humming lullabies. Tante Sandra couldn't play the invalid forever, though. With several days to spare before her next meeting with Jono, she resumed normal activity and asked Opa for the money. Finding a plausible pretext was easy: A good friend was heading to Paris, and Tante Sandra wanted to ask her to buy something from Chanel on her behalf.

"There wasn't even the slightest hint that your opa thought I was lying," our aunt said with a bitter laugh. "Or that he knew about Jono at all. I was so naive back then. Such a stupid, stupid fool."

She waited in the coffee shop for Jono for a full two hours. He never came. Her initial anger turned to worry. What if the loan shark had done something to him? What if her help had come too late? She went back home and stayed on alert, waiting for him to call her. Days passed. Noth-ing. She forgot how upset their last encounter had made her and started panicking instead. She imagined, at best, that he was in the hospital with broken bones. She imagined, at worst, his throat slit and his body thrown into a canal. Unable to stand it any longer, after dinner one evening, she jumped in the car and told the driver to take her to Jono's address.

She didn't think she'd had any expectations of what his home would look like. He'd never spoken about it. Nor was she familiar enough with the city's humbler neighborhoods to draw any conclusions from the mailing address he'd given her before he'd left Australia for good. The car circled the area for half an hour before she eventually told the driver to wind down the window and ask people on the street for directions. A man pulling a wooden cart full of trash directed them to a narrow alleyway barely large enough for the car to squeeze through. They rolled down it, and the driver made inquiries again when they reached a small snack-and-sundries stand cobbled together from plywood planks. The shopkeeper shook her head when the driver asked about the address, but our aunt called out Jono's name from the back seat, as well as the names of his siblings, which she miraculously remembered. The shopkeeper pointed a finger down an even narrower lane bordering her stand.

There was no way the car would fit. Tante Sandra ordered the driver to wait and walked down the lane, into a world that she knew existed but had never encountered firsthand: narrow dwellings of crumbling concrete and exposed brick pressed together in tight rows; windows and eaves hung with lines of laundry and curtained with cheap fabric or yellowed lace; gates of rusted iron and peeling paint, or sheets of corrugated zinc; tiny verandas of cracked tile crowded with birdcages and plants in plastic buckets. She was dimly aware that these living conditions were more than respectable— those of the city's lower middle class. But the spoiled rich girl within her kept hissing, *Poor. This is what it's like to be poor.* The shopkeeper sent a boy running after her to show her where to go. Overtaking her, he trotted to a stop in front of a house with two green plastic chairs out front. He lingered expectantly. She fished around in her purse for a coin and pressed it into his palm.

It was Jono himself who came to the door when she called out her awkward "Hello" instead of the "*As-salamu 'alaikum*" she'd overheard Muslims use. He had a split lip and a swollen black eye. There were gashes on his forehead and cheeks.

She asked him what had happened, even though she thought she knew. The loan shark had obviously sent his goons. Jono stared at her and said nothing. She reached into her purse and pulled out the envelope of cash. Was it too late to give him the money? she asked. She apologized for not trying to find him sooner when he had missed their appointment.

He still didn't say anything, still kept staring at her, as if he were trying to make up his mind about something. At long last he spoke, the words dripping with disgust: She could keep her money.

Her blood froze. What did he mean? she asked.

He laughed. She didn't know? he sneered before proceeding to enlighten her: an ambush on the way home from the restaurant the night before they were supposed to meet. A blindfold. The back of a van. Four men in army uniforms. And once the beating had finally stopped, a warning on behalf of Pak Irwan Sulinado to find some other rich girl to milk for cash.

She'd better go, he told her. Then he tried to close the door.

She pushed it back open, tears streaming down her face, swearing she hadn't known, that it wasn't her fault.

If she really wanted to help, he yelled, she would leave him alone. Then he shoved her away and slammed the door shut.

She sat down in one of the green plastic chairs and cried some more. From inside the house a woman's croak drifted, thick with phlegm. It must have been Jono's mother. It sounded fearful: Who was it and did it have anything to do with those bad men? No, just some crazy woman who had the wrong house, he said. And that seemed to be the end of that.

A crazy woman. She did feel like she'd gone crazy. How could her father have done this to Jono? For that matter, how did her father even find out about their relationship? She'd never told any of the family about him; it had simply never come up.

"At least, that's what I told myself then," Tante Sandra confessed to my sister and me. "Once I found out the truth about him, I must have known on some level that the family would disapprove, even if we had just been friends." She shook her head mournfully. "Friends. Not even that. It turned out I was his enemy. Worse. And I had no clue. That was the unforgivable part. I had no clue at all."

That hadn't been the end of it. Once she'd calmed herself down and wiped away most of the tears, our young aunt ran back to the car. Home, she ordered the driver with some urgency, and, startled, he put the car into reverse.

A crunch. A scream. Followed by more screams—of the shopkeeper on the corner and of children. Both the driver and Sandra sprang out of the car. They had backed into a young girl. Her calf lay at an awkward angle, but she was still conscious and shrieking in pain. A teenage boy was cradling her in his lap and screaming at the top of his lungs.

"My brother! Get my brother!" he told one of the other kids in the group, who raced off down the lane, crying, "Mas Jono! Mas Jono! Your sister's been hit by a car!"

It was a nightmare. It had to be. She crouched by Jono's brother and sister and tried to soothe the girl. Jono came sprinting up.

"The driver didn't see her! It was an accident," our aunt babbled. "Let me take her to the hospital—"

"You've done enough," Jono snarled. "Just go!" And he raised his hand as if to strike.

An older man with a mustache grabbed his arm. "You'll get in trouble," he whispered to Jono. "Look at her. She's rich. And Chinese too. Their kind won't have mercy when it comes to people like us."

Our aunt fled then. She had no alternative. But she thrust the envelope full of cash into Jono's hands before she did. The driver, a nervous sort by nature, was in a high state of panic. He quickly shifted gears, stepped on the accelerator, and left the cluster of people in a cloud of dust.

The sense of it all being a bad dream refused to recede, even once she was safely home, the car gliding into the garage as smoothly as a boat sailing into port. As she entered the house she'd grown up in, she felt as if she were walking into someone else's life. Was this really where she belonged—unchanged despite the horror of that other world she had wandered into and wrecked? Her parents had evidently turned in for the night; almost all the lights were off. The silhouettes of her mother's beloved objects loomed menacing and numerous, walling her in on all sides.

Out of the corner of her eye, she saw one of the maids dart up the stairs and back down—to tell her parents of her return, she suspected. Sure enough, her father appeared soon afterward at the top of the stairs, the hardness of his face unsoftened by his pajamas and slippers. He observed, simply, that she was back. She nodded. They stared at each other in silence. She should choose her friends carefully from now on, he added. There were a lot of bad men around. Then he said good night and returned to his room.

"How did he even find out about Jono?" I asked, breaking the story's spell.

Our aunt snorted. "Turned out they'd known about him since we'd started dating. One of my Indonesian friends mentioned it to her mother during a phone call home. Her mother knew my mother. As if I should have been surprised. Rich Chinese-Indonesians. Everyone knows each other. They told the driver to spy on me when I came back."

Estella frowned. "*They* told the driver to spy on you?"

Our aunt flashed us a chilling grin.

Maddeningly, instead of elaborating, Tante Sandra picked up her story from where she'd left off: with her younger self plagued with remorse over how she had smashed up Jono's life; haunted by all that Jono had said, both outright and implied, about "her people" and "her kind," the truth of it evinced by the ruins of his life. The ensuing months only made it worse, his way of seeing things slowly seeping into hers.

Our aunt had always been exceptionally conscious of our family's dysfunction, not to mention the way we coped with it—by ignoring it, by gilding over it with gold. Our faults had roused in her sadness, compassion, sympathy, but never antipathy. The incident with Jono stirred in her, for the first time, alienation.

"I couldn't identify with the family anymore," she stated unapologetically. "The whole thing with Jono altered my perception entirely. Made me see the bigger picture."

In other words, she began to see us through his eyes: the decadent world we had cocooned ourselves in, we filthy rich Chinese, and the heartlessness with which we built it up and defended it from "outsiders" like him. On one level, she knew perfectly well how simplistic his assessment of the situation was. And yet she couldn't help but see it mirrored in the life our family led.

Shortly after the visit to Jono's house, the whole family took a trip to Monte Carlo (Tante Sandra in a hotel bathrobe weeping—I hadn't misremembered the scene). There was nothing unusual about any of it: the well-appointed suites, the hotel limousines at our disposal, the shopping sprees, the eight-course dinners, the wines, and, at night, the baccarat table (the family's game of choice). But for the first time, our aunt found herself sickened by the matter-of-course extravagance. *Your people do well for themselves*, she heard Jono's voice say, and she couldn't deny it.

A month after the family's return, Tante Sandra started work—as junior director of the clove and tobacco subsidiary of the family conglomerate. Even though she felt her eyes had been opened wide, the inherent shadiness of business as usual in Indonesia peeled her eyelids back further than she'd imagined possible. All the proper authorities had to be well-oiled to get permits renewed and misdemeanors overlooked. Ironically, squeaky wheels received a different sort of treatment: In her second month on the job she was tasked by her sister Sarah with firing the organizers of a laborers' strike before the protests had even begun.

"It's no big deal," our mother assured her, which only served to horrify Sandra even more. Though she knew everyone got their hands dirty doing business in Indonesia, not just "her people," as Jono had alleged, it was nonetheless undeniable that her family did it without blinking an eye. And now she was helping them.

"With each passing day," Tante Sandra told us, "I could feel myself becoming more and more what Jono despised."

Obviously, Estella and I had always known how different Tante Sandra had been from the rest of the family—pure and guileless, vulnerable and honest—and we had idolized her. But up to that point, I don't think either Estella or I had ever realized just *how* innocent our young aunt had been—how at twenty-two she could have been so ignorant about what it took to get rich and stay rich in our country. Knowing the extent of this innocence made its loss all the more tragic to me—as if something sacred had been violated.

"So that's why you ran away?" Estella asked. "You didn't want to become—" The absent word materialized despite the words trailing off: *us*.

Our aunt contemplated this, then shook her head. "I might not have run away. Even then." She chewed her lip and hesitated before speaking again. "If you must know, your oma was the real reason I did it."

"You mean, she helped you disappear," I said by way of clarification, but our aunt shook her head again. Her gaze was heavy as it rested on us, perching, then pressing down.

"You have no idea who she was, do you?" she declared finally.

She took our puzzled silence, correctly, as assent.

After a year or so, our aunt told us, her loathing of family and self had ripened to unbearable proportions. It demanded excision; she needed to unburden herself, but to whom? Who among her family and friends, the very objects of her contempt, would ever understand? Out of desperation, Tante Sandra turned to her mother, and it made perfect sense to me why she would—our sweet, gentle oma with her billowy housedresses and rose-and-butter scent, the soft matriarchal yin to Opa's stern patriarch yang. Tante Sandra didn't expect Oma to comprehend fully, any more than one might expect, say, a kitten to comprehend grief. But she also wasn't prepared for the revelation that came next; nor were Estella and I when we heard it from our aunt more than twenty years later.

Tante Sandra had finally poured out her heart on a Saturday, in the kitchen, while Oma had been baking for a family tea. (Fond memories of those afternoons sprang to mind, mingling with my aunt's words: of Estella and me and our cousins playing tag in the garden between bouts of gorging on Oma's treats.) Tante Sandra waited until the cakes were cooking in the steamer before she launched into her tearful account—of the friendship with Jono and its souring, of the beating ordered by Opa, of the door slammed in her face and the girl's crushed leg. Enfolding her in her arms, Oma hushed her sobs away (a remedy I remembered well—the pillowy bosom, the comforting sensation of having one's hair stroked).

And then those words: "Don't cry, my darling. I asked your father to take care of it. That boy won't bother you again."

At first, what Oma said made little sense to our aunt, groggy with the grief of revisiting the traumatic events. But gradually, the fog lifted. What did she mean? she asked, pulling herself out of her mother's embrace. Who'd taken care of what? The ominousness of that last sentence hit home. What had been done?

The kitchen timer rang and Oma bustled over to the stove, explaining almost absentmindedly as she went: There'd been no choice, the driver had told her all about the accident with the sister. The risk of the boy taking revenge was far too high, and she'd acted fast in order to prevent retaliation.

Tante Sandra's head spun, even as the tone in which her mother delivered this information remained the same as the one she'd been using to soothe her just moments before—as if that terrible piece of news was meant to comfort her too. Oma kept speaking as she transferred the cakes onto a platter, testing with the tip of her tongs the spring in each chocolate-marbled creation: She and Opa had acted without their daughter's knowledge because they hadn't wanted to cause her any further distress. That boy had made her so unhappy. It was their fault as parents, in a way—they'd let the relationship go on for far too long. But they'd wanted to give her room to be an adult, to make her own mistakes. At least, such had been Opa's line of reasoning; if it had been up to Oma, she would have nipped it in the bud—paid off the boy earlier, before things had gotten so bad. Before he began trying to get money out of her, before they'd had to have him thrashed, before they'd had to do worse. Oma shook her head. She felt terrible for the fellow's family. In any case, Sandra had nothing to fear. That awful boy was gone for good. Sandra was lucky to come from a family with enough money to protect her. My, look at how beautifully the cakes had turned out. She should eat one while they were warm.

"You came running in then," our aunt told us. "Do you remember? You and your uncle Benny's youngest two: Theresa and . . . Richie?"

My sister corrected her. "Ricky," she said, her voice as faint as I felt.

First our aunt, now our oma. The last of our idols had been felled. Oma's scent as I remembered it seemed to sour into rot. Those pearls of wisdom she used to utter, passed down to her from her father, took on a sinister sheen: *Feelings, ideas . . . they're reliable as the wind. Gold, on the other hand, and land . . . keep you and your loved ones healthy and alive.*

My memories of our grandmother reconfigured themselves immediately, exposing her virtues as vice. Her penchant for ornate furniture and knickknacks—a weakness for extravagance and excess. Her innocent housewifely simplicity—an unreflecting and dangerous obliviousness.

How ironic. We had embarked on this mission to save the family from darkness, only to discover that we ourselves were darkness through and through.

"That's when I knew I had to leave," said Tante Sandra. "I wanted nothing to do with the family anymore. I hated them."

"And Oma helped you run away?" my sister asked, dull-eyed, ash-voiced. I knew how she felt. The hope had bled out of me too.

"Yes and no," our aunt replied. "I started making plans myself, but then your oma found out. At first she tried to talk me out of it, but I threatened to tell people what they did to Jono if she didn't let me leave."

"And that worked?" asked Estella.

A strange smile crossed Tante Sandra's face. "It did. But you know something? I don't think your oma understood why I was so upset. She seemed hurt, if you'd believe it—they had only been trying to protect me, she said." Our aunt shrugged. "It worked out for the best. I wouldn't have been able to pull it off without her help. If I'd done it alone, there would have been search parties, police, private investigators, the works."

The plan had been astonishingly simple. She and Oma had taken a trip to Bali for the weekend. The other siblings, busy with their own lives and dimly aware that "something" had gone on with their kid sister—boy trouble of some sort, it was assumed—figured it was an attempt at recuperation from a broken heart. Opa drew the same conclusion about the trip's purpose, knowing what he did about the "trouble" with the boy, and gave his consent without giving it a second thought.

Oma had chartered a boat to take them out to sea. In the middle of the ocean, they met another boat and Tante Sandra hopped on. Mother and daughter said good-bye. It was as easy as that.

The men Oma had hired were top-of-the-line: Tante Sandra was well on her way to the Philippines by the time the Indonesian coast guard started their search. No one had much confidence that she would be found alive, not after hearing Oma's account. She had been flipping through a magazine as her daughter snorkeled near the boat. She'd waved at her daughter, then looked down. By the time she'd looked up again, the girl had disappeared. The crew corroborated Oma's account: One second she was there and the next she was gone.

The authorities continued to comb the waters over the course of several days as a Sandra Lee (née Sulinado), brand-new passport in hand, left the Philippines, changed planes in Tokyo and again in Hawaii, before finally arriving in Los Angeles. She'd wandered around California for a few weeks before settling on Bakersfield—no chance there of running into anyone she knew.

She used the money Oma had wired to her new US bank account to set up house, most of it going to the purchase of a studio apartment and a convenience store.

"I never used family money to do anything else ever again," she declared with some pride.

I can see that, I thought, her shabbiness and that of her furnishings striking me afresh.

It was an immigrant-makes-good-in-America story straight out of the movies from that point on: She worked hard and the store did well; she bought a house and leased the apartment to tenants; ten years later, she took over a Chinese takeout place in the downtown district.

"The food is awful," she stated baldly. "Still, our customers don't seem to care."

Night had fallen, but in the course of telling her story, Tante Sandra had neglected to turn on any lights. The darkened house depressed me, but I also found it consoling to be spared the burden of sight. I wanted to deny any of it existed—our ruined family, our ruined aunt, our ruined grandmother. Swathed in the soft folds of darkness, I could forget these ruins and finally deceive myself, as most of our family seemed to do with little effort.

It was too good to last. Our aunt turned the knob on the lamp next to the sofa and the low-watt lighting cast her and everything else in a seedy jack-o'-lantern glow.

"I won't go back," she said as if we'd asked her to. "Over there you have no choice about what you become. It's all laid out for you, by family, by race, by money and status. There's a set role you have to play, and if you go off script it all comes falling down. It's different in the West. I don't have to be a monster here. I'm free to be whatever I want. I like it this way."

Our aunt's satisfaction with the life she'd built was both touching and terrifying—a doll sitting in a doll's house, boasting about the vastness of her domain. It might have been inspiring if she'd escaped to pursue a truly virtuous life, but she appeared to have achieved nothing more than insipid moral neutrality. And as for her claim about being free—I recognized (thanks to Ray Chan) that she'd merely traded one costume for another. If she'd been forced back home to conform to a stereotype—coldhearted and clannish, haughty and rich—here, she'd merely become typically "Chinese" on American terms: pragmatic, industrious, well-to-do, and thrifty. She hadn't shown us much of her life, but we'd seen more than enough: her frumpy blouse and ill-fitting jeans, the cheap refreshments and tacky curios, the off-brand suitcase and the plastic bags from Payless and Bargains-R-Us near the front door. The woman ran a convenience store and a takeout place, for crying out loud.

"So, you live alone?" I found myself asking, which was the politest way I knew of confirming the apparent.

Tante Sandra nodded. "I prefer it," she said with a practiced defensiveness. "I'm freer this way. Besides, with two businesses I don't have time for that sort of thing."

My immediate reaction was one of pity, but I quickly suppressed it: Who was I to judge in such matters? Me, thirty-three and also alone, also professing to be happily married to my career.

Fear gripped me: To what extent was I merely a rendition of our aunt as she now was? Come to think of it, to what extent was Estella merely a reprise of our aunt's younger, naive self? Were these the limited options open to us: Tante Sandra as she once was or Tante Sandra middle-aged? Hopeful ignorance or detached contempt? Not so much options as different stages of a single life: caterpillar and butterfly, silkworm and silkmoth?

"What happened to your neck?" I asked abruptly, as if by changing the subject I could steer myself away from such unpleasant thoughts.

"Grease burn," she said with a wry smile. "It was my first time deep-frying anything. Hazard of living your whole life with maids and cooks."

Then, suddenly: "Why are you here?"

Tante Sandra's question was angry—more like a demand. With a jolt, I became aware of what she'd probably just realized herself. We hadn't told her the reason for our visit and she hadn't yet thought to ask.

I took the cowardly way out and shot a glance at my sister. After all, the whole mission had been her idea.

Estella's face colored as she worked out what to say. "I thought finding you might save us," she finally managed. "Save the family, I mean. There's so much wrong with us. You of all people know that."

Our aunt stared at us as if we were mad. "How would finding me help?"

Estella and I were silent. What on earth could we say? That we'd counted on finding someone else entirely? A breath of fresh air? Drops of dew? My sister and I had set out to resurrect a savior and bring her home. She would reform us, or at least temper us—so we'd thought. And now here she was, unearthed and scornful, and not what we'd wanted at all.

How would finding me help? Our aunt's question mocked us. We had no answer to give.

Again, that unnervingly pretty giggle from our aunt—and in its wake: "Nothing can save the family. You're beyond help."

❖   ❖   ❖

It was late when Estella and I left Tante Sandra's house, and, having abstained from the cookies, I was starving. Our aunt hadn't offered us any dinner, and we hadn't suggested staying for one. The thought of sharing a meal with her made me feel ill, for reasons I wasn't entirely sure of. All I knew was that I wanted to get out of there as quickly as possible. We wished each other well and said our good-byes, Tante Sandra stationing herself on the porch to see us off. She looked neither happy that we'd come nor sad that we were leaving, and I imagined that Estella and I must have looked pretty much the same way. We were already speeding down the interstate back to LA when I realized that no desire had been expressed on her part or ours ever to contact each other again.

Estella drove like a demon, weaving in and out of lanes whenever there was traffic, breaking a hundred miles an hour on the more deserted stretches of road. My suggestion that we make a quick stop for a bite to eat went unheeded, as did my observation a little later that drive-through fast food might be a good option if we really didn't want to lose any time.

I was about to remark that our flight back to Jakarta was not until tomorrow and that it didn't matter if we stopped to eat before heading back to the hotel, when she anticipated me, snapping, "How can you think of food after what just happened?"

Her tears then came rolling down each cheek, leaving trails, like tiny skiers on a snowy slope.

"There's nothing left, Doll," she whispered hoarsely. "No one left standing, not a single one. Not Tante Sandra. Not even Oma. My God, we don't even have Oma to believe in anymore."

The engine roared and the speedometer crept over 110.

"Stell, calm down," I said, trying to keep the alarm out of my voice, confining it to the fingers gripping the edge of my seat.

"Easy for you to say!" she exploded. "What do you care? You checked out when you started Bagatelle!"

"I do care," I replied, my voice rising in response to hers. "I'm here, aren't I? On this failure of a mission that was *your* stupid idea!"

My sister's voice dripped sarcasm. "Well, thank you for gracing me with your presence! You shouldn't have!"

"You're right, I shouldn't," I rejoined. "But if you'll recall, you were the one who begged me to come along."

The knives were drawn now. Defeated, and hungry to boot, we turned on each other, precisely because turning anywhere else wasn't an option.

"Anyway," I continued, "you have no right to hold Bagatelle against me. You've always encouraged me to go ahead with it alone although I've asked you repeatedly to come on board."

"Only because someone has to be responsible and try to save the family!" my sister yelled. "We can't all retreat from reality and devote our time to fashioning glorified trinkets out of bugs."

Hurt, I slashed wildly, "As if you're in a position to save them. As if you didn't kill your own husband."

"As if *you're* not just as bad. As if you didn't help me do it."

"You didn't have to act on my advice," I shot back.

"Or administer the poison you gave me for the occasion?"

My voice died in my throat. She had a point. The poison had been mine—one of the failed attempts at creating Bagatelle's patented serum before my fleet of scientists had got it right.

"You're so self-righteous." Estella sneered. "Now that you're in business for yourself, you think you can pretend our sins aren't yours? We share a history, Doll—you, me, *our* family. You're part of us whether you like it or not."

I didn't answer, just kept my eyes on the illuminated asphalt of the road ahead. She was only speaking the truth. My autonomy was an illusion—I would always be one of them.

"You know, Doll," my sister murmured reflectively, "I thought Bagatelle would be a good outlet for you—and me by proxy; that's why I was so supportive. But in hindsight I'm not so sure. You're too out of touch with real life."

"Is that so bad?" I found the strength to croak.

She frowned, her anger gone, channeled into what appeared to be grave concern. "Maybe it is. I know you're proud of Bagatelle—I am too—but it's making you live too much in your own little world."

Here she paused. "And I need you," she added. "You know that. I always have."

Our truce was unspoken. We drove the rest of the way in silence. In fact, we barely spoke for what little remained of the trip. I think we were afraid we'd end up discussing what we'd discovered—not just about our aunt or Oma, but ourselves.

Or myself, rather. I'd worked so hard to put the past behind me that my role in Leonard's murder seemed positively surreal. A bad dream I'd stashed away, now seeping from the confines of its sodden box. Or maybe it was the reverse: reality's poison dripping into the fairy tale my life had become.

Poison. The one I'd offered my sister to kill Leonard was the perfect agent. Genetically modified fungal extract, concocted in my labs. Therefore unknown, therefore untraceable. That particular version had produced death, not dormancy, so Bagatelle's scientists had kept on tinkering. But it had been ideal for ridding us of my brother-in-law once and for all. An antidote, one might have called it. Yes, a lethal cure for the disease that was Leonard. The love that my sister persisted in feeling for him would have no choice but to stop short at the grave. Even now, I knew I would have murdered Leonard again, to save her once and for all, to avenge what he had done to her and me.

As I sat in that car, speeding through the dark, something else frightened me too: the way Estella had criticized Bagatelle for removing me from the real world when she needed me. She had spoken as if she were the one who had permitted Bagatelle to come into being, and as if she were deciding whether it should continue to exist. In short, she acted as if I didn't have a say at all, which I knew wasn't true, but it unnerved me nonetheless. All through the flight home I was plagued by the sense that something terrible had been set in motion, and that it couldn't be stopped.

❖ ❖ ❖

When we landed in Jakarta and parted ways, I was relieved to say goodbye, though I tried not to show it. I buried myself in Bagatelle-related work, almost as if to affirm that it was really mine, that I was in charge. So what if Estella had been right about how it had become my escape from reality? What was wrong with that? Estella tried to ring me, but I ignored her calls. And her texts. Sunday came and went without us meeting for the brunch that had become a ritual of ours. I still couldn't rid myself of the nameless and irrational fear that had sprung up inside me on the drive back from our aunt's house.

A little over a week passed. There were three days left until Opa's big birthday bash. I'd just eaten dinner and was curled up in my living room with a stack of Bagatelle sales reports and a half bottle of Montrachet. When the knocking on the door commenced, loud and sharp, I was startled; the twenty-four-hour concierge and intercom system downstairs were supposed to prevent visitors from being a surprise. I called for the maid, but to my annoyance the pounding continued. Where was she? Had she fallen asleep? With some reluctance I rose and went to answer the door.

"Who is it?" I demanded to know. I certainly wasn't stupid enough to let someone in without asking. But there was no reply, just another series of insistent raps.

"Who is it?" I called again, trying to sound not the least bit scared.

Then there came another sound—of a key turning in the lock.

Whose key? Mine? I glanced at the hall table next to me. My set of keys was still there.

The door swung open. I leapt back and snatched up an umbrella—the nearest weapon to hand.

"Oh, for God's sake, Doll, it's only me."

Indeed, it was. Estella.

"STELL? WHERE DID you get a key?"

"Don't be stupid, Doll. I've always had one." And with that, my sister pushed past me, deposited her purse on the hall table, and kicked off her shoes.

Of course she'd always had a key; she'd just never used it. I felt silly immediately. And also alarmed. The initial relief I'd felt at finding Estella, not a burglar, at my door vanished, and the overwhelming desire to avoid my sister reasserted itself. Especially since her mere presence had revealed yet another fact I'd decided to repress for some reason. I could understand why I'd chosen to forget painful things like my crush on Ray Chan and the exact role I had played in poisoning Leonard. *But why forget that Estella has a key?* I wondered, my heart beating just a little faster.

"Care for a drink?" I asked—unnecessarily. She'd already found the wine and claimed my glass as hers. You'd think she owned the place, the way she was taking my spot on the sofa, flipping briefly through the sales reports before tossing them aside in a flutter-storm of loose paper.

"Hey," I exclaimed. "Those were in order!"

"It doesn't matter," she said. "I've come to a decision. You have to move on from Bagatelle. It's distracting you."

"From what?" I scoffed.

"From helping me, of course. That was its original intent. But now Bagatelle has become an obstacle—that much became obvious on our trip."

"What are you talking about?" I asked.

"Don't you think you're too immersed in your own world, Doll?"

She'd said the same thing on the drive back from Tante Sandra's house:

You live too much in your own little world. Before I could respond, my sister stood up and began to circle the living room. She drank in its handsomeness: the dark woods and plush fabrics; the authoritative furniture, made especially, it seemed, for rich old men to sit in or lean on as they smoked expensive cigars. Yet there was an oddly wistful note to her admiration—as if everything in the apartment was about to be packed away.

"It's a gorgeous world, I have to admit," she said, "but it's served its purpose, and now it's doing far more harm than good."

I sighed. "I don't have time for this, Stell. Please just tell me what this is about."

She chuckled. "Yes, you're right. It's better to be frank. I guess it doesn't come naturally—we're part of the family, after all."

She took one last sip of wine and motioned for me to follow her around the corner and down the corridor to where my bedroom and dressing room were located. By the time I'd caught up with her, she was standing at the end of the hallway, facing the wall. She made a motion, as if turning the handle of a door, and the next thing I knew, a brass knob appeared in her hand. The door itself materialized soon after, swinging open.

"After you," said Estella, standing to one side, motioning for me to enter.

"Wh-where . . . ?" I managed to stammer, breaking into a cold sweat. How had Estella done that?

"Don't be scared, Doll," Estella said, giving me a reassuring pat on the back and shoving me through. "It's just one of the labs at Bagatelle."

◆　◆　◆

She was right. The room was instantly familiar: the blinding white of the walls and floor; the broad stainless-steel countertops; the lights in neat luminescent rows overhead. To our left were the mesh-topped glass terrariums housing the test subjects for the new serum. I shook my head in an attempt to clear it, to wake myself up.

Impossible. This couldn't be happening.

"And yet it is," said Estella, reading my mind.

"How are you doing this?" I demanded, grabbing her by the arm.

She only laughed. "Shouldn't you check on the silkworms? See how they're faring?"

Her mere suggestion had the effect of a magic spell. I released her immediately and ran over to examine the terrariums. The mulberry leaves were in desperate need of changing, and the floors were piled high with leaf debris and droppings—and carcasses. Almost every silkworm was dead. For a moment I forgot about Estella, mesmerized by the fungal tentacles poking out of their bodies, splitting apart the fleshy segments as adeptly as someone might peel and partition an orange.

"Aren't you going to ask why we're here?" said Estella, standing behind me.

I whirled around to face her. "Why are we here?" I asked in a trembling voice.

"To shut down Bagatelle. It's taking up far too much of your energy and I need you for something else."

"And what would that be?" I said, wincing. My head had suddenly begun to ache.

"We have to do something about our family."

"We tried. We're beyond redemption, remember?"

She drew close. "Don't worry, Doll. I'm not talking about redemption anymore. The time for that has long since passed. But we can't leave the family as it is either. We're sick, Doll. Gravely ill."

She peered into one of the terrariums. "We're infected. Like these silkworms," she said, "but worse. When it comes to us, there's no end in sight.

We keep on feeding, keep on thriving even as the corruption keeps on circulating inside us. Remember what you said on the flight to LA? 'We're so good at hiding the bad stuff, we manage to fool ourselves'?"

I nodded weakly.

"That's the problem with us: The bad stuff remains hidden, entrenched. And none of us know we're diseased, or if we do, we don't know how dire it is."

Sliding the mesh top off one of the terrariums, my sister reached in and extracted a twig. At least a dozen silkworms had crawled up its length and clamped themselves there—a symptom of the final stage of the fungal disease. A few still twitched, but the majority were dead. Out of the latter grew orange stalks, fat and tuber-like and knobbed.

"They're like us," she murmured contemplatively. "Trying to crawl away, clinging on for dear life, not knowing it's the infection itself that makes us crawl and cling. We think we can escape, but we can't: Leonard trying to 'flee from sin,' as he called it, and Tante Sandra running away. You and me too, Doll: The fungus is inside us. Even though we know about it, there's nothing we can do."

I struggled to follow her train of thought. The pulsing in my head was getting worse. "The fungus . . ." I repeated, pressing my forehead to my hands. "You mean . . ."

"Fooling ourselves about how bad we are. And if there's anything I've learned from our trip, it's that we're very bad. And that we're very skilled at deceiving ourselves that we're actually good. You look awful, Doll. Have a seat."

Estella wheeled an office chair out from underneath one of the countertops and pressed me into it by the shoulders. I tried to push her away, but I was too weak with pain.

She continued: "I was upset about how our trip turned out, obviously. But I don't think it was for naught. On the contrary, all that reminiscing you and I did—it made me realize how much I'd buried. The ambient vices that Leonard tried to cleanse us of: corruption, excess, materialism, greed. We do what we do because we have to, or because everyone else does it, but that doesn't make it right."

I began to have a sense of where this talk was heading. I wanted to protest, but I felt as if my skull was about to crack. I gripped the armrests of my chair. Estella kept speaking, ignoring my agony.

"I don't blame us, Doll," she said. "It's not our fault we're rotten—no more than being infected is the fault of these poor silkworms you experiment on. That's just the way it is. Attribute it to whatever you want: sin, environment, upbringing, culture. But the fact that we hide it from ourselves, that's what makes it really tragic. Not to mention dangerous. And that's the real reason we need to be stopped."

"Stopped . . ." I murmured, suddenly aware I'd been reduced to an echo, aware I couldn't feel my limbs, though my hands were still anchored to the chair. *What have you done?* I wanted to cry, but couldn't. I recalled the silkworm test subjects—how the fungus would take control of their bodies toward the very end.

Stop, I wanted to say. "Stopped," I repeated instead.

My effort seemed to amuse Estella. "Exactly. I'll say it again too," she said. "We need to be stopped. Think of all the harm we inflict on each other and the world because we're convinced that we're not deadly: Ma and the family pushing me into marriage with Leonard and genuinely doing it out of love; and Ba even, standing by, hands in pockets, letting everyone else do what they think best. Shall I go on? How about our family and Leonard's conspiring to kill him, citing the sake of the greater good? And Leonard himself, frantic and blind as a bull in a frenzy, goring me, then turning on his family until we put him down?

"Then there's Tante Sandra—wrecking that guy's life, inadvertently ending it, clueless about what she was doing all the while; hiding out now in the Central Valley, dead on the inside but still leaking poison. You and I won't ever recover from that visit, will we?

"And Oma—" (Here, my sister's voice faltered.) "Maybe it's better that we'll never know entirely what she really was. After all, she didn't know it herself. None of us know ourselves. Perhaps you the least of all."

"You . . ." I echoed.

She reached out and stroked my hair. "Yes, you. Actually, you're not that different from Tante Sandra: she, taking refuge in Bakersfield; you, seeking sanctuary in Bagatelle. But as I said, it's time you pulled your head out of the sand, Doll. You're going to help me put an end to us once and for all. And by 'us,' I also mean the Angsonos, the Sukamtos—all the guests at Opa's birthday party. They're just as bad as us, make no mistake."

Despite my paralysis, the throbbing in my brain had escalated into a sharp, stabbing pain. An attempt to shake my head in refusal proved fruitless, as did an attempt to utter a horrified "No."

Estella understood me perfectly nonetheless. "My dear Gwendolyn, you hardly have a choice."

As she spoke, our surroundings began to change. The room was no longer gleaming white or state-of-the-art. The air smelled musty. Clutter appeared on the counters: papers and petri dishes, vials and pens strewn about. The room looked more—the word forced itself on me—*real*. Through a pain-induced haze, I recalled a snippet from a conversation long ago: *We're expecting a shipment for the new factory lab*. It was what Estella had told Leonard one morning over breakfast. I made the connection, hardly believing it as I did.

We weren't in Bagatelle's laboratories; we were in Mutiara.

A peculiar sensation came over me—as if I'd been inhabiting a compartment designed to look like reality, and now the walls were dissolving, revealing what lay beyond.

My face was wet. I was crying. I don't understand, I thought.

My sister was still talking, still stroking my hair, gently, lovingly. "I don't know what I would have done without Bagatelle—having you dream it, plan it, then see it through to success. You of all people know the difficult times I've been through. Without you and Bagatelle, I'd never have been able to cope.

"You were baffled about why I kept my distance the way I did, why I insisted on not getting directly involved. But you must see now that I genuinely couldn't: To do so would have been to destroy Bagatelle altogether. No, no. It had to stay separate, well away from my disaster of a life. It had to be kept as a world all its own."

My memory, like our surroundings, shifted with my sister's words. Scenes from Estella's life mingled with scenes from my own. More than that—they merged, as if our colors had run and we'd bled together, until she and I fused into one. Our late-night squabble during college when I'd warned her to stay away from Leonard became Estella lying in bed alone, wrestling with her better judgment. My sister crying in the kitchen in Berkeley, telling me we couldn't be together anymore, became Estella saying good-bye to the side of her Leonard hated so much.

The altered memories came faster and thicker, in no particular order. Two sisters fleeing together to Monterey—a lone woman attempting to reclaim independence. Our family's stubborn refusal to acknowledge Bagatelle—completely understandable given that Bagatelle didn't actually exist. Those weeks in Paris immediately after Leonard's death—Estella's withdrawal into a fantasy realm, so severe that it left her flesh to wither on the bone.

I found I could speak freely again. "I'm *you*," I whispered, the truth finally breaking like dawn.

" 'My better half' might be more accurate," said Estella, circling me where I sat captive in my chair. "The woman I've always wanted to be—speaking your mind, standing up for yourself, pursuing your dreams. I know you take the blame for letting Leonard come between us, but actually, I was the one who let you go. I felt I had to submerge you if Leonard and I were going to stand a chance.

"How was I to know it wouldn't make a difference? It was terrible without you, Doll. You recall what Leonard was like back then. I felt so helpless, so utterly alone. My only consolation was that I'd imagine you leading the life I wasn't: doing well in classes; pinning insects; dating, even—before Leonard, I used to have a crush on Ray Chan.

"Then you and I ran away to see the monarchs, and it felt like we'd never been apart. We came up with Bagatelle on that trip, remember? And you began drawing up plans. Daydreaming—that's what it was when I was doing it. But when you did it, Bagatelle became not fiction but fact . . . at least to me. Then came Leonard's decline—the decline of his whole family—and I was free again, or at least able to give free rein to you.

"The family put me in charge of Mutiara, and I began tinkering with silkworms and Cordyceps fungi in this lab. It was my way of compensating for what I missed out on at Berkeley, and it's just as well Mutiara didn't require much attention from me. I spent a lot of time reading about silkworms, and when I found out that people use them in medicinal Cordyceps cultivation, I began doing some dabbling of my own—though not seriously, just in a childish, mad-scientist kind of way. But it was enough: It gave me the idea for Bagatelle's serum, and you picked it up and ran with it from there.

"Your world provided the escape I needed in order to tolerate what my life had become. Your strength was my strength—*is* my strength. And that's why I need you to help me now."

I struggled to resist her. "I won't," I managed to gasp.

My sister overpowered me as easily as someone brushing away a fly. "As I said, Doll, you don't have a choice. We can't be allowed to carry on in our diseased condition. Think of it as a kindness—to us and the world at large."

The throbbing in my head ceased. Something in me gave way. As it burst open, it engulfed us in a searing white light.

❖   ❖   ❖

Estella and I are walking, no, striding down a long corridor, approaching a realm of clanking and clanging and terse shouts. A bespectacled man in a tuxedo—the manager—hurries over and we dispel his concerns with a smile. He beats a simpering retreat. There is smoke and steam and flames. There are woks swiveling and steamers puffing away in great sweating stacks.

We pull the vial of poison from our collar—the "serum" we've developed in Mutiara's lab. It doesn't control insects or extend their life spans, but it's deadly. And it's even more concentrated than the one we used on Leonard.

One flourish and the deed is done. We head back to our table, where we sit with our cousins, our parents strategically scattered throughout the ballroom among the more important guests. Opa and New Oma sit next to Om Benny and Tante Soon Gek at a table reserved for the most venerable of their fellow tycoons. Opa's behavior these days is such that his children don't dare to leave him unchaperoned.

Ricky's on our right, stuffing himself with buns—rehab makes him hungry, he says. If possible, he's even fatter than when we saw him last. Marina on our left, ever the watchful mother, is glancing at the kids' table. Ricky gives us a knowing wink, reaches across us, and steals a sip of her champagne. It's been a while since all us cousins have had a chance to congregate like this. We all reminisce boisterously about childhood days, ignoring the puzzled looks of our spouses. The first course—crisp-skinned slices of suckling pig—is served and cleared before we know it, and soon we're passing around the red vinegar to splash into our bowls of shark's fin soup.

The band in the corner stops playing. The emcee—a pleasantly plump woman in a sparkly cocktail dress—announces a special treat, and the photos selected by Estella and me play on screen to Barbra Streisand's "The Way

We Were." The show concludes with a series of family portraits, ranging from Opa and Oma's wedding shot to pictures of them with their kids, to the formal photo Estella and I had chuckled about by Marina's pool. Tante Margaret's double chin is still there, along with Om Peter's finger up his nose. We all look less than our best—our father's slouch, and Tante Betty's stray lock of hair; the empty space between our mother and Om Benny, as if someone is missing (Tante Sandra, of course); and the unflattering lighting that gives us all a shifty, sinister air. Even Oma, despite claiming this was the best photo of the lot, has a menacing gleam in her eyes. Then again, it's hard to tell which of these things are visible only to Estella and me.

The slideshow ends; the music starts up again. Our empty bowls are whisked away and replaced with braised abalone in pools of velvety brown sauce. Ricky sneaks some wine. Benedict rolls his eyes and hands him his glass, saying, "At least it's not cocaine," at which his sister Jennifer punches his shoulder, and everyone else laughs.

There was a time when Estella and I might have been softened by this conviviality. "We're not so bad," we might have been tempted to say, our heart mellowed by happy memories and rich food. That time is past.

Now my sister and I are united and clear-eyed and resolute. It's nice that we can all share one last meal together, but it's all an illusion and it has to stop.

The Peking duck arrives, done to perfection, the flayed skins glistening atop translucent pancake rounds. The wails begin, and then the screams, followed by the retching and twitching and collapsing. The ballroom has been transformed into a sea of writhing, pain-racked bodies—our family and closest friends, and my sister and I, equally damned, writhe along.

It is for this suffering that our contorted image, reflected in one of the enormous mirrors on the wall of the ballroom, asks forgiveness: not for what we have done but, rather, the violence of its execution.

CODA

I WONDER IF, with every stop on the journey, each pause on the way to the promised land, the monarchs have any inkling of remembrance: that somewhere along the ancestral timeline they have been there before; that it is not an arrival in strange lands, but a pilgrimage to the old country.

I wonder how they must feel. Whether it occurs to them that the universe has played them for fools. Imagine: to settle at last on the branch of a tree and congratulate oneself on having gained fresh ground only to find oneself haunted by the faint impression—something in the muscles—that the neighboring twig appears very familiar indeed.

Or maybe they are proud of fluttering in the well-worn flight paths of preceding generations, of weighing down in their vast numbers the very same branches from which their ancestors too hung like fruit.

Or maybe they turn philosophical, pondering not just the purpose of this rite of passage but also the compromise inflicted on their individual selves. Is each of them merely a part incomplete? A fragment of a whole? Then what is one to make of the infinitude of one's own memories, one's own emotions, one's being?

I'm part of Estella. Yet she's dead, and I remain—as do certain memories that refuse to be accounted for, that bear stubborn testament to my life as my own.

The pounding of my seven-year-old heart as I sit knees to chest on the floor of our mother's closet, waiting for Estella to finish counting to a hundred so she can come find me. It's dark. The hems of the dresses tickle my nose. I hear her voice, distant and clear, "Ready or not, here I come!"

Oma lets me lick cake batter from a wooden spoon while Estella lies in bed recovering from chicken pox. She's making a chocolate sponge cake: my favorite. The batter gets onto my hands, so I lick them. I want to bring some batter up to Estella, but Oma tells me I shouldn't disturb her. I get chocolate all over Oma's housedress and giggle because it looks like poo.

I'm sitting on Indian Rock in Berkeley, watching the sunset. I'm alone, but nobody else is. In front of me, I see a girl from one of my economics classes necking with someone I assume is her boyfriend. They remind me of Estella and Leonard, who are probably doing the same thing while watching a movie on our couch. The sunset starts pink, flames orange, and blazes out in violet. I graze my knee during my careless clamber down and wince in pain.

It's graduation day. The sweltering heat of the sun is made even more unbearable by the heat of the several hundred polyester-robed bodies hemming me in on all sides. Our row finally stands and shuffles to the edge of the stage. They call my name. I walk across the stage and catch sight of my parents sheltered bravely under a golf umbrella. Ma is waving. Ba is taking pictures with his free hand. I remember Estella and wish she were here as well.

It's our first trip to Monterey. I'm getting a little sleepy even though I'm driving, so I turn down the heat and lower the window a smidge. The cool air slides in and wakes me up. I look at Estella out of the corner of my eye and see that she is out cold. I note the trickle of spit sliding from her mouth onto her chin, then hanging off it and bouncing like a yo-yo. I snigger to myself.

I'm in Paris. It's the day after Bagatelle's debut, but my breathing still turns shallow at the excitement of it all. I wake up at four because I'm so happy I can't sleep anymore. I pull on my boots and my trench coat and go out walking. The birds are beginning to chirp. I sit on a bench across from a patisserie and watch the workers bustling about inside, shaping dough into baguettes and folding buttery sheets into crescents and rolls. I watch the empty baskets fill with fresh loaves and the cakes and pastries multiply row by row in the glass display case. And then I swoop in and seize my prize. As I walk back to the hotel, sucking my oily fingers and brushing the flakes from my scarf, I think about what the future holds and squeal out loud with delight. That morning, the world is new and the world is mine, all mine.

You understand, then, why I find it so difficult to accept the truth of my circumstances. I'm Gwendolyn. I have to be.

I hear footsteps now, followed by the swish of curtains. It's a nurse, but there's someone else as well. Whoever it is lowers into a seat at my side—I hear the chair creak. I wonder who it is.

"Estella," a voice sighs. It's a woman. Tante Sandra.

Not Estella, I want to say, but can't. Despite everything, I'm touched that she's come all this way.

Someone else approaches. "Ma'am," he says, addressing my aunt. "We need you to speak with the doctor about your niece first. Then you can sign the consent form. Please follow me."

The chair creaks again as my aunt rises and the two of them walk away. I wonder what the consent form consents to, though I can make an educated guess.

I don't mind that they're going to pull the plug. Now that I've solved my mystery, there isn't much purpose to life.

I've been having dreams lately. All variations on the same theme: I am swimming through caverns half filled with water, sometimes floating on my back. It's cool and the sound of lapping waves echoes against the rock. Every now and then, I take a deep breath and dive underwater and find I am not alone. Ma drifts past me, spritzing herself with perfume, followed by Ba, smiling his ironic smile. Ricky, his hands folded behind his head, snoozes away on a passing current. Leonard kneels, suspended in prayer, and I even see Tante Sandra with a man I imagine to be Jono. They're picnicking on a plaid blanket that glides through the water like a flying carpet through the sky. Opa is there too, and New Oma—both watching TV—and a shadow soars over everyone's heads. It's Oma, her colorful housedress billowing out like the wings of a stingray, a tray of cakes in her hands.

Something brushes against my arm. I turn. It's Estella. She clasps my hand and we dive down. She looks so serene, I don't think she remembers anything of what has passed, what she has done. And in these dreams, I too forget.

ACKNOWLEDGMENTS

DEEPEST THANKS TO Boey Wah Fong, Carl Olsen, Keri Glastonbury, and Helen Mangham for taking the time to read an early draft of this novel. I'm not sure this book would have made it without their feedback and encouragement. Many thanks also to my agents Jayapriya Vasudevan and Helen at Jacaranda Literary Agency—for championing my work and reassuring me whenever I begin to panic. And to Daniel Lazar at Writers House, who helped bring this book to the attention of publishers in the US.

My gratitude to Cate Blake and Meaghan Amor at Penguin Random House Australia for their superhuman editing skills and patience. And for pushing me to make this novel into the best version of itself. I am likewise grateful to my editor at Atria Books, Rakesh Satyal, and my copyeditor Mary Beth Constant for helping me fine-tune this North American edition.

For assistance in establishing various facts and historic details, I am indebted to my mother and father, Jan Getson from the Monash University Archives, and Peter Oboyski from the Essig Museum of Entomology.

A thank-you to Julie Koh for helping me rework an extract of this novel for inclusion in *BooksActually's Gold Standard 2016*.

And last but not least, three cheers for those who stepped in to provide extra childcare so I could have time to write and revise: my mother, my father, Justin, Lian, my mother-in-law, and John and Judy Baker.

ABOUT THE AUTHOR

TIFFANY TSAO was born in San Diego, California, and lived in Singapore and Indonesia through her childhood. She is a graduate of Wellesley College and received her PhD in English from the University of California, Berkeley. She lives in Sydney, Australia, with her husband and two children.